Praise for Jane Porter's Novels
Flirting with Forty

"A powerhouse of a novel . . . By turns funny, thrilling, and poignant, this story is always compelling and ultimately empowering . . . Jackie is a character who will resonate with readers long after the end of this great tale."

—LoveRomancesAndMore.com

"Fits the bill as a calorie-free accompaniment for a poolside daiquiri."

—*Publishers Weekly*

"Don't miss the sexy story of Jackie, a forty-year-old divorced mother who finds a romance she wasn't even looking for with a much younger man."

—*Complete Woman*

"An outstanding novel and an RRT Perfect 10. Whether you are a voracious reader or only read one book a year, I highly recommend FLIRTING WITH FORTY. Jackie's struggle to redefine her life is heartbreaking and, at the same time, uplifting and hopeful. Her journey is one that touched me and made me remember that there is more to life than routine and the daily struggle—there is laughter, and love, and hope for more."

—Rom

"Incredibly true to life . . . this introspective novel explores the true meaning of happiness. The plot is fresh . . . Jane Porter is an author to keep on your *must buy* list."

—BookLoons.com

"A May-December (maybe September would be more descriptive) romance between two individuals who must defy societal relationship taboos of the older woman and much younger man. Readers will want the best for Jackie . . . fans will enjoy this fine book as Jackie gets her groove (or does she?)."

—*Midwest Book Review*

"A great read . . . Tears, laughter, desires, and hopes are a part of everyone's life and this book captures them from the perspective of a woman's middle life crisis."

—MyShelf.com

Odd Mom Out

"Funny and poignant . . . delightful. Jane Porter knows how to scoop the reader into the palm of her hand. She knows her characters intimately and makes sure the readers get to know them, too."

—Stella Cameron, *New York Times*
bestselling author

"Nobody understands the agony and ecstasy of single parenting better than Jane Porter. Alternately funny and touching, *Odd Mom Out* champions a woman's right to be herself, even at a PTA meeting."

—Vicki Lewis Thompson, *New York Times*
bestselling author

"Fresh, fun, and real, Jane Porter's writing is a delight!"

—Carly Phillips, *New York Times* bestselling author

The Frog Prince

"Witty, smart, sophisticated . . . I loved this book!"
—Christine Feehan, *New York Times*
bestselling author

"Witty and fun."
—*San Francisco Chronicle*

"A painfully funny, utterly true story for every woman who has ever wondered what happens after the fairy tale ends. I absolutely loved this book!"
—Susan Wiggs,
USA Today bestselling author

"Entertaining and witty . . . tugs the heartstrings in a big way."
—*Booklist*

"Porter . . . has a great ear for dialogue. She offers a fresh twist on the 'broken heart and personal renaissance' theme of so many chick-lit novels."
—*Seattle Times*

"Filled with vibrant, interesting characters, the world of *The Frog Prince* leaps off the page and keeps readers enthralled."
—Kristin Harmel, author of
The Art of French Kissing

"There's real heart in this book . . . enjoyable reading for those wondering what comes after the happily ever after."
—*Romantic Times BOOKreviews Magazine*

"A winner! It will make you stand up and cheer."
—WritersUnlimited.com

Also by Jane Porter

The Frog Prince

Odd Mom Out

flirting
with
forty

Jane Porter

NEW YORK   BOSTON

Copyright © 2006 by Jane Porter
All rights reserved. Except as permitted under the U.S. Copyright Act of 1976, no part of this publication may be reproduced, distributed, or transmitted in any form or by any means, or stored in a database or retrieval system, without the prior written permission of the publisher.

5 Spot
Hachette Book Group USA
237 Park Avenue
New York, NY 10017

Visit our Web site at www.5-spot.com.

5 Spot is an imprint of Grand Central Publishing.
The 5 Spot name and logo is a trademark of Hachette Book Group USA, Inc.

Printed in the United States of America

Originally published in Trade Paperback by Hachette Book Group USA
First Mass Market Edition: May 2008

10 9 8 7 6 5 4 3 2 1

ATTENTION CORPORATIONS AND ORGANIZATIONS:
Most HACHETTE BOOK GROUP USA books are available at quantity discounts with bulk purchase for educational, business, or sales promotional use. For information, please call or write:
**Special Markets Department, Hachette Book Group USA
237 Park Avenue, New York, NY 10017
Telephone: 1-800-222-6747 Fax: 1-800-477-5925**

For Ty Gurney
Thank you

Some books are meticulously crafted, painstakingly pieced together, while others arrive in an adrenaline rush of ifs and maybes. *Flirting with Forty* was the latter, coming to me in one swoop while I sat poolside at the Halekulani in Hawaii. The idea came to me as though I were watching the trailer of a movie, a colorful teaser with a beginning, middle, and end. But a movie trailer isn't a movie, and a premise and sample chapters do not make a book. Grateful appreciation to my agent, Karen Solem, for her constant support and encouragement as I find my footing in every book, and admiration and gratitude to my gifted editor at Grand Central Publishing, Karen Kosztolnyik, for her invaluable thoughts, editing, and insight. I love working with people who care about books and stories as passionately as I do. Thank you.

As this is a book about friendship and women, I must thank a few of the women who have taught me what I know about friendship today: my two best friends from high school, Cyndi Johnson and Anne Morse; and my gal pals in Bellevue, Washington, Lisa Johnson, Sinclair Sawhney, and Joan Lambert.

And final thanks to my children, Jake and Ty Gaskins, who have taught me the meaning of humility, compassion, courage, and love.

flirting
with
forty

one

~~~~~~~~~~

Ah, Christmas. The most wonderful time of the year.
Not. Not if you're a newly single mom.

People say crowds at the malls or lines at the post office ruin Christmas. I say it's the damn Christmas tree.

The whole Christmas tree thing is miserable, wasn't designed for women, and certainly not for women with young children.

Christmas trees require a man, or a gaggle of women friends, but when you're my age and *Time* magazine calls your generation "soccer moms," you know your friends will go to lunch with you, have a girls' night out (which means expensive cocktails at a swanky place), or indulge in a manicure/pedicure spa date, but they don't go Christmas tree shopping with you, and they won't do the lifting, hauling, tying, untying, hauling, and lifting that's required to get the tree from lot onto car, home, and then into stand.

I'm no weakling—I work out—but I've yet to meet a full, fresh noble fir that's, well . . . light.

Which reminds me. Last year—the first year Daniel

and I were living apart before we actually filed for divorce—the nice man at the Christmas tree lot near the Arboretum sold me a tree with—I love this—a double trunk.

A double trunk.

That tree had to have weighed ninety pounds at least. Maybe a hundred. Getting it home and into a stand was unreal. (Horrible.) I've learned my lesson. I will feel every tree up and down before I let the guy with the chainsaw buzz inches off the bottom, making a tree officially mine.

Now it's a year later, and here I am again with my children shopping for a tree, albeit at a different tree lot. And my mood's low, I admit. December's the hardest month in the year for me being single—not because I need a man, but because all family traditions I worked so hard to create now bite me. But today is going to be fun. I swear. We're going to have fun right now.

Right now, I insist silently, jamming my hands deeper into my trench coat pockets, shoulders hunched to ward off the December Seattle rain.

I'm trying hard not to let the rain get to me. Contrary to popular opinion, it doesn't rain every day in Seattle, and I seriously doubt we have the highest suicide rate in the country. That's absurd. *Sleepless in Seattle* was set here. This isn't a depressing place. In fact, we here in the Pacific Northwest blithely refer to our wet weather patterns as drizzle, mist, droplets, light showers, scattered clouds, scattered rain, afternoon clearing, and reported sunspots.

How is that depressing?

But I will tell you I'm less than thrilled to be shopping

for a tree right now. The rain isn't exactly pelting us, but it's got a nice clipped tempo, and it's cold out, and the lot is muddy and the trees are wet and the kids are now wet and I just want to go home.

But I promised them (Mom, a promise is a promise), and they came home from school excited, so here we are.

"How about this one, Mom?" William shouts from a thicket of green that easily tops ten or eleven feet.

"That's a beautiful tree," the guy from the lot says, baseball cap pulled low on his forehead, hiding his face and sparse ponytail.

"It's got to be ten feet," I say, trying to keep the exasperation from my voice. How does he think I'm going to pack and carry a ten-foot tree on my midsize SUV?

"It's twelve, ma'am. And a really nice tree. You won't see many that pretty."

I shoot him a long look. I'm an interior designer. Ceiling heights are my thing. "My ceilings are barely eight feet."

"We can always take something off at the bottom."

Like what? Four and a half feet? And they charge you by the foot when you buy a tree? Sure. That's fiscally wise.

I turn away, push wet bangs off my forehead, as the hood on my coat doesn't quite cover my face. I'm cold, tired, wet, and grouchy and would give almost anything right now for a tall, nonfat, sugar-free vanilla latte. Or just a plain old cup of coffee would do.

"William. Jessica," I call, trying to inject some enthusiasm into my voice. "Come and help me find a *six*-foot tree."

Jessica comes skipping out of the drippy pine tree forest, her lavender sweatshirt soaked, her long blond hair matted.

"Where's your coat, Jessica?"

She stops, gazes back, around, blue eyes wide. "I don't know."

"Honey, go get it."

"I'm hot."

"Jess, it's raining."

"I'm *hot*."

I will say this for children born in the Pacific Northwest: They're not wimps. Fog and rain don't slow them down any. "It's forty degrees, Jess. Get your coat on or we go." I warm to the threat. I like this threat. I'd love to go home right now. "If you can't cooperate, then we're heading home."

William, my nine-year-old, has heard this last part, and he comes stumbling out of the trees in protest. "But you said, Mom, you said—"

"I know what I said, but I'm not going to fight with you or your sister, not today. Getting the Christmas tree is supposed to be special. I want this to be fun, not a hassle." *Right.*

And there are times (like now) when I wonder where I got all this parent-speak from. Is it something inherited? Something transmitted in the XY chromosome? Because sometimes (like now) my mouth moves and words come out and I hear my voice, and the tone, and I am a nag. A *mother*.

William turns to his sister, who is conveniently three and a half years younger and continues to live up to her status as the baby in the family. "Knock it off, Jess," he hisses. "Get your coat and do what Mom says or we'll go home and we won't have a Christmas tree and there won't be any presents and Santa won't come and it'll be all your fault."

Jessica gets her coat.

I look at William, my handsome firstborn who is thicker around the middle than he used to be, putting on size where I didn't know size would go, and silently congratulate him on getting the job done. These days I'll take all the help I can get.

Reaching up to wipe my face dry again, I think of the two umbrellas in my car that have been there for two years and never been used. Odd to live in a place that rains so much and yet never use an umbrella. It's just that most of us who live here don't pull out umbrellas for something as insignificant as showers. We're, well . . . tough . . . tougher.

Or maybe just stupid. Stupider.

I feel stupider right now, walking through wet, mushy soil to stare at staked trees. We're the only ones at the lot. Yes, it is a Monday at four in the afternoon, but surely there must be other parents who promised their kids they'd buy a tree today if they were good.

If they were good. Glancing at my two, I see Jessica take a swing at William. Jessica with her blond hair and blue eyes and great dimples may look like an angel but is the devil incarnate. She's hell on wheels, and I wish I could blame it all on Daniel, but word has it I was difficult at five, too.

And six. Seven. Eight. But who's counting?

Certainly not me, because I just want to go home.

"How about this one?" I say, pointing to a relatively attractive fir that's in the five-to-six-foot-tall range.

Both Jessica and William shake their heads. "It's short," Jessica says.

"It's ugly," William adds, moving his hand in one of the tree's huge holey pockets. "There's nothing here. How will you hang ornaments if there's nothing to hang them on?"

He has a good point, but I've seen the price tag. The tree is sixty-five dollars, twenty less than the better-groomed brothers in the seven-foot row. "We can put something special there," I say.

"Like what? A piñata?"

He's getting funny in his old age. I can only imagine the excitement of adolescence. "It's not perfect, but it's a nice tree."

He harrumphs at me, much the way his father used to do, and then finds the tree we end up buying. While Jessica splashes in puddles in her best shoes (why didn't I see she was wearing her best shoes earlier?) and then cries the whole way home that she's cold.

The good news is that we have a tree tied to our roof and we're in our car heading home.

The bad news is that it's only step one. Swiftly I review the other steps—

Step one: Buy tree & tie on car.
Step two: Drive home without losing tree.
Step three: Get tree off car.
Step four: Get tree in house and in stand.

We're home soon—I like step two, I feel really good about step two, and congratulate myself for a job well done. Now it's time for three.

I send William into the kitchen for my utility scissors while I open the various car doors, positioning for my climb toward the roof. William hands me the scissors, and I cut the twine on this side and then the other and the other until the tree's freed. The kids cheer me on in the dark, as twilight has given way to night at only four-thirty in the afternoon. The rain is still coming down in a nice, steady splat, splat, splat, and bless my kids, they never once mention the rain, don't think to complain, and I know it's because they think all children live like this.

It doesn't even cross their minds that right now, this very minute, it's sunny somewhere else in the United States.

That places like Phoenix, Orlando, Los Angeles, and Denver all have sun. That Palm Springs is perfect this time of year. Hawaii sublime. Miami a total hot spot.

No, they're innocent. They don't realize if we just moved south, we'd move to blue skies and sun year-round.

Which is why we try not to take them out of state too often. It just makes them wish for drier pastures (notice, I did not say "greener," as the only place possibly greener than Seattle is Ireland), and they're not getting drier pastures until they go away to college.

"Okay, William, Jessica, stand back." I hang on to the SUV's roof rack. "I'm going to drag the tree to the edge and then drop it down."

I scoot the tree across the roof, cringing as the branches

squeak and scratch. Lifting the base of the tree, I feel the sticky ooze of sap. I make a mental note to be careful of sap. I have sap stains from last year's mammoth double trunk on one of my favorite sweatshirts still.

Even though this isn't a double-trunk tree this year, it's still heavier than expected, and suddenly it's caught on one of the rack rails. I tug, the tree doesn't budge; I check the twine, it's cut; I check the tree, the branches aren't caught. The tree is just too heavy to knock off the roof.

"William, I'm going to need a hand. Be careful."

He's eager to help. He jumps up on the driver's seat, reaches for the top part of the tree.

"Why can't I help?" Jessica protests. "Why does William get to do everything?"

"You're helping, Jess." I grunt as fresh noble fir branches slap my face. Another good hard yank and I should have the tree off. "Stand back. William—yank it your way and then try to catch it before it falls."

Yes, I know. Not the smartest thing to say or expect him to do. Looking back, I should have just let the tree fall. To hell with the car. To hell with the asphalt. To hell with protecting the tree.

I should have protected the son.

Fortunately, there's no blood. And he's not crying. But in the house he lifts his T-shirt, and he's got a huge red welt running from his shoulder past his sternum to his lower ribs.

"I'm sorry, baby," I say, giving him a huge, guilty hug. But at least step three's accomplished.

On to step four.

I get a bottle of water from the fridge, twist off the top,

and take a long, fortifying drink as I mentally review my strategy for getting tree into stand.

Even with Daniel, getting the tree into the stand is a series of four-letter expletives strung together.

Now, without Daniel here, I'm determined we're going to do this and keep it fun. I'm an adult. I've had two babies—one of them nine pounds—I've carried six grocery bags at one time. I can do this.

And the kids, bless them. They're looking at me with all the confidence in the world.

I put on a CD of Nat King Cole's Christmas carols, do a little stretching—okay, feeling vaguely like Owen Wilson in *Shanghai Noon*, but that's fine. Anything to keep this fun.

Jess, William, and I fling open all the doors, grab a piece of tree, and drag-carry our increasingly less noble noble fir into the living room.

We get it there, and it lies in the middle of the floor, hogging space. I know the man at the lot said it was only seven feet, but I didn't really think about girth. It's a big wide tree. Wow. It's sure going to look good when it's decorated.

I stand back, rub sap off my hands. William plucks at his shirt. Sap. Jessica's lavender sweatshirt. Sap. *Good.* It's a *healthy* big wide tree.

Still rubbing my hands, I share the plan: "We're going to slide the tree into the stand while it's still on the ground. And then together we'll lift it. Then while you guys hold it steady, I'll tighten the screws and we can start decorating."

It's a good plan. It should work.

It doesn't.

And of course it doesn't. Nothing about Christmas is easy. It's the most wonderful—cut, edit, paste—*stressful* time of year.

The tree's lower branches won't let us get the tree stand ring high enough around the trunk to hold the tree upright in the stand. And as nice as the tree looks horizontal on my carpet, I worry about twenty-some days of sap leekage.

We lower the tree, and screws are loosened with great difficulty (I shouldn't have been so zealous with the pliers until I knew the tree would fit).

We're going to have to cut branches. And of course, I don't have any tools for cutting branches.

In the divorce Daniel got the second house, the Porsche, the new young girlfriend, and the old saw we used for things like this.

I should have bought a saw. I bought a toolbox when Daniel and I separated—a nice red-painted box packed with tools—but a saw wasn't in it. And in case you're wondering, I'm the kind of designer who has good ideas, not the kind who's crafty herself. A pity, I think now, because maybe if I were more crafty and better with my hands, my tree would be standing up properly right now.

"How about scissors?" Jessica suggests.

"Scissors will break," I answer, sitting on my heels. I hear Nat croon, but it's not helping. I'm not happy. I'm really not happy. We left for the tree lot at four. It's now past six. The kids haven't had dinner, done homework. And the tree is still prone, a massive green whale on my cream thick-pile carpet.

"How about a knife?" William offers.

"Sure." I'm battling here for warmth and charm. It's December, Christmas, fun, family fun, make it fun, make it special for the kids. "Get the bread knife, though. That's the long one with the serrated edge—" I see his blank look, break off. "Never mind. I'll get it."

One bread knife later, I'm sawing at the slim lower branches that seem to have sprung up all over the tree base. It takes minutes to cut just one. There are at least ten more. My God. This could go on all night.

The tree is rapidly getting on my bad side. It's not a helpful tree. It's not cooperating.

Good trees should practically leap into their stands, nice and straight, and wait while one tightens the base. This tree doesn't even care if my kids get fed.

I'm still sawing away, swearing under my breath. I take a rest.

"Mom, let me do it. I can do it. I'm strong."

I look at William, my William, who at nine has become the new man in the family, and I see how big he has become. My nine-pound baby on his way to adulthood. "I don't want you hurt."

"I won't get hurt."

"You got hurt outside."

"That's because you dropped the tree on me."

Mmmm. Good point. But still. Knives are different. "I'd hate for you to get cut—"

"I won't." He takes the knife from me. "Stand back."

Stand back. I almost cry. Little boys shouldn't have to ever take care of their mothers. "You can try, just for a minute," I say, crouching close by in case he slices off a few fingers and I have to run fast to get them on ice.

Nothing will go wrong, I tell myself. Why would anything go wrong? This whole tree thing has been a roaring success.

William saws and hacks away at the tree. Carpenters and contractors on home improvement shows would be appalled at our crafts skills, but we're a family, and we hack and saw like a family. "How's it going?" I ask him.

"Good, Mom."

Jessica's crouching close now, too. "My turn."

"No, Jessica. You're not going to use the knife."

"Why not? William is."

"William's almost four years older."

"So?"

"Knives are dangerous—"

"You let him do everything and you don't let me do anything."

"You're right." I sit back, hands on thighs. "I should have let you get crushed by the tree instead of William. He's ninety pounds and you're what? Forty? You can handle it."

She rolls her eyes at me. "I wouldn't get crushed. That's an exaggeration. Daddy says you always exaggerate."

Oh, I love Daniel. I love him sooooo much.

"William, that's good," I say, beginning to get uneasy the longer he saws at the tree. I'm just waiting for the knife to slip, fingers to fly, blood spurting. And I'm seriously not good with blood. Even when I was a kid, the TV show *Emergency* made me queasy.

"But, Mom, I've almost got it."

"No."

"Mom—"

"*No!* Give me the knife."

He looks like a dog that's just been kicked. But he hands me the knife.

Jessica, however, eyes me with five-year-old contempt. "You didn't have to yell at him, Mom. He was just trying to help."

"Jessica . . ."

"Why are you always so mean?" She glares at me. "Melinda's not mean."

Melinda being her daddy's legal eagle girlfriend in Silicon Valley. *She's smart, Jacqueline. Ambitious. Princeton grad, MBA from Brown, we've got so much in common.* Hooray, Daniel. I'm so glad for you.

He and sexy, sleek Melinda practically live together, while I can't even think about dating.

It's not that I hate men, I just don't want anything to do with them. I've been divorced a year now, and I'm still dead inside. I have nothing left to give anyone, and the men I do meet are looking for wife number two to replace wife number one, which means (like me) they come complete with houses, children, and ex-spouses. And I'm not ready for that. I can barely deal with my own kids; how can I possibly deal with anyone else's?

No. After eleven years of being a good corporate wife and (part-time) interior designer, all I want are my kids, my friends, and my business to thrive.

The friends are easy, the work is challenging, and taking in Jessica's mulish expression, I think at least one of the kids is impossible.

"Because Melinda's not your mother," I answer. "She's your daddy's girlfriend."

"So?"

Thank God I had William first, because if Jessica had been the firstborn, there would have been no other children. "So Melinda isn't responsible for you. I am. And it's my job to make sure you grow up healthy, safe, and *polite.*"

Twenty minutes later, we're ready to try to stand the tree again. William and I are holding the tree and trying to shake it all the way down to the bottom of the stand, but we can't get it down no matter how hard we try.

I stand back to see what it looks like, while William is buried in the tree, holding it steady. "Maybe it's okay like this," he mumbles around a mouthful of pine.

I'm thinking he's right. It looks straight. Enough.

"Keep holding the tree, and I'll tighten the screws the rest of the way." I've located a second pair of pliers, and with pliers in hand I wiggle on my stomach beneath the tree, heading in face-first, as if I'm auditioning for the staged version of Desert Storm. Jessica's crawling in from the other side with her pliers, and together we bang and clank on the screws while William shouts encouragements.

"You've got it," he says. "Looks great. I think it's going to work."

"Mom, I've got this side," Jessica says.

And finally, sappy and red faced, I crawl back out. The tree looks okay.

"Are we going to decorate now?" Jess asks, putting the pliers to bookends and drawer knobs and anything that protrudes.

"You guys need dinner."

"No, we don't." William already has the strings of lights coming out of the boxes.

I rub the back of my neck and try not to see how William is getting the light strings in knots. "You do. You'll be starving and won't sleep."

Jessica kneels to clamp a light with the pliers. "*Jess,*" I warn.

She looks up at me, all wide-eyed innocence. "What?"

"Those bulbs are glass."

"Uh-huh."

"They'll break." And *snap*. She shatters one. Bright bits of red glass shards in the carpet.

Jess drops the pliers. "It broke."

William shakes his head. "You did that deliberately."

"I didn't."

"You did."

"I didn't!"

"Guys." I stand between them, a restraining hand on each. "Come on. We've got lots to do." I send Jessica for the vacuum, William for the phone to call Domino's, and I pop two Advil. This is going to be a really long night.

Three hours later, the kids are finally in bed and I'm sitting with a Santa mug of mulled wine in the darkened living room, staring at the tree, the red and green and blue and gold lights glowing and my favorite old Neil Diamond Christmas album playing. Daniel hated my Neil Diamond Christmas album, as well as the Barry Manilow, Carpenters, and Barbra Streisand albums, but he's not here anymore and I can damn well play what I want.

And Neil Diamond is such a guilty pleasure.

"Song Sung Blue."

"Cherry, Cherry."

"I am . . . I said." Or something like that.

I sip the spiced mulled wine, a recipe I've made every year for the past thirteen years. It was one of Daniel's and my first traditions. Pizza, mulled wine, and tree.

Daniel probably doesn't even remember why I started making mulled wine. The mulled wine was to coax him into helping put up the tree after work. He'd be tired, and not festive, but I'd make the wine and put on some carols, and after a few cups he'd be in the spirit. It always worked. By cup three he was singing along with the Neil Diamond CD I snuck into shuffle mode.

I miss him. We can't be married anymore—we just grew too far apart—but I do miss the traditions, the fun times, the family times. I think that's what I miss most.

The kids will never have Mom and Dad in the same house.

They'll never have a traditional Christmas again.

And it's such a hard thought, so grim and unsettling, that I get up, pull the plug on the tree lights, return the Santa mug to the kitchen, and head upstairs for bed.

I'm just through washing my face when I hear a horrible splintering crash from downstairs. I go cold everywhere and for a second can't move. I just stand there with a sick, icy feeling in my middle. I can see myself in the mirror, puffy shower cap still on my head, traces of foamy soapsuds at the hairline, and I know what it is, that thud punctuated by breaking glass.

The tree.

It's just gone down.

two

~~~~~~~~~

It's been twenty days since that happy occasion, but we've made it. Tonight's Christmas Eve. And you know what that means: Showtime!

This is it. No more shopping, no more wrapping, no more frantic last trips to the grocery store. Instead it's time to pull out all the stops and make it happen. Big dinner, roaring fire, carols, family, friends, and that all-important late night visit from Santa, of course.

I've invited my closest friends to join us for Christmas Eve dinner. I have three tight friends, Kristine, Nic, and Anne, and I know their kids and husbands as if we're all an extended family. And maybe we are. Kristine doesn't have family in state. Nic has only her mom, who lives in Portland, a four-hour drive away. Anne has parents locally, but they're a lot like mine (my mom and dad live in Spokane, comfortably distanced by the hulking Cascade Mountains), which means they're always traveling, busy doing what retirees with AARP cards do.

It's a treat for me to have everyone over, and I might not be able to get a tree in a stand, but I can host a party that puts Martha Stewart to shame. This is a Whiting skill, Whiting being my maiden name. The women in my family can cook and set a table and create an atmosphere that makes people just want to pull up a chair and stay.

Tonight's menu comes from an old issue of *Gourmet* magazine—ham, turkey, roasted chestnut stuffing, smooth brown gravy with a hint of champagne, mashed potatoes, glazed sweet potatoes, homemade rolls, cranberry salad, pomegranate-and-avocado-laced spinach salad—sublime. This is my traditional Christmas Eve feast, and everything is as it's always been. Except for Daniel missing.

And just thinking, remembering, I feel my insides do another free fall, one of those maneuvers that takes my breath away and leaves me shaken, filled with too much adrenaline.

I miss my life. I miss the family we had more than I can say.

But Daniel and I aren't married anymore, and I can't go back, can only go forward. So I put him out of my mind, knowing he's with Melinda tonight. He's fine. I'm fine. Everybody's fine. Besides, I don't have time to feel sad. I've got seventeen people arriving in minutes, eight of them kids, plus some visiting relatives my friends couldn't leave home, seeing as they'd flown into Seattle for the holidays.

Showered but not completely dressed, I run around the house lighting all the candles, then dim the lights, put a match to the Duraflame log in the living room (Duraflames are a gift to the single woman), turn on the CD player already loaded with carols, and we're almost ready. I just have to finish my makeup, button the back of my blouse, and get shoes on.

Upstairs again, I'm throwing makeup on my face as if this is a game of paintball—beige splat; gold splat; gray splat; red splat. Thank God I know my face pretty well now. I can point and shoot, and the makeup hits the target with ninety percent accuracy.

I'm just spritzing perfume when the doorbell rings. They're here.

Anne, her surgeon husband, Philip, and her brood of three are the first to arrive.

"Merry Christmas!" Anne cries, giving me a hug as they enter the house and begin peeling off coats. "You look great. I don't remember those pants. Are they new?"

I accept a kiss from Philip and point their kids upstairs, where my two are playing in the bonus room. "Yeah. I was tired of you always giving me such a hard time for wearing baggy clothes."

Philip's already heading to the kitchen with the bottle of wine they brought, while Anne and I hang up coats in the hall closet.

"It's about time you bought yourself something sexy," Anne continues as I shut the closet door. "You have a great figure, Jack. Show it off." Anne's been on a diet for the last year. She loses weight, and then three months later it comes back.

"You'll lose the weight, Anne. You always do."

"Just to gain it back."

"Well, you can always try my weight-loss program," I say lightly, sliding a hanger into the last coat. "Get divorced, break your heart, cry yourself sick for a month or two, and the weight will just melt off."

"You did get skinny."

"Annie, you're happily married. You have three gorgeous kids. Five or ten extra pounds shouldn't change your self-worth."

"Shouldn't, no. But they do."

And isn't this the truth? We do see our value in terms of our weight, our hair, our physical desirability. Shouldn't be so, but is.

The doorbell rings again. Nic and Kristine and their families have arrived all at once, and suddenly the house is bursting at the seams as kids pound up and down the stairs and the men gather round the bar I've set up in the dining room.

"Everything looks fabulous," Kristine compliments, smoothing her tailored black trousers. Once a lawyer, always a lawyer, and even at Christmas Kris has a practical, no-nonsense approach to wardrobe.

"Thanks."

"Is that the infamous tree?" Nic asks, nodding at my problem Christmas tree in the corner of the living room.

"It is." I accept the poinsettia Nic has brought, place it on the antique console in the hall. "Wine? Champagne? What sounds good?"

Champagne seems to be the drink of choice tonight, and we head for the kitchen, where the kids have already devoured half the crackers and nearly all the grapes from the cheese tray.

Anne, seeing my lavish appetizer buffet on the granite counter—cheese platter, pâté, chilled dill shrimp, hot crab dip, smoked-salmon spread—turns and looks at me with an arched eyebrow. "What?" she asks, deadpan. "No Cocoa Puffs?"

This is a little inside joke. A few years back, Anne and I got into a tense standoff—about nutrition, no less. Anne's a great cook, very healthy, into organic foods, and she once said that maybe if I didn't feed my kids so much sugar, Jessica might be calmer and William not so husky. I took offense.

I don't feed my kids crap. It's not as if I pour Kool-Aid down their throats. I make healthy dinners. Yes, we do have Chips Ahoy! cookies in the pantry, Eggo waffles in the freezer, and kid-friendly cereals for breakfast—but so does most of America, so leave me alone.

I said as much, too, and I don't know if it was my delivery or the fact that I was really hurt, but it took us a few weeks to work through that. We can joke about it now, but I wouldn't want to fight with her again. It's hard enough fighting with your spouse. You don't want to fight with your friends.

"I don't know how you do it, Jackie," Nic says slightly enviously as she takes in the miniature decorated tree on the counter, the appetizers, the burning candles, the crisp pink-, red-, and green-striped cocktail napkins. "I can barely get my teeth brushed sometimes, and here you are, looking amazing, hosting a glamorous party on your own. How do you do it?"

I shrug, flattered but uncomfortable. I've spent days doing this, days I should have been working at my desk, but sometimes my priorities get mixed up. Sometimes I want everyone to be so happy because then I think I'll be happy. I know it doesn't work like that, but I can't seem to change.

"Talked to Daniel lately?" Kristine asks. Kristine, the

former lawyer (her husband is still a lawyer), is also a mother, homemaker, and now nonprofit volunteer extra-ordinaire. Kristine's always co-chairing a fund-raiser, calls me usually on her way to or from one of her committee meetings.

Kristine learned early in our friendship that I don't do committees. I'm happy to donate my time, do a job, cut a check—just don't make me sit around with a bunch of women who look like me and talk like me and try to come to a joint consensus.

"It's been a few days," I say, struggling to pop the cork on the champagne and finally succeeding.

"How is that?"

"Fine, I suppose." I pour everyone flutes of champagne. "We don't talk long. It's stilted again. I don't know why."

"At least you're talking again," Nic answers. Nic's sensitive and wants everyone to always be happy. She was a teacher before she had kids and stays home now with hers.

"I'm trying." I watch the bubbles fizz and pop in my flute. "I think he's trying, too. We both love the kids."

"Is he still talking about moving to San Jose?" Kristine asks.

I shake my head. "Not lately. His girlfriend's spending more time up here."

For a moment no one says anything, and then Nic volunteers that she bumped into Daniel and Melinda at Whole Foods yesterday. "She seems really nice," Nic concludes awkwardly.

I say nothing, as I don't know what to say. After being

with Daniel nearly fifteen years, I know him so well, but what I know—what worked—doesn't work anymore. As an ex-spouse, you're familiar and not, known and yet criticized. Once loved but now rejected.

"Do you ever think you'll get back together?" Nic asks hopefully. She's probably my one friend who would like to see a reunion romance. I don't know if it's her Catholic upbringing (she taught both public and parochial school) or the statistics she shared with me about children of divorce (they're more likely to get divorced than children raised in stable nuclear families), but she's taken our divorce quite hard.

"No," I answer bluntly, smiling tightly, not wanting to think of those statistics, hating to imagine Jessica or William going through what I'm going through. "Have to move forward. Can't go back."

Then suddenly I'm looking ahead, thinking of all the holidays and Christmases to come. Next year, I won't have the kids for Christmas. The first time I will not be with my kids for Christmas since William's birth nine years ago. How can I not have my kids at Christmas? How could Daniel and I have divided up the holidays this way?

I'm scared, I think, so scared. What will I do without the kids for Christmas? What will Christmas morning be like without stockings?

"So you don't have any regrets?" Nic persists, leaning across the counter to snag a chip and wedge of cheese.

Stomach in knots, I watch as Anne spreads warm baked Brie in my flaky pastry crust on an apple slice. The reason I've lost weight is that I can't eat, can't swallow, can't do much but feel like shit for putting the children through this.

"Of course there are always regrets," I force myself to say, "but the worst regrets are when I need help and there's no one to offload on. When I can't call Daniel and say, 'Grab William from baseball,' or, 'Stop by the store and get milk.' But we're learning. Adapting. If we're out of milk, I pack up the kids and we go to the store. Or we go without."

Anne sighs heavily, dramatically, going for a laugh. "Which would mean no Cocoa Puffs."

She gets the laugh. I'm laughing, at least. "Shut up about the damn Cocoa Puffs."

Everyone joins in the laughter, and the tension's broken. We drift into a new discussion and stand around the island, snacking and sipping champagne. Time passes, and it's so relaxed and happy and easy that I'm jolted when Kris's husband appears in the kitchen with his coat, saying that they have to go.

What does he mean, they have to go? Why do they have to go? But before I can protest, everyone's mobilized, charging around, gathering kids and purses, locating sweaters and missing socks.

Watching the move toward the door, I feel only pain and panic. They can't be going now. They can't all leave at once. No one's even eaten dinner!

"You don't have to go yet, do you?" I plead, blocking the coat closet, arms outstretched. "It's early still. Not even nine, and I have so much food—"

"Jack, my turkey is still in the oven," Kris interrupts gently. "The kids wanted their traditional dinner at home, so we just pushed our meal back."

I look at her and feel foolish, even more foolish as tears fill my eyes. "You have a turkey at home?"

"I thought you knew we were coming just for drinks."

Right. Turning, I look at Nic and Anne. "Do you guys have to leave, too?"

"My mom's tired," Nic says. "She only drove up from Portland tonight."

Right.

And the tears in my eyes are nothing compared to the pressure in my chest. It's all gone, the life I had, isn't it? The family, the traditions, the security. There's nothing left, and suddenly the tears are falling.

I miss my old life, and I'm not quite sure what my new life is.

It's just so confusing.

I've been a wife and mom so long that I'm not sure how not to be a wife anymore. I'm not sure how to be a woman anymore.

I'm not even sure what a woman is or what a woman does.

"Oh, Jack," Nic says, moving forward to hug me. "Don't cry. Everything's good. Everyone had a lovely time."

I nod against her shoulder. Everyone did seem happy; the kids ran around, and I heard them laughing as they raced upstairs and downstairs and into the kitchen for more grapes and apples. But I made dinner, real dinner, the "sit down around a table and be a family" kind of dinner.

"I just . . ." And I pull back, wipe beneath my eyes, catching the tears before they can ruin my mascara. "I just thought you were all going to be here longer."

"It's Christmas, Jackie." Kris is trying to be gentle, but it doesn't help.

That's exactly the problem. It *is* Christmas. And it doesn't feel the way Christmas is supposed to feel. Nothing feels the way it's supposed to feel.

"I know," I say. "I know—" My voice breaks, and I feel my face cracking, tears springing. I hate this feeling of losing control. But it's too late. The control's gone. All that's left is exhaustion. "I'm sorry. I'm sorry. It's not you guys. It's not anything you've done. I'm so glad you all came. Really glad."

"No reason to apologize," Anne says as Kris fumbles in her purse for a tissue. "Christmas is a really hard time for everyone. It's bound to be extra difficult for you."

I nod and mop my eyes and pray the men won't walk in at this moment. The husbands are still good friends with Daniel, and I couldn't bear it if they saw me standing in my own hallway sobbing in front of the coat closet. "I can't believe I'm crying like this. I'm so embarrassed. Here it's Christmas and it's supposed to be happy and I wanted everything perfect—"

Nic gives me another hug. "It is perfect. You're perfect."

And it just makes it worse. I'm not perfect, but the fact that my friends love me anyway undoes me. I cry harder. My God. I honestly didn't know it'd still be this hard. I didn't know I'd feel so . . . so everything. It's been a year since the divorce.

The tears are falling madly, and I turn from Nic to take another tissue from Kris, and yet I'm still losing it. They all have husbands to go home with tonight. I used to. I used to before I decided I wanted, needed, more. But I'm so afraid there is no more. I'm so afraid this is it and I'm screwed. I can't see having a new husband, they're far too much work. And yet living alone with kids and running between mommy mode and designer mode and trying to keep everything functioning, and the bills paid, and the homework done and the carpools run . . . I'm just shot.

I'm gone.

I've got this outside-me with the great hair and the Rembrandt-whitened teeth, the classy wardrobe, and all the facial creams a woman turning forty could want. But I don't have me.

Where have I gone?

"You're doing great, Jack." Anne sees Philip in the door, motions frantically for him to go back into the other room before continuing. "You're through the worst, Jackie, you really are. You've got the kids moved, settled in your new house. They're happier than they were a year ago. You're happier, too. You're just tired. You need a break."

But that's the problem. There is no break. We may have joint custody, but the kids are with me the majority of the time, and the work is endless. William's homework takes hours after school every day, and then there's his sports and the carpools and the running them from here to there.

"Maybe it's time to hire a sitter. Sneak away for a few days," Kristine says. "You and Daniel used to have weekend getaways. There's no reason you can't still escape and do something nice for yourself for a few days.

Visit a spa. Check into a posh hotel and just sleep in, order room service—"

"Kris, I'd hate it. It'd be lonelier than hell." I make a face, wipe my eyes with the tissue. "I'm alone too much as it is."

For a moment no one says anything, everyone bundled in their winter coats, and I'm suddenly embarrassed to have said so much. "But of course I'm alone more," I add quickly, dabbing now at my nose. "It's to be expected. I'm not married anymore, and most of the time I'm good with it. I thought I'd be lonely at night. I'm not. I'd much rather sleep alone than next to someone who doesn't even care if I'm there. It's just the other stuff . . . the work stuff, you know, sharing responsibilities. I think that's the hardest part."

They murmur assent, saying properly comforting things. But the sound of children squabbling reaches us, and the energy has shifted. It really is time for them to go. I hug everyone good-bye, thank the husbands for coming tonight, and then they're all gone.

I shut the door.

My kids are standing on the stairs. I smile, banish the blues. "You guys hungry? Ready for some dinner?"

Jessica shakes her head, yawns. William shrugs. "Not really."

Great.

"Not even a little turkey sandwich?"

"Maybe tomorrow, Mom," William says.

"Okay." I am not going to cry just because no one ate my dinner. "You're ready for bed, then?"

"Santa's coming, Mommy." Jessica is suddenly her

angelic self. "We have to go to bed so he can bring us lots of presents."

My angel's always thinking. "All right." I give up. They win. No one needs turkey and chestnut stuffing and champagne-laced gravy. "Go change into your jammies. I'll read you a quick story—"

"*Santa Mouse*?" Jessica interrupts hopefully.

"Sure."

By ten o'clock, my kids are asleep, and after changing into sweats, I head back downstairs to confront the mess.

Dishes are piled in the sink. Sticky punch cups are stacked on the counter, while trays of dried-out appetizers jostle with dirty wineglasses. Red candles on the granite counter have melted into puddles of wax.

The dining room is even worse. The table is still crammed with platters and hot plates, serving dishes and bowls. The turkey is intact, drumsticks untouched. Only a dozen slices are missing from the nine-pound ham. The sweet potatoes are still glazed and dotted with bits of brown sugar. There's a mound of rolls, with three dozen more still warming in the kitchen warming drawer.

I had food for an army—well, maybe fifty—and I don't know why I cooked so much. I always do this. I go overboard. My mother and grandmother did this, too. Not the cooking too much, but making sure everything was just right.

My family has this thing about food. Meals. Unity. Don't know if it's a German-Scottish thing or just the good old midwestern background showing, but neither my mom nor her mother worked outside the home. Their job, their labor of love, was family. Family, my late grandma Whiting used to say, is everything.

I miss my grandma—we were close—but I'm glad she died before Daniel and I divorced. She wouldn't have understood. Grandma Whiting never cared about Daniel's title at work, how much my business made, or where we went on our vacations. She was more concerned with our spiritual lives. Were we still going to church every Sunday? Were we sitting down for dinner every night as a family? Did the children say prayers at night before bed?

No, no, and no, I think, starting to clear the table.

In the kitchen I toss out some food, try to find homes for other items in my mismatched plastic storage containers. Spotting an open bottle of champagne floating in the silver bucket, I pull out the champagne, fill a flute, take a sip, and get back to work.

As I dump the wilted pomegranate salad, I turn on the garbage disposal and think about breakfast. What will I make in the morning? My traditional ham-and-cheese strata? Homemade cinnamon rolls?

Or how about a few frozen Eggo waffles?

After turning off the disposal, I reach for my champagne glass and crack a reluctant smile. I'd *never* serve Eggo waffles on Christmas morning. I couldn't serve Eggo waffles on Christmas. Grandma Whiting would turn over in her grave.

Christmas is special. Christmas is the most wonderful time of the year.

The day after Christmas, Daniel picks up the kids for their week in Palm Springs. Anne calls later in the day to see if I have time for coffee that evening. She'll pick me up after she gets the kids to bed.

At eight p.m. the phone rings. Anne's on her way. I'm at the door when I see her headlights flash in the driveway.

We head to the nearest Starbucks in Madison Park, her Audi wagon's headlights shining on and through the massive trees lining the narrow road.

At Starbucks we order before finding a comfortable table near the fireplace. "You okay?" Anne asks as we settle in. "You were pretty sad Christmas Eve."

"I was just tired."

"We're all worried about you, Jack."

"I'm okay—"

"You're not. You're exhausted. And blue. You need some R and R."

"I don't want to go away and be alone."

"You won't be alone." Anne cups her coffee. "You'll be with me. We'll have a girls' weekend, celebrate your birthday."

I hate being reminded about my birthday. Nothing in me feels like celebrating this birthday. Forty and divorced? Now there's a fun concept. "Even if I wanted to celebrate my birthday, Philip would never let you go away for a girls' trip. You know how he is—"

"He's not that bad."

"He doesn't like you going out for dinner and drinks with your friends. He's not going to want you taking off for a weekend."

"He said I could do something for my birthday."

"With *him*."

Anne's blond hair falls forward, covering half her face. "Philip can't get away. Work's too busy. They're short staffed on his rotation right now."

"They've been short staffed on his rotation since I met you." Which was roughly six years ago, not that anyone's counting. I just always remember because I met her shortly after discovering I was pregnant with Jessica and still in that "I'm going to barf any minute" stage.

"Blame insurance companies and lawsuit-happy people. Hospitals don't want to go broke. It's just too expensive these days." She sighs. "Sometimes I wish he'd just get out of medicine altogether. What's the point of being a brilliant surgeon if you can't pay your bills?"

"You can pay your bills."

"It's definitely tighter. When we first married Phil made seventy, seventy-five thousand more than he does now."

I see her lips compress, jaw firming, and this is what I mean about everyone having problems. Anne married relatively late, made up for lost time by having three babies in quick succession, and tried for a fourth, only to miscarry at the beginning of the fifth month. Since the miscarriage two years ago, Anne's struggled to lose the weight she'd gained with that final pregnancy, and the extra weight literally weighs heavy on her heart.

She doesn't feel the same about herself, not fifteen pounds heavier (or twenty, as she claims), but I don't see the extra pounds. I just see Anne, an amazing person, a true-blue friend, despite her antisugar and organic food fetish.

"I could use the break, too," she says softly, tucking a

thick blond lock behind her ear. "I don't feel like myself anymore. I don't know what's wrong."

"You're busy. You've got three kids and they're all very active and a husband that works long hours."

Anne makes a hoarse sound and looks up at me, blue eyes wide, intent. "When you were a kid, did you ever think this is what life would be like?"

"No," I say softly.

She nods slowly. We finish our coffee.

Later in the car, as we're heading home, Anne again brings up the need to get away. "I'm going to book the trip," she says firmly. "We're going to go away. We're going to do it. You need it. I need it. We'll do it together."

"Annie—"

"It's your fortieth birthday, Jack. We have to do something special. This is a major milestone."

"I wish you wouldn't keep reminding me."

"I'm serious." Her hands tighten on the steering wheel. "Philip can manage without me for one weekend. I haven't been away without the kids in . . . well, forever. We'll go somewhere sunny and warm, where we can sit by the pool and sip tall, frosty blender drinks." She shoots me a quick side glance, and she's smiling now. "Drinks served by a sexy young thing."

I smile reluctantly. "Sounds delightful." But I know we're not going to go, and I won't get my hopes up. No point in getting my hopes up. I love Anne, and she's been there for me this past year every time I needed a friend.

"Where do you want to go?" She hasn't dropped the fantasy. "Mexico? Arizona? Hawaii?"

"I don't care."

"It's *your* birthday."

"I never asked to be forty."

"Better than the alternative."

"Without a doubt. But wouldn't it be nice if somebody had consulted us regarding the aging process? Kris says her eyes are already going. She can't even read a menu anymore. What's that about?"

Anne laughs. "You don't have to worry about that yet. She's forty-two."

"Ha ha, very funny." Only two years from now I get to squint and hold menus and prescription bottles at arm's length to read the fine print.

"Where's it going to be?" Anne persists. "Mexico? Hawaii?"

I won't rain on her parade. "Surprise me." I smile a little, and then the smile fades as Anne turns onto my street and I see my house at the end. It's a nice two-story house. Not fancy, but proper. A Beaver Cleaver home in a Beaver Cleaver neighborhood, but I'm no June Cleaver. I know that much.

And some of my social world has let me know, too. This year at Christmas there weren't any invitations to parties. The kids don't get asked to sleepovers much anymore. Kristine says it's because people don't want to take sides. But they don't have to take sides, and they don't have to have me over. Just don't exclude the children.

Parked in my driveway, Anne leans over to hug me. "I'll call you tomorrow with the details," she says. "Last week of January, right?"

"You're not serious."

"I am. We're going to do this. We've talked about it for years. Let's just go do it."

"Okay." I'm excited.

Anne grins, and her deep dimples flash. "We're going to party. We're going to paaaarty," she chants, cranking her arms around the steering wheel and doing her best seated-hip-hop dance. For a white girl who's popped out three babies, she's still got some moves.

New Year's Eve day, I head to Sea-Tac Airport to collect my kids from their Alaska Airlines flight. Daniel sent the kids back a day early so he and Melinda could attend the gala New Year's Eve party tonight at his favorite golf country club in Palm Springs. I didn't have plans tonight, so getting the kids a day early is a treat.

I reach my house in time to see Anne backing out of my driveway. I brake, roll down my window. She does the same from her Audi wagon. "What are you doing?" I ask.

"Dropped something off on your doorstep. Check it out and give me a call."

"What?"

"You'll see." She beams, waves, and drives away.

I park in the garage and carry the kids' luggage into the house, William shouldering his backpack and Jessica's while Jessica pushes past, empty-handed, freeloader, intent on reaching the TV and her beloved Cartoon Network.

Inside the house, I put the suitcases in the laundry room while William goes to the front door, opens it, and brings a large white envelope to me. "Stellar Travel," he says, reading the blue logo in the upper left corner.

I open the envelope, and inside there are brochures and computer printouts listing flight itineraries and hotel confirmation.

"What is it, Mom?"

I'm smiling, shaking my head. She did it. Anne booked the trip for the last week of January. "My birthday present." I grin wider. Anne and I are going to *paaaarty.*

three

Last week of January, the kids are at Daniel's for the next five days and I'm at the airport, but Anne's not with me. She's on the phone.

"I'm sorry, I'm sorry," Anne repeats for what seems like the fiftieth time since calling me minutes ago. "God, Jack, I'm sorry to do this to you at the last moment. I feel horrible."

My stomach has bottomed out. My mouth is dry, and I can't seem to swallow to get it wet. "It's fine," I say, throat scratchy as reality sets in. Anne's not going to Hawaii. The trip's over before it ever began. "If Phil's sick, there's nothing you can do."

"He was up all night, Jack. Sicker than a dog. If he hadn't passed out, slumped on the toilet, I'd still go, but he's out cold—"

"I understand, Annie. I do." But he's faking it, I think. I know he's faking it. I just can't say so. If our friendship suffered over a Cocoa Puffs comment, it wouldn't benefit from a spousal slight.

Anne hesitates at the other end of the phone line. "You're going to still go, aren't you?"

I glance around the airport terminal, where I'm in line with people decked out in tropical threads even though it's a cold, wet, windy Seattle morning. "I don't know."

The disappointment is huge. Significant. "What am I going to do there on my own, Annie?" I'm already picturing the hotel pool, the young waiters in shorts, the couples and families having fun, and me by myself. And I've had enough of being by myself this year, thank you very much.

"What are you going to do there?" Anne's voice rises, incredulous. "You're going to soak up the sun, drink great blender drinks, ogle cute guys. Jack, it's Hawaii!" She takes a quick breath. "And need I remind you that the weather *sucks* here? It's supposed to rain all week. Again."

This is a good point, I think, nudging my suitcase forward with one toe as everyone in line slowly moves up. A really good point. We've had the wettest, coldest, yuckiest winter in years, and I don't even know what blue sky looks like anymore.

"And if you don't go, you'll end up running yourself ragged again this weekend. Let Daniel keep the kids and you get on the plane and just relax."

But I so don't want to go alone. I so don't want to do a girls' weekend without another girl. "What if we postpone the trip? Wait until you can go?"

"I wish we could, but it's a package vacation. The hotel is nonrefundable, and it's a swanky hotel, Jack, deluxe ocean-view room, right on the beach. Paradise guaranteed."

I say nothing, knuckles pressed to my mouth, and I'm scared. *Scared.* I haven't been anywhere in years on my own. Yes, there have been short business trips and buying trips, but I've always stayed at the corporate-style hotel, and there was a purpose to the trips. This is just vacation. I don't know *how* to vacation on my own. I'm an almost forty-year-old woman, mother of a nine-year-old and a five-year-old, and I don't want to go on a vacation if it's not with my kids or friends.

"Jack . . ." Anne's voice is gentle. "You'll have a good time. Just get on the plane. A driver's waiting in Honolulu. He'll have a sign. Go to the hotel, check in, put on your swimsuit, head to the pool, and drink a banana daiquiri for me."

I laugh even as I fight a faint sob. I *am* scared. That's exactly what's happening here. I'm scared of a long weekend on my own. I'm scared of being alone with my thoughts, scared that the exhaustion isn't exhaustion but maybe depression. And I don't need to go away to be depressed—I can be depressed right here at home.

"Call me once you get there," Anne says. "Give me all the details. Make me green with envy."

I look around the crowded airport, see far too many bright, smiley faces, and wonder how people can be so cheerful when it's still dark outside. I should have had coffee before I left. Maybe if I'd had coffee, I'd be happy now, too. "You're sure you can't join me later? Exchange your ticket . . . fly out as soon as Phil's better?"

She sighs. "I don't see it happening, Jack."

Because Philip never wanted her to go in the first place.

Because Philip still can't accept that Daniel and I aren't together anymore. Philip fought the divorce, tried to counsel us, tried to support us. And I respect him for trying to save our marriage; but Daniel and I didn't divorce after eleven years of marriage because Daniel likes blue and I like pink. We divorced because there were huge, painful, insurmountable differences between us, and our kids were caught in the middle, and the kids were suffering, too.

"You can do this, Jack."

"I know. I'll be fine." And to hell with all of them, I think, squaring my shoulders. I am going to go. And I am going to have a good time. There's no reason I can't go and have a good time.

Even if I will be celebrating forty on my own.

For a second I feel sick, heartsick, and disappointed. Not in Anne, but in me.

Forty and divorced and very much alone for this birthday. If there's a bright spot in this picture, it's that now I don't have to broadcast the fact that the eggs in my ovaries have begun their final decline.

"You're sure?" Anne's desperate for reassurance. Nic's the sensitive, creative one; Kristine's unbelievably competent; and Anne's the Earth Mother. Warm, funny, kind, and patient. Must be the Taurus in her.

"I'm sure," I say, feeling her worry, seeing it in her face. Anne has a great face, a heart-shaped face, strong eyebrows, and thick blond hair that she can't keep her hands out of. She's probably dragging her hand through her hair as we speak, creating wild, worried waves, while my hair is pulled back now in a sleek, hopefully sophisticated ponytail. My red hair's naturally curly, but I blow it out and then flat-iron it for good measure. And maybe that's the best way to describe us—by our hair. Anne's warm, relaxed, and outgoing, while I'm always trying for a cool and calm look I don't feel.

Anne and I met years ago at a hospital fund-raiser. Daniel was on the board—he's big money here in Seattle and sits on every important board—and Anne's surgeon husband, Philip, was speaking at the Virginia Mason hospital fund-raiser, and we were all seated together. Our husbands hit it off first—I actually thought Anne was a little too into the whole natural mother thing that night (she'd brought her baby to a black-tie event), but in the end, Anne and I became tight friends and our husbands ended up seeing each other only on the golf course.

But that's to be expected.

Men don't talk. Won't share feelings. Generally won't pick up the phone.

It's the women who knit families, communities, together. It's the women who sustain the ties. And it's not always easy, not a pressure women need, but there it is.

"I'll call you after I check in," I promise, tugging on my ponytail now, stomach in knots. "You go take care of Phil and the kids."

The phone call from Anne saying she can't make it is a very bad surprise.

Happily, my next surprise is good. I've been bumped to first class. I may be traveling alone, but I'm going in style.

I have an aisle seat in row three, and as I slide my carry-on bag beneath my seat, the flight attendant arrives to take my coat. "Would you like a glass of champagne or a mai tai?" she asks, slipping a hanger inside my coat.

Alcohol at eight in the morning? I'm about to say no and then immediately wonder, Why not? Why can't I have a glass of bubbly? This trip isn't a death sentence. I'm not going to jail. I'm going to Hawaii.

"Champagne, please," I answer, leaning back in my wide leather seat and crossing my legs. It was brutal rushing to the airport without coffee in the pitch black of morning—that early alarm is always so jarring—but now I'm beginning to feel human.

The flight attendant returns with my champagne in a real glass flute, and we chitchat for a moment about my trip. She wonders if I'm traveling on business, and when I tell her this is a vacation, she immediately wants to know who I'm going with.

"No one. I'm on my own," I answer, sipping madly at the champagne, trying to get it down before we push away from the gate.

"You're not married?" she asks.

"Divorced."

"Kids?"

"Two. Nine-year-old boy. Five-year-old girl."

"Where are they now?"

"With their dad."

The flight attendant nods, pats my shoulder, and moves on. I distract myself by watching passengers board, including a family of four trying to settle into their seats in first class.

The children are excited, and they're talking a mile a minute, asking endless questions as the mother tries to get them buckled into their seats. The father is already seated, and he's pulling out his newspapers, drinking his mai tai, while the mother crouches next to the kids, scrambling to get them organized, pulling out a variety of Beanie Babies, blankets, coloring books, and games.

The family reminds me of us before the divorce. The husband could be Daniel immersed in his *Wall Street Journal* with his cocktail at his elbow. The kids could be William and Jessica at a younger age. And I could be the flushed, frazzled woman kneeling in the aisle, tucking loose bits of hair behind my ear as I struggle to get everything taken care of before I'm forced to my own seat for takeoff.

I feel a little pang but quickly suppress it. No bad feelings, no sad feelings, no recriminations. I'm going to enjoy this trip. I really am.

It's not long now until the cabin door closes and the flight attendants walk down the aisle collecting glasses and napkins for takeoff. The jet has pushed back from the gate at Sea-Tac, and we lumber slowly toward the runway. I feel a few butterflies in my stomach. This is crazy. It's been so long since I went anywhere on my own. I'm scared and exhilarated and flying in first class. I should be happy. I want to be happy. But I also suddenly miss the kids.

The captain announces we're next in line for takeoff. I grip the armrest in anticipation. There's a momentary pause, and then we're moving, faster and faster, and the jet vibrates, a powerful shake as wheels rumble and engines roar, and we're hurtling toward the end of the runway and finally up, surging up.

We're off.

I'm off.

* * *

Six hours later, we touch down. The landing is so smooth that I barely feel a bump, and we deplane quickly, first class exiting first.

It's warm and humid as I leave the jet rampway and enter the Honolulu terminal. Greeters stand with strings of flower leis, and the heavy sweet fragrance is overpowering. And just as Anne said, in baggage claim a driver waits for me, sign in hand. Together we claim my luggage, and then it's off in the back of his white limousine for my hotel in downtown Waikiki.

I get a glimpse of the ocean as the limousine travels the freeway, and then again as we exit the freeway for town. I feel more butterflies in my middle. I'm on *holiday*. I'm feeling a little giddy. Maybe, just maybe, this could be fun.

The hotel is modern on the outside, sleek, with high white walls and little bits of roof visible. But once inside the foyer the hotel falls away, the walls disappearing, and the open-air lobby is all quiet native woods and elegance.

My room is ready, and it's enormous, not exactly a suite but luxuriously spacious, with a sitting area, a separate desk, and a Carrera marble bathroom the size of a studio apartment.

I change into a swimsuit and cover-up, pack my straw bag with suntan lotion, books, and sunglasses, and set off for the pool. I'm met poolside by a tan man in short navy shorts, a white polo T-shirt, and white tennis shoes.

He's the towel boy, but not exactly a boy, and he grabs an armful of blue-and-white-striped towels and then guides me around the pool until I find the right chair in the right amount of sun.

"This is good," I say, setting my straw bag next to a

pair of empty lounge chairs not far from the wall separating pool from beach.

"Excellent." He gets to work. *Pfoosh,* towel spread on lounger. *Pfft,* umbrella raised, providing perfect shade.

And then towel boy-man is stepping back, hands folded behind his back in an unnervingly militaryesque pose. "Is there anything else I can help you with?"

"No, thank you." And I settle into my lounger to see what the rest of the day brings.

It brings the cocktail waiter.

Keith, another very tan boy-man in shorts and a white short-sleeved polo, circles the pool, which has begun to get crowded as the afternoon progresses. But I'm not ready to order a drink yet.

Under the semishade of my umbrella, I study the pool area. Today seems heavy with men, mostly middle-aged men with rounded bellies, gray curling hair on their chests and in their goatees.

Watching the clusters of men, shiny with suntan oil, I wonder if this is my future.

No, I answer just as quickly. Absolutely not. *Can't be.*

I try to concentrate on my book, but I can't resist people watching, and I pick up bits and pieces of conversations. There's an elderly couple with European accents in front of me. Another older couple from Canada. A family of five from Switzerland, and I know the family's from Switzerland only because the woman—Marcelle? Marcella?—stops to speak to the European couple near me even as two slim Asian women are seated in lounge chairs one row behind me.

There are also Americans here; the women are poured into their suits, and a few are in remarkable shape. The men aren't very tanned, not like their wives, who've discovered Mystic Tan, and they're thick around the middle, with varying degrees of hair loss.

No one here to get excited about. Not that I'm planning on getting excited.

I try to lose myself in my book again, and I do for another hour until Keith comes by to see if I want that fun tropical drink yet.

I check my watch. Three o'clock. Why not? I had champagne at eight a.m., why can't I have a blended drink at three?

As Keith returns with my drink, I notice two men in dark blue blazers conferring in the corner beneath a tall palm tree. They have little earpieces and discreet name tags. I ask Keith about them.

"It's hotel security," he says, setting the drink on the table next to me.

This is definitely a posh place, a place Daniel would like because it's service oriented. "Can I sign the drink to my room?" I ask.

"It's already been taken care of."

"It has?"

"You have an admirer."

I immediately picture my fantasy guy, someone handsome, charming, someone like Pierce Brosnan, but Keith is gesturing across the pool at a cluster of three very sunburned men, bald or seriously balding, with big bellies.

Ah, my future. Right.

I don't very much like my future at all. "Will you please give my admirer my thanks?"

Keith nods. "He also wants to know, since he sees that you're alone, if you'd like to join him."

I glance at my admirer and his friends again (although I'm not exactly sure which is my actual admirer), and I'm sure they're nice people, very nice men, but I'm not sure I like even very nice men all that much anymore.

"Keith, could you let him know I've just arrived and still unwinding, but maybe I'll stop by later and say hello?"

But my admirer is more persistent than that.

An hour later, my admirer leaves his friends and approaches me, crouching next to me. "I'm Butch," he says, sticking out his hand.

"I'm Jacqueline," I say, pushing up my sunglasses and shaking his hand.

"And you're perfect, baby."

His enthusiasm is a little excessive, but I let it go. "Thanks for the piña colada. That was very nice of you."

"Can I get you another?"

Up close like this, Butch isn't unattractive. He actually has good bone structure and lively blue eyes, and he has a very nice voice. "No, thank you. I don't drink too much."

"But your body's perfect."

I flush. "Actually, I just don't like liquor that much."

Butch pats his round belly. "I wish I didn't. I wouldn't have this." He motions to the empty lounge chair next to me. "Mind if I sit down? The crouching thing's hard on the knees." He takes the lounge chair before I can say yes or no, and he's looking at me closely and shaking his head. "Man, you're beautiful, baby. Just gorgeous. So natural, too."

I think Butch means well, but he's making me really uncomfortable. "Here on vacation?" I ask, knowing it's inane, but it's a topic that has nothing to do with me and the way I look.

"Yeah. From Las Vegas. Originally San Diego. You?"

"Seattle."

"Seattle." He makes a face, runs his hand across his jaw, which hasn't been shaved in a day or two. "God, that place is miserable. Always rains there, doesn't it?"

"Sometimes." Butch isn't making a lot of points with me right now.

"Doesn't it have the highest suicide rate in the country?"

"Haven't heard that," I lie, hating when people knock Seattle right off the bat. Oh, the rain, the gray, blah blah blah. Well, it rains in Paris even more than Seattle, and you don't hear people taking about the suicide rate there, do you?

"What are you reading?" he asks, pushing my book up to see the cover.

"A Patterson novel," I say, letting him study the cover.

"Any good?"

"Very good."

He nods. "I don't read much anymore. Just don't have the time for it. Work's too intense. I'm a developer, build the really big hotels in Vegas, and business is booming. It's been like this for nearly ten years. You like Vegas?"

"Don't go that much," I answer honestly. With the

house in Palm Springs and Nic's place in Scottsdale, there was no reason to go to Las Vegas for sun; and since Daniel and I weren't gamblers, there was no point to go for the casinos, either.

"Vegas is all about food. Did you know that? People don't realize that Las Vegas draws some of the top chefs now. I could show you Vegas like you've never seen it."

I do like good food. All our friends in Seattle used to enjoy going out to eat, trying new restaurants, pretending we were foodies. It was one of the things we did together as couples and one of the things I miss most. "Sounds wonderful."

He looks around. "So you're not here with anyone?"

"Nope." He seems to be waiting for more information, and I reluctantly fill him in. "I was supposed to be here with a girlfriend, but at the last moment her husband got sick and couldn't watch the kids, so here I am."

"On your own."

"I don't mind," I say quickly, not liking the way he made being on my own sound.

"You're not married?"

"Was."

"Me, too." He smiles ruefully. "Four times. And after the last I've decided I'm not going to marry again. Just have girlfriends."

"Sounds sensible."

"And you? Married just that once?"

God, yes. How many husbands should someone my age have collected? "Just one."

"Kids?"

"Two."

"I don't have kids," Butch says, shaking his head. "Never wanted them before—"

"Your wives didn't?" I can't help interrupting.

"One and two might have, but three and four, no. Especially not after they had work done. They wouldn't want to risk ruining the surgeries."

"Ah."

Butch leans closer, still staring at me intently. "Have you had anything done? Well, not a boob job, obviously, but anything to your face?"

So he's saying I'm flat chested. Lovely. "No, it's all my own face. Wrinkles, scars, and all."

"I don't see any wrinkles, and you've got a great nose."

"Thanks."

"Are those your green eyes or contact lenses?"

"My eyes, but I think they're hazel."

"They look pretty green to me, baby."

For a moment there's silence, and I can feel Butch's gaze sliding over me, weighing, weighting, examining. He's an expert in female flesh, and as someone who obviously hasn't had a boob job, I'm beginning to feel a little lacking and decide it's time to go. I begin gathering my things, thrusting lotion, sunglasses, and book into my tote bag.

"Let me take you to dinner," Butch says. "There are some great places here in Honolulu. You just have to know where to find them."

I'm on my feet but can't find one sandal. "You're probably right."

"You haven't been out of the hotel yet, have you?"

Distractedly, I search for the missing sandal, wanting to escape, needing to escape, but trapped by the shoe situation. "Not yet, but will soon."

"I'd love to take you out tonight, show you some of my favorite places."

I tuck a strand of hair behind my ear, fight a wave of frustration. Where the hell did that shoe go? "That's a really nice offer, but I have plans for tonight."

He looks surprised. "You do?"

I nod and spy the sandal underneath Butch's lounge chair. Right underneath his butt. Right where I won't go. I want my shoe, but I'm not going to reach between his legs to get it. "Butch, can you grab my sandal? It's under your chair."

He huffs a little as he leans between his knees and retrieves my sandal. "I'll make you a deal. Your shoe for dinner."

"I've got five more pairs upstairs," I say, smiling a little and holding out my hand for my shoe. Having kids has helped me deal with persistent men. Maternal charm and teacherlike authority.

"This is an expensive shoe."

"*Butch.*"

Reluctantly he gives me the shoe. "A drink tomorrow?"

"That might work. We'll see."

In my room, the light on my phone is blinking and I check messages. Anne's called. I sit on my bed and quickly dial her number.

"So?" she demands the moment she hears my voice. "How's it going? Having fun?"

I picture Butch the developer, who just got me running

back to my room, but Anne doesn't need to know that. "Great. It's gorgeous. The hotel is gorgeous."

"Does the room have a good view?"

"Amazing. You can see everything, the whole beach, the hotels on the strip, and all of Diamond Head."

Anne sighs. "God, I'm jealous. It's horrible here. Cold and wet. The rain hasn't let up since you left."

That's encouraging. Suddenly four hundred a night doesn't sound so revolting. "Is Philip better?"

"Much." Anne sighs again. "He was better within a few hours of you leaving."

Not surprising. I'm sure Philip could have managed to deal with the kids if he'd wanted. At the very least, he could have tried to get a sitter and let Anne go on the trip with me.

"You could still jump on a plane," I say, thinking that a few days would be better than nothing. But Anne immediately makes a negative sound, and even though she's on the other end of the phone, I can see her shaking her head.

"I can't. I think Philip has passed the bug to the kids."

She's such a good mom, such a good wife.

And for a moment I think I should have stayed with Daniel, even though we weren't happy anymore. It would have been the better thing to do. Better for the kids, at least.

Which reminds me, I should call Daniel, let him know I've arrived. Not that he'll pick up my call. He'll see my number and let it go into voice mail.

"Have you met anyone interesting?" Anne asks.

I picture Butch again and his hairy belly and his

stories about Vegas restaurants and surgically enhanced women. "No."

"No one?"

"No one interesting."

Anne hesitates. "Maybe your standards are too high."

"Maybe I'm still not ready to date."

"Then don't date. Just have fun. You're in Hawaii, for heaven's sake!"

"I'm fine. Having fun."

"Okay then," Anne says, relenting. "Just promise me you're not sitting around the hotel room by yourself, because I'll feel terrible then."

"I'm not sitting around my room."

"And you're going to go out? Do things?"

"I'll do things."

"And take pictures? Because I want to see all the photos when you get back."

I roll my eyes. "Don't be such a mom."

"I am a mom."

I know. So am I. And maybe this is the problem.

four

~~~~~~~~~

After saying good-bye to Anne, I make that call to Daniel, and he doesn't answer, and I go to voice mail. I leave a brief message, letting him know I've arrived safely and to give the kids my love. I don't mention that Anne hasn't come. I don't know why. Is it because I don't want him to worry—or I don't want his censure? Even though we've been divorced a year, I still feel the bonds of marriage—responsibility—duty. I still hear his voice in my head, still anticipate his criticism and disappointment.

Isn't that sad? He was my husband for nearly twelve years, in my life for fifteen, and all I can feel is failure.

Failure.

It doesn't matter that I did my best, tried so hard, nurtured us. It doesn't matter, when the divorce negates everything we were . . . everything we believed.

I don't like the restlessness inside me, don't want to be alone with thoughts like these, so I shower, change, blow-dry my hair, and dress in a slim black skirt and a simple black blouse that ties at my waist. I apply a little makeup, add gold bangles to my wrist, then leave my room in search of a glass of wine and maybe dinner.

The concierge sends me to the hotel's restaurant, an elegant dining room fronting the ocean, and I'm seated just as the sun begins to set.

Catamarans pull from the shore and surfers walk away from the beach, boards on their shoulders and heads, even as the fading sun streaks the horizon purple and reddish gold.

I see a couple standing on the beach, arms around each other, watching the sunset. Their heads are tipped close together, and as the sun sinks, disappearing into the sea, he turns and kisses her. I feel a pang—deep, sharp, hard. What did I do wrong? Where did I lose Daniel?

Blinking back tears, I smile up at the waiter as my first course is served.

"Having a good time?" he asks, putting the crab cakes in front of me.

I nod, reach up, wipe away a tear. "Yes."

"Beautiful sunset."

"Gorgeous."

"Is there anything else I can get you?"

I shake my head. "No. This is perfect."

But as he moves away, I don't feel perfect, don't feel even close to perfect. There's so much about marriage I miss. So much about the life I knew, the life I loved. If I hadn't found those e-mails between Daniel and Melinda, would we still be married today? If I hadn't known he'd been unfaithful, would our lives be the same?

As my main course is served, night has fallen and it's darker. Far offshore I can see the moving lights of freighters and cruise ships sailing past.

The rising moon dances on the water, and the voices of the other diners blend with the dull roar of the ocean, the break of waves against sand, the music coming from the hotel bar next door.

The wind kicks up and the breeze makes the torches whisper and flame, each torch blowing, flickering in a different direction; light plays everywhere, on the dinner tables, on the beach, on the water.

I return to my room. It's only eight here, but it's eleven at home. I'm tired, exhausted, but can't seem to fall asleep. Too many thoughts. Too many emotions. Too much on my mind.

After turning the light back on, I grab the TV remote and flick through the pay-per-view movies until I find something light, easy to watch, a film for the preteen set. The romantic comedy is predictable and sweet, like pink cotton candy, and as soon as it ends I fall asleep because I don't want to think, and right now I think I'd love to be loved again someday.

I wake up close to five, and it's pitch dark out. I splash water on my face, put on my running shoes. I don't know my way around, but I figure if I stick to the main road, which seems to be Kalakaua, I won't get lost.

There are a few other early morning runners like me, people who haven't adjusted to the time change, and I run until the designer shops and storefronts disappear and the street curves along a park and gives unobstructed views of the ocean. When the street begins to creep up-hill, I stop, stretch, and jog slowly back.

It's hot out and humid. Far more humid than I'm used

to in Seattle, and I'm sweating profusely as I approach the hotel. I grew up in Spokane, where summers are long and hot, but I've been on the other side of the mountains far too long and can barely tolerate the heat anymore.

The sun rises as I reach the Halekulani, the sky the palest shade of lavender gray. In front of my hotel tower, I'm sweating and walking in circles, waiting for the elevator.

As I'm walking, hands on hips, feet appear in my peripheral vision. Looking up, I see Butch.

"I've been waiting for you," he says.

I smile, drag an arm across my damp brow. "Hope you didn't have to wait long."

"I saw you go."

"So what are you doing today?" I ask, wiping sweat on the back of my shorts.

"Hoping I can convince you to go do something with me." His eyes are narrowed, and he's inspecting me again, looking me up and down. "God, you're perfect, baby. Just look at you. I haven't seen a woman this natural in . . . well . . . ever."

"I should go shower."

"How about a helicopter tour later?"

"I don't think so."

"A dinner cruise?"

"Butch."

"What, baby?"

"I thought we were just going to have a drink by the pool. Keep it low-key. I'm here to relax, take it easy this week."

"Baby, I just want you happy."

"I'll be happy if you don't pressure me."

He raises his hands. "No pressure. Just a drink and sun and fun."

The elevator arrives, and I get in and think I could strangle Anne right now. She should be here, dealing with Butch. She should be fighting off his moves, not me.

At the pool, I try to get into my book before I can be disturbed. I'm not going to look up, I vow, not going to make eye contact.

Look bitchy, I tell myself, look mean and unapproachable.

But Butch must like mean and unapproachable because he and his cronies are spreading their towels and magazines and bottles of suntan lotion on lounge chairs all around me.

I smile politely at Butch before returning my attention to my book, thinking maybe, just maybe, I can convince him to leave me alone if I don't respond to him.

I didn't come to Hawaii to meet a man. This was a girls' escape. Anne and I were going to chill. Relax. Celebrate my (ugh) birthday.

We were going to lie in the sun and read all the novels we've been collecting by our beds, get massages, facials, enjoy glasses of wine over late dinners. It was going to be fun, but girls' fun, and now without Anne I'm struggling to redefine that fun.

I'm staying at a luxe hotel filled with luxe people, and this, I think, turning a page in my book, is what my world has become—a lifestyle. Polished, expensive people who love polished, expensive things.

Nothing rough or rustic anymore.

Nothing unplanned, unexpected, unpalatable. Only the best money can buy.

Including my divorce.

I go to lunch and return to find that Butch has pulled his lounge chair even closer to mine. I pretend not to notice and immediately settle back down with my book, closing my eyes when I sense Butch looking at me.

I've now spent the better part of the last hour with my eyes closed so I don't have to make conversation, but Butch and his buddies are drinking and their voices just keep getting louder with every cocktail.

This is so not the holiday I imagined.

And I'm contemplating how to escape Butch and the claustrophobic atmosphere here at the pool when Marcelle, the French-Swiss woman who has climbed in and out of the pool in her diamonds with her fabulous figure, shouts, "Thanks, Kai, for the surf lesson. That was fabulous."

Marcelle went surfing?

I open an eye, peer in Marcelle's direction (Butch is always looking in her direction), and see her patting herself dry next to her lounge chair as she says good-bye to someone who is far more interesting than anyone else here at the pool.

He's young, and virtually naked, except for a plain white towel wrapped around his very narrow, muscular waist.

The rest of him is bare. And tan. Darkly tan. His hair is dark, wet, combed sleekly back from his face. And he has a really nice face, too.

I watch as he walks around the pool toward my lounge chair, and I sit up higher to get a better look as he nears me.

He must feel me staring because he turns his head and glances in my direction, and my eyes lock with his.

Wow.

Handsome isn't even the half of it.

I swallow hard. I should look away. I must look away. I can't.

He's almost past now, he's going to be leaving the pool, returning to wherever he came from, and I sit all the way up, wrap an arm around my knees. "You teach surfing," I say just as he passes in front of my chair.

He—this surfer, Kai—pauses and turns to look back at me. The corner of his mouth curves, rises. "Yeah."

I feel everything go fizzy inside me, and I look up into his eyes. They're blue, very, very blue. And his face with its square jaw and strong cheekbones is very, very tan. I think he's one of the most beautiful men I've ever seen.

"Interested in surfing?" he asks, taking a step back toward me even as he unwraps his white towel, revealing red board shorts, washboard abs, and a tattoo between his navel and shorts that makes me want to lean closer to get a better look. Is that a dog inked on his flat belly? Or something else?

I realize I'm staring dangerously close to his crotch and look up abruptly, straight into his eyes, and he's rewrapping his towel tighter around his waist. "No."

"Why not?"

"I don't know."

Dimly I think Butch is saying something to me, but I

haven't a clue what. I can't focus on anything but all the hard muscle and very tan skin just inches from my eyes. Nervously I reach for my piña colada, which has been sitting next to my chair melting for the past hour, and take a watery sip.

"Have you ever tried to surf?" surfer Kai asks.

I shake my head and put my glass back down. "No. I— No. Not the surfer type," I say, aware that Butch and his friends are listening.

"Why not?"

"Much too hard."

"Surfing's easy."

"For athletic people, maybe."

Kai smiles. "You're athletic." His blue gaze settles on me, a slow, provocative inspection that makes me blush and gets Butch shifting noisily on his lounge chair.

"I used to surf," Butch says, swinging his legs to the ground and flexing a little. "Down in San Diego. Del Mar. You know where that is?"

"I know the area," Kai answers, his gaze leaving me briefly, to take in Butch, before returning to me. "What's your name?"

"Jacqueline."

"Jacqueline," he repeats, then stretches out his hand. "Kai."

"Kai as in sky?" I have to lean forward to take his hand.

"Kai as in sky, but spelled a-i."

"Ah."

His hand closes around mine, and his skin is warm, his grip firm. I feel my pulse leap.

"Sure you don't want to try?" he asks, releasing my hand. "I guarantee I can get you up. Or your money back."

My heart's hammering, and it has nothing to do with surf lessons. "I'm sure."

"Okay." He nods, shrugs, smiles that fleeting mysterious smile. "But if you ever change your mind, find me."

Kai's gone only five, ten minutes before I feel absolute panic set in.

Don't leave me here, I think. He's the first interesting person I've seen since I arrived, and I hated watching him go, but I force myself to read. Or at least I try to read. But I can't get into the story, not when everything feels so tight and hard inside of me. It's as if I've been shot full of anxiety or adrenaline. I'm restless. Reckless. *Hungry.*

I suddenly want to go. Do. Explore.

But explore what? Do what? I haven't a clue, but I'm suddenly rushing, jamming my feet into my sandals and wrapping my sarong around my waist.

Butch sits up. "Hey, baby, where are you going?"

"Out," I say. I can't seriously be chasing after Kai. That would be stupid.

"Want company?" he offers, rising.

"No, no." And I'm off, because chasing after Kai is exactly what I'm doing.

And if I find him? I wonder as my feet and sandals sink into warm, soft sand. What then? What will I say? What do I want?

For a moment I can't move. I feel a sense of helplessness, almost hopelessness, and then I shake it off. I'm not going to feel that way. I'm thirty-nine. An adult. A woman. I can do what I want.

Can't I?

To the left of the hotel, I see a shaded beach services desk with a bright blue awning advertising surf lessons. I stop at the desk and ask about the lessons offered, and the guy behind the desk, wearing a sleek silver name tag ("Tommy") is handsome, muscular, and tan, *and* has an English accent.

The effect, I think, looking at him yet again, is disgustingly, disarmingly attractive. "You're from the U.K.?"

"Leeds," he answers.

"I didn't know Leeds was a surfing hot spot."

Tommy laughs. "Not the best surf conditions, no." He points to the rate sheet. "Have anything in mind, love? Private, semiprivate, group lessons?"

I stare blindly at the rate sheet, wishing Kai would appear and save me from this because I don't want a surf lesson at all. I just want to talk to him again. I want to feel whatever it is I felt at the pool, and what I felt was warm and hopeful and dizzying.

I liked the dizzying part immensely.

"Um, private?" I say, because I can't think what else to tell him when I'm trying so hard to find a way to ask about Kai.

He taps his pen at the rate sheet. "It'll be seventy for an hour. Is there a particular instructor in mind?"

"No."

"Then I'll sign you up with Kent. He's free—"

"Actually, I did meet someone." I'm blushing. It's so immature, and I feel so immature. But there you have it.

He waits, his expression betraying nothing, yet I think I can't be the only woman who stumbles to the desk in search of some bronzed, handsome surf god. "Kai," I whisper, willing my voice to be stronger. "His name is Kai."

Tommy from Leeds doesn't openly crack a smile, but there's a glimmer of something in his eyes. "Right. Kai." Tommy doesn't look surprised that I've mentioned Kai, and he peruses the schedule. "Well, your friend Kai's all booked for the rest of the day. Let me see how tomorrow looks." He turns a page, studies the next schedule. "Ah, Kai's a popular one—he's an elegant surfer, you see, has class—and he's booked all day tomorrow, too. Anyone else you have in mind, love?"

No. Just Kai.

I shake my head, and I must look pitiful because charming Tommy from Leeds makes little clucking sounds.

"If I weren't busy, I'd take you out myself."

My blush returns, deepening. I now feel embarrassed as well as ridiculous. "It's okay. I was more curious than anything. Thanks."

As I start to turn away, Tommy puts out his hand. "What's your name, love?"

Love. Hmmm. So long since I felt like anyone's love. "Jackie. Jacqueline."

"Right. I'll tell Kai you stopped by, Jacqueline."

I'm blushing more furiously, shaking my head. I feel awash in emotions, a return to geeky adolescence. "Don't tell him. I don't want to bother him."

"It's not a bother, Jackie."

I shake my head harder, feel hot from my chin to my forehead, hot everywhere the sun touches me. "Really. It's okay." And before I can dig myself into a deeper, more embarrassing hole, I hurry away, on down the beach, in the opposite direction of my hotel. Because Butch is waiting at the hotel, and I can't handle Butch. Not now. Not when I feel like this. Not when I want something so bad and I've no idea what it is.

I walk and walk, all the way down the beach until the sand runs out and there's a seawall and what looks like a minicoliseum—although I haven't a clue what that is—and then I turn around and slowly start back even as the dull panic returns.

In forty-eight hours I go back to Seattle. In just two days I go back to my life, yet there's all the things I've never done. All the things I wish I'd done.

The catamaran sunset cruise.

The surf lesson.

Not to mention the sexy young surf instructor . . .

The sun's dropping in the sky. I must have walked for nearly an hour, and I'm tired. And hot. And thirsty.

Not far from my hotel I hear music, and I stop at one of the outdoor restaurants on the beach. I recognize the name of it; Butch has been talking about it. Duke's.

I stand at the edge of Duke's patio to check out the live band playing. The patio is crowded with tables, and the tables are all full. And with the sun long and warm, casting bright gold rays on everyone and everything, I feel so apart. So alone.

I watch everyone sitting there, girls, guys, groups sprawled everywhere, and they're golden in the warm, late afternoon sun. The girls have such long, easy hair, straight, shimmering in the sun, flat stomachs untouched by age or childbirth.

I hitch my sarong higher on my waist, hiding my post-baby tummy, which is flattish when I stand but has a roll when I sit—it's a tummy that will never be the same short of surgery—and I feel old. I don't remember growing old. I don't remember changing. Aging.

I do remember the wedding vows, the first house, the first baby. I remember waking up at night every two hours, I remember walking with a colicky, screaming newborn when I couldn't put another foot in front of the other. I remember trying to get infant cereal in my stubborn infant's mouth. I remember diaper rashes and ointment, teething, first teetering steps, and potty training. I remember the tearful first days of preschool and night terrors and the artwork brought home that I taped to the refrigerator. I remember the wet kisses, the baby hugs, the tantrums in the middle of the grocery store.

I remember loving my husband and children. I remember loving them, and somewhere I must have stopped loving me—because I look at these people on the patio, in the sun, and I don't feel anything like them anymore. Or if I ever did.

And standing there at Duke's, I want it all back. The me that doesn't exist anymore, the me that doesn't laugh as much or know how to sit back in a chair and just relax.

I want to smile. I want to laugh. I want to stop looking at my watch and worrying about the time. Worrying about losing time. Worrying about not getting enough done and still being overwhelmed.

I have worked so hard my entire life, so why do I feel as if there's always so much more to do, as if what I've done is never good enough?

How does one find peace?

Satisfaction?

Contentment?

How does one stop pushing so hard, because what is on the other side of achievement? What is success if it means nothing? What do I want that I don't already have?

And I know that answer, it's the same one that let me walk away from Daniel when the marriage turned sour.

I want more. More happiness. More love. More laughter. More sex. More of everything.

I want to be a lover and a mother. Sexy, not just maternal. I want to be everything I know I am.

Everything I've never let myself be.

I'm just about to leave when a group of guys enter Duke's, and the guys are gorgeous. Mind-blowingly gorgeous. All *GQ* models or something equally otherworldly and so not part of my Seattle world, where we're attractive but settled, solid, dependable, and rapidly reaching forty and above.

These guys are nowhere near forty and appear to be from Beautiful Planet, and I wonder if they're here for a bachelor's party. You know, maybe one last fling of the young and free before the marriage noose tightens.

They settle into chairs, stretch out long legs, and the late afternoon sun plays gold havoc on the tops of their heads. As the young, pretty cocktail waitress in a tight white top and little shorts hurries over, I know I was never that young or beautiful. I was pretty, maybe am still pretty, but the pretty I am now is settled. Rooted. And that should be okay, right?

But here on the beach at the edge of Duke's patio, I want something that isn't settled, predetermined, predefined. I want new. And interesting. I want different and surprising.

Anne really should have come on this vacation with me. Anne would have saved me from thoughts like these.

One minute I'm watching the beautiful people, and the next minute I realize one of the beautiful people is watching me.

Shirtless. Tan. Muscular. Handsome. Oh, so very handsome.

It's *Kai*. Our eyes lock, and one of his eyebrows lifts. Flustered, I look away.

I was staring, openly staring. Flushing, I'm not sure what to do with myself. There's nothing wrong with looking at a man, but Kai is young, and he must think I'm some lecherous old woman chasing him down the beach, drooling over him.

I was drooling a little, but that's hardly the point.

One of the waitresses stops in front of me. "Would you like a table, hon? I've got one opening up. I can save it for you."

"No. Thank you. I was just . . . uh, people watching."

She winks at me. "Good place to do it." And she turns and walks away.

I look up again and catch Kai's eye once more. He's got his beer now, and he's leaning back in his chair, staring at me, the corner of his mouth slightly tilted.

As I look at him, broad shouldered, bare chested, muscles hard and cut, with a tattoo around his thick right bicep, I think I've lost my mind. I've chased a sexy surfer down the beach, cornered him at Duke's. What the hell am I thinking?

But Kai's staring pointedly at me, and I don't know where to look, what to do. I try to look away but can't. His expression is fixed, intent, intense, and for someone so beautiful, he's very direct. Bold.

Kai wiggles a finger, signals to me, beckoning me over.

Right. Like I'm going to saunter over to a crowd of twenty-something-year-old men to see what gorgeous Kai has to say. Don't think so. I shake my head, muster a faint smile.

His smile is white and warm, and the warmth burrows all the way into me.

Kai says something to them, rises, his abdomen contracts, muscle after muscle knotting until his stomach is one of those washboards of definition. He has that other tattoo lower on his belly, sandwiched between shorts and navel, the one that looks like a growling bulldog.

He's left the table and is walking toward me. My breath catches in my throat, and I don't know what to do. I pull my sarong tighter, making sure the fabric is wrapped securely around my waist.

"Hey, girl," Kai says, standing before me. The sun is dropping in the sky and slanting long across the ocean, the reddish gold rays nearly blinding.

I lift a hand to shadow my eyes. "Hi."

"Looking for me?" he asks, and I blush and sputter and shake my head.

"No."

He laughs, and it's warm and husky, just like his smile. The man's gorgeous and confident, possibly arrogant, but he's also intriguing. "Just out for a walk," I say.

"Did you see anything interesting?"

"Just this place. Duke's."

"Quite a scene," he says.

"Makes me feel really old."

His grin makes his eyes even bluer. "You're not old."

"I'm definitely a lot older than you."

He shrugs. "Why does age matter?"

Suddenly I see what I've never seen before, and it's so clear that it makes me want to scream.

I've grown old waiting for life and happiness to find me.

I thought marriage and babies, keeping house and decorating the vacation home, would fulfill me. And maybe it did, for a while.

But the newness wore off, and even though I love my children more than life itself, they're going to grow up and go. They're going to become adults and move away. And then what?

What happens to the me that's more mother than woman? What happens to the female in me?

I don't have an answer for that, and I turn away, out toward the beach where catamarans are anchored and filling with tourists with tickets for the last sail of the day, the sunset cruise.

"Have you ever been on one of those?" I point to the nearest sleek boat.

"All the time. I used to work on the *Outrigger* part-time."

"Are they fast?"

"Can be, if you catch a good wind. You haven't been out yet?"

I shake my head.

"What have you done here?" Kai asks.

I shake my head again. "Not much of anything."

"Why not?"

"I've been here on my own."

"So that fat hairy guy back by the pool isn't your husband?"

I laugh at Kai's description of Butch. "Not my husband. No. I came on my own."

"Left your husband home?"

I slant him a sideways glance. "I don't have a husband. I'm divorced." I take a breath, get the rest of the words out quickly. "And I have two kids. A nine-year-old boy and a five-year-old girl."

"Where are they now?"

"With their dad."

Kai nods and tips his head, looks long and consideringly at me. "Miss them?"

And his question nearly undoes me. A huge lump fills my throat. Tears start to my eyes, and I have to turn away, stare out at the water, and I know why I haven't left the Halekulani pool until now. It's because there are kids all over the beach, playing in the sand, jumping waves in the surf, and I'm not very good watching other people's kids while missing mine. And I miss mine. "Tremendously."

"You want to go for a sail, then? I can probably get us on the *Outrigger* or the *Mai Tai*. I have friends that work on both."

I hesitate.

"Or are you anxious to get back to the hotel?" Kai asks.

I grimace. "No. And I'm sure Butch—"

"Butch?"

"The hairy old guy from the pool—would like to spend the evening with me, but it's not going to happen."

"What will happen?"

"I'll probably go up to my room and watch another expensive pay-per-view movie."

"So let's go for a sail."

"Now?"

"Now."

"But I don't have a wallet with me."

"You don't need a wallet. If they've got space, they'll let us on for free."

"I can pay—"

"No, no. They're friends. We look out for each other." And as he says "No, no," his hands go out, a casual gesture but one that speaks volumes. He's so relaxed, so comfortable in his own skin. And there's quite a bit of skin—tan, taut, sleek skin—and I feel something jump inside me. Desire as well as despair. I have become so much older than I ever hoped to be. And I'm not talking about the outside or chronological age, but the inside me, the one that feels weary and practical and resigned.

I don't want to be resigned to life. Don't want to blindly accept fate. There's still this wild girl inside of me that craves change and needs risk and wants everything. But how does one get everything without losing what one already has?

"Okay," I say, my insides nervous as hell. "Let's go."

five

~~~~~~~~~

Kai whistles to his friends at the table, signals that he's taking off with me, and I see the guys he was sitting with smile. I look away, feeling vaguely uncomfortable. How often does Kai do this sort of thing? Adopt a woman? Take a lonely tourist under his wing?

But I don't ask, and we walk down the beach to the catamarans. Kai talks to the captain of one, who gives us the go-ahead to board.

The sky behind the boat is bright yellow deepening to a fiery orange red. It's going to be another dramatic sunset.

One of the *Outrigger*'s crew reaches down and pulls me up the stairs, and Kai follows behind.

Most of the seats are taken, so we stand at the side of the catamaran, half leaning against the lightweight railing.

As the boat pulls out, one of the ship's hands blows a conch shell, a bellow of sound. Halfway out in the bay, the sails are loosened, snap up, and the wind catches us, sending us swiftly on our way.

My hair is blowing in every direction, and the water

sprays. Laughing, I try to catch my hair in one hand, wishing now I had a hair elastic or something to keep it from whipping every which way.

Kai leans forward to take the two mai tai cocktails from a crew member who is filling drink orders, and I take my pinkish punch and clink plastic tumblers with Kai. "To adventure," I say, smiling nervously.

One of his eyebrows lifts as he taps his cup against mine. "To adventure."

We drink and turn to watch the sun drop lower, the sky shades of orange, violet, and red. "So where are you from, Jacqueline?"

His question, lazily put, makes me smile. I can't help remembering the commercial on TV, the one where the woman is getting some serious one-on-one instruction from two very yummy surf instructors while the husband flounders in the distance without any surf help.

"I've heard all about guys like you," I say, and I think it comes out far more prudish than I like.

He's not worried. "And what have you heard?"

"That beach boys are playboys."

His eyebrows rise.

I swallow, compelled to continue. "That girls throw themselves at you."

He's still looking at me, but he's smiling faintly. He's amused. And probably pleased.

Men are such bastards. Especially the young, gorgeous ones.

The corners of his mouth curve upward. "You're getting all worked up."

I glare at him. He's right. I am. Why? Why do I care

that men can sleep with anyone and everyone and it's perfectly acceptable in our culture—while women are supposed to stay home and keep the house tidy and a warm fire burning in the hearth?

"All I did was ask where you're from," he adds, lifting his plastic tumbler and looking at me. He's making fun of me. Me and my worry. Me and my anxiety. Me and my guilt.

Is every woman my age as tied up in knots as I am?

And I can't help thinking of the things I do well and the things I do badly and the consequences. Because there are always consequences.

"Seattle," I answer now, making a small face. "And I'm sorry . . ." My voice drifts off, and I don't know what to say, what I was going to say. He just waits, not rushing in to fill the silence. "It's been a hard year," I conclude.

His jaw shifts, eyes narrowing. He has blue eyes, intensely blue, and I have to look down, look away, because I'm feeling all the crazy things I didn't think I knew how to feel anymore.

Hope.

Desire.

Desire.

I exhale slowly and look up at him, thinking maybe the blue eyes and the attraction is all a trick of my imagination. He's still looking at me, and the effect is the same.

Me, girl.

You, boy.

I look down again, drag my finger through the moisture

beading the cup. What were we talking about, anyway? Where's my brain?

God, I feel like I'm turning into a teenage boy. I'm thinking of things lusty and lustful, and instead of shame, I feel . . . strong.

"Where are you from?" I ask, rubbing more moisture from the outside of the cup, the tip of my finger going back and forth, over and over on the same cold wet spot. God, I'm nervous. And excited. And nervous.

He's too young.

He's too young.

He's waaaay too young, and I'm too old. And I'm a mother. I have children. Little girl and little boy. I can't . . . can't—what?

Be attracted to a man?

I'd like to tell myself he's not a man, but when I look up at him and he's looking back—all blue eyes in sun-tanned face, all high, hard cheekbones and perfect jaw with lips that belong on a movie star hunk instead of a surf instructor—I know he's not a kid. He's a man.

And that's why I'm nervous. Because he's a very sexual man, and every time I look at him, I think—feel—sex. And it's been forever since I thought about sex. Forever since I felt sexual.

"Florida," Kai answers. "Fort Lauderdale."

"What are you doing here?"

"Having a life."

"You couldn't do that in Florida?"

"No."

"Why not?"

He shrugs. "People love their things too much."

I'm suddenly aware of the hulking five-star hotel we've just left behind with its long rectangular pool that sparkles in the perfect tropical sunshine, the soft swish and sway of palm trees, and the discreet cocktail service provided by charming, uniformed cabana boys. "What's wrong with things?"

"Nothing if you don't mind being owned by them."

I say nothing, feeling a little defensive. This has been an ungodly expensive vacation here, and so far it hasn't necessarily been all that much fun, and I don't need some Florida beach bum telling me what's what. "I like being able to afford to travel."

"Yes indeed."

He sounds serious, yet there's a glint to his eyes, and I know he's not agreeing with me at all.

"Poverty is overrated," I say with great dignity, grateful for once that I know something about something. I do remember what it was like in those early years when Daniel and I struggled with all those student loans, the car payments, the first mortgage that ate nearly every penny we earned. We both worked so hard those first few years we were married, and then William came and I stopped working for a few years to stay home with him. Then baby Jessica came, and it was William and Jessie and me killing time every day until Daddy came home from work.

And then I'd thrust the kids at him and want to escape out on my own. Of course, Daniel—even though he loved the kids—didn't want them shoved on him. I couldn't help it. Two kids under five and my mind going crazy, wanting something to think about other than chicken nuggets, Barney the purple dinosaur, and wiping little toddler bottoms. And then Daniel suggests that maybe we might want another.

Another what? Another lobotomy or a breakdown?

I force my mind away from the past and all that I can't change. Futility is so depressing. "When's the last time you went home?" I ask instead.

Kai shrugs. "Couple years."

"Years?"

"I don't go back to the mainland. I live here."

"Yes, but . . ." My voice trails off, and I try to imagine living in a place this small, this isolated, this . . . casual. No four seasons. No real city life. No professional sports. "You don't get bored?"

"Bored in Hawaii?" Kai sounds incredulous. "I'm never bored here. I get bored on the mainland, but here, everyone's in a good mood. Everyone comes to Hawaii for a good time. You don't come here unless you want to have fun. Rich women come, poor women who've saved and scraped, and everyone wants the same thing—to escape. To relax. To feel good."

Yes, but I haven't relaxed yet. This hasn't been an escape, and I still very much want to feel good.

"Have you thought more about the surf lesson?" he asks. "Free. No strings attached. You'll have fun."

The idea of me actually surfing is laughable. Me in my expensive Lycra Miracle suit that hugs the tummy and slims the waist and lifts the fanny, surfing? Right. "You mean, you'll find it funny. I could never surf— couldn't get up—"

"I get everyone up." Kai wasn't bragging. It was just a statement of fact. "But that's what surf instructors are paid to do. We're paid to get you up, make sure you have a good time. It's part of the surf school guarantee."

Part of me is so intrigued, part of me would love to do something different—daring—would love to go home and feel that I've had a real adventure. Maybe if Kai were closer to my age, and less gorgeous, and less sexy and interesting, I could do it. Try it. But I don't want to look more foolish than I am. Than I have.

I clutch my mai tai and feel my stomach free-fall and sink, just as the sun sinks every night into the dark blue sea. "I can't." My voice is a whisper, and it's fear I feel clawing inside me. Fear and fear and fear. Everything's changed in the past year and a half. I've changed. I'm not Daniel's wife. I'm a single mom. I don't know what that means, though. I don't really know who I am.

But Kai won't let it go. "Why?" he asks, and he leans close, close enough that I can see the texture of his beard, the curve of cheekbone beneath tanned skin, the translucent edge of his front tooth.

"I'd fall," I blurt. I've had just enough to drink—one mai tai and half of a second—and my head feels a trifle woozy. I flex my fingers, testing them, and even they feel stiff. But it's also good. It's been a long time since I felt like this—almost like a teenager, not quite in control of all my faculties. "I'd look like an idiot."

"Why are you so hard on yourself?"

His question silences me. I bite my lower lip, feel the air in my chest constrict. I'm close to tears, and I don't even know why.

"You're beautiful, Jackie. Smart, interesting, fun. Why beat yourself up?"

The tears are there behind my eyes, and I concentrate on the horizon to hold them back. "Because it's what we women do after we hit a certain age." I'm trying to be funny, but it doesn't sound funny at all. "We become specialists in self-ridicule."

"Why?"

I turn, glance at him. There's curiosity in his blue eyes, but also concern. "I don't know if it's life, motherhood, or marriage, but women start giving pieces of themselves up. Little by little, year after year, and then one day you wake up and you're not even there anymore. All the things that made you fun and fiery and hopeful . . . are gone."

My eyes prickle and burn, and it's a battle to keep them dry. I blink, take a quick breath, force a smile. "This wasn't who I was fifteen years ago. I used to live overseas. I had my own place in Paris. Had an apartment in Italy. I was so adventurous. Took so many risks. And yet now I'm . . ." And my voice fades because I can't say it, can't admit that I'm like Casper the Friendly Ghost. I'm gone. I'm not even there anymore.

He doesn't speak and I don't try, and I'm feeling hot and miserable for saying so much. I shouldn't say these things, not to a man, not to a younger, fun-loving man. God, I wish I weren't so intense, so emotional, so full of thoughts and regrets.

The regrets will bury me someday.

"How long have you been divorced?" Kai asks after a moment as the catamaran lifts and drops on a wave, water splashing everywhere.

"A year," I answer. "A year this week."

"You're dating?"

"A little. I do get asked out, but it's different."

"You don't sound like you're having fun."

"I don't find dating at my age . . . fun."

"Your age." Kai laughs softly, runs a hand through his dark hair, his blue eyes creased in his very handsome, very tan face. "That's funny."

"What's funny?"

"You're very hung up on age."

"Most women my—" I break off, flushing.

"Your age?" he guesses, nearly downing the rest of his cocktail. "Are you afraid if you don't keep reminding me of your age that I might, what? Come on to you?"

I don't answer because he's right. That's exactly what I'm afraid of.

Almost as afraid that he won't hit on me.

After the cocktail cruise ends, we stand on the beach for a moment. I'm trying to find a way to say good-bye but the words don't come, not easily or gracefully. "I should go," I say, yet even I hear the reluctance in my voice.

"Your friends are probably waiting for you," he agrees.

"Friends?"

"Buzz."

I grin. "Butch." My smile fades a little. "Not that I'm eager to see him again."

Kai laughs. "He's loaded. Have you seen the diamond rings that guy's wearing?"

"Yes. But it's a little too bling-bling for me."

"You don't like bling?"

"I live in Seattle, Kai. We're not very bling-blingy."

"What are you into in Seattle?"

"Rain." My answer makes him laugh, and I add, "Coffee. Sports. Labradors. I swear, everyone has a blond Lab where I live."

"If you're not in a hurry to get back, let's get another drink."

I've probably had more to drink than I need, but I nod, because I'm not ready for the night to end. We head down the beach a little, cut through the sand up to the back of a pink hotel, and then in through the wrought-iron gate to the outdoor beach bar.

"I recognize this hotel," I say, dropping into a seat at the small round table. "It's about the only thing I recognize from my first trip here."

"When was that?"

I shoot Kai a side glance. "Probably the year you were born."

"That's right. You're closing in on fifty."

I laugh, amused that he's playing me at my own game. "Sixty, actually."

"So what was it like here in the Dark Ages?"

"Dark. They didn't have many buildings then. And just a few streetcars. Lots of horses, of course. Tourists found it hard to get around."

He smiles and leans forward and touches my cheek briefly with the backs of his fingers. "You're beautiful, Jackie. Film star beautiful—"

I roll my eyes. "Please."

"It's true." He nods for emphasis. "And you know who you look like? Debra Messing. From *Will and Grace*."

I shake my head, but of course I'm secretly, deeply

flattered. Debra Messing is gorgeous. "Thanks, but we're on two different galaxies, Debra and me."

"Not to me."

"Have you ever seen a celebrity?"

"Many." Kai leans back in his chair and smiles, but his expression is interesting. Watchful. As well as guarded. "I take a lot of celebrities out."

The moon's high and full, and the torches flame bright orange against the night. I lean forward, elbows resting on the metal table. I'm tempted to ask for a list of his celebrity clientele, but the cocktail waitress has appeared at the table for our order, and since I don't want to be seen as overly nosy, I let the subject drop.

It's not until Kai walks me back to my hotel and we weave through Waikiki, which has come alive with noise and cars and bright lights, that I ask him about his job again.

"You really like being a surf instructor?"

"What's not to like? I meet all kinds of people, and every week's new and different. I'm in the water, get paid to surf. It's a dream job."

"So who takes to surfing the easiest?"

He doesn't even hesitate. "Kids. And anyone who just wants to have fun."

I study him, trying to be dispassionate and failing miserably. "And who has the hardest time?"

"Women who don't let go."

I laugh, shake my head. "You're making that up."

"You should let go."

"And what? Let hell break loose?"

He shakes his head in frustration, and we've reached

my hotel. Kai faces the Halekulani. "You know who stays here, don't you?"

A dark-suited security guard stands in the shadows, and Kai and I both see him. "No."

"The newly wed and the newly dead."

I laugh because I've seen lots of both here and Kai's right about a lot of things. "It's a great hotel. Great service."

"Because that's so important."

"It is."

"Why?"

And I'm stumped. I don't have an answer. Instead I reach for my room key and suddenly remember I've nothing with me. No wallet, beach bag, nothing. I'd left everything by the pool. And the pool is definitely closed. "Damn. I left everything by the pool earlier. Now I'll have to find out what they did with my things."

"I'll say good night here, then," Kai answers. "The beach boys aren't allowed inside."

I glance at the hotel's discreet whitewashed walls. "Why not?"

"Riffraff."

"You're riffraff?" I arch an eyebrow. "Because you're a surf instructor?"

"Because we entertain the tourists."

I get the picture. "Ah. The ladies."

He shrugs. "Lots of beautiful women come to Hawaii looking for a good time."

I make a disgusted sound. "You sound like a gigolo."

He laughs, not at all insulted. In fact, nothing seems to ruffle him. "I didn't say I slept with them all. Until recently I had a long-term girlfriend."

"Still."

"It's the way it is here, girl." Kai glances over his shoulder as a limousine pulls into the hotel's covered driveway. "So what about that surf lesson tomorrow? Going to give it a shot?"

"I'll be terrible."

"You'll do great."

"I'll never get up."

"You'll get up the first time."

I laugh. "Kai, I'm not one of your sweet young things just out of college."

"I know. You're a mother. Divorced. Two kids. Non-athletic. Have I left anything out?"

"Just my Suburban."

"You have a Suburban?"

"Everyone does in Seattle."

"Jesus," he mutters, raking a hand through his hair. "Why?"

"Wet weather. Four-wheel-drive vehicles can head to the mountains for skiing, tow boats, carry a lot of equipment."

"You ski?"

"The family does."

"You don't?"

"Not very well."

"Why not?"

"I hate going too fast."

He laughs, shakes his head. "All right. Eleven o'clock tomorrow. Go to the beach desk where you were earlier today inquiring about lessons with me—"

"You know?" I feel heat rush through me, warming my face.

"Yeah. Tommy told me."

I just stare at Kai, mortified. "Why didn't you say anything earlier?"

"I thought it was cute. Didn't want to embarrass you."

"And you do now?"

Kai's white teeth flash. "So I'll see you at eleven."

"You're already booked tomorrow for eleven."

"I'll work it out."

"Kai—"

"Eleven." He turns, not giving me a chance to argue, and walks away. And I stand there and watch him go and feel like I'm all of sixteen again.

six

~~~~~~~~~~~~

The next morning I'm on the beach early, hours before my eleven o'clock lesson, partly to escape Butch and partly because I'm curious about how the surf lessons work.

I hide behind big sunglasses and a blue beach umbrella to watch Kai and the other instructors give the first lesson of the morning.

My insides do a funny jump when I first spot Kai, wearing his now familiar red board shorts and carrying surfboards, three at a time, out to the sand. He carries the long boards effortlessly, as each of the muscles in his back pop and every line and curve of his bicep and tricep muscles grow distinct.

Muscles, tan, and tattoos. Makes me nervous just looking at him.

As he drops boards into the sand, a bevy of high school girls walk by in bikinis that barely hold in their pert breasts, and they give Kai bold, giggling glances. He sees. The corner of his mouth lifts. Why shouldn't he smile? He could have his pick of women.

Why would he want me?

He wouldn't, I tell myself, circling my knees with my arms. This isn't TV. You're not going to get an island romance.

But as he goes through the dry land instruction (my God, am I going to have to lie facedown on my surfboard on the sand with my big white dimpled ass in the air and practice jumping to my feet?), I can't quite give up on that excited little girl inside me, the one who's hoping for something good, hoping for someone to still like me. Enjoy me.

Kai's first morning lesson consists of two girls in their early twenties. They're medium height and pretty, and like the high school girls moments ago, they, too, look great in bikinis. Finally I know who buys all the bikinis in the stores. Not women my age—and if we do, we buy those conservative Miracle slim-kinis with underwire, gel-padded push-up tops, and Lycra-and-spandex bottoms that pull up the droopy butt, press in the fuller stomach, and use fabric, patterns, gold chain, and mesh to draw the eye up, down, and all around—anywhere but at the faded, age-spotted body that doesn't look quite so hot anymore.

Now, I don't have any freckles or age spots yet. And my stomach isn't as big as it was before the divorce and the annihilation of my appetite. But even unspeckled and less plump, my body is not what I would call bikini worthy. Which is why I haven't worn a bikini since before William was born. Grandma was right. Some things are better left to the imagination.

Not that these two sassy coeds are interested in leaving anything to the imagination.

At Kai's instruction, they're stretching onto their stomachs on the blue soft-top surfboards resting on the sand. Kai motions for them to inch forward on their boards, and as the girls creep forward, I notice how their Brazilian thongs ride between their tanned butt cheeks, reminding me uncomfortably of a beach peep show: "All Live! All Ass! All the Time!"

Kai must hate his job.

I press my lips together in disapproval. I hate the disapproval, too. The truth is, I don't disapprove of them—or miserable, long-suffering Kai—I'm just jealous. I'd *love* to have the girls' confidence. But not just their confidence. I want a firm round tan ass that doesn't dimple and sprawl like well-worn cushions on a thrift store sofa.

Kai kneels in front of his lesson, thighs hard, quads flexed, and he cups his hands, shows them how to paddle. The girls mimic him. He then shows them how to push up on the board, kind of a football straight-arm thing, and the girls copy that, too.

This is who Kai should be out with. Young, toned, tan. I'm none of the above.

I wrap my arms tighter around my knees, feel my tummy bulge, and have never felt like such a single mom. I don't feel girlish, or feminine, or physically appealing. I just feel . . . maternal. Asexual. As if I'm a workhorse and not a woman.

And I've pretty much felt that way since William was born.

I can't do this, can't go out on a lesson, can't make a bigger fool of myself than I already have. Sure, women surf. Lots of wonderful, athletic, tennis-playing, golfing, volleyball-loving women surf. But I didn't grow up near the ocean. I grew up in Spokane, and our version of summer vacation was heading to the lake and floating on rafts and inner tubes.

Kai's got his lesson on their feet, both girls giggling and pretending to balance Gidget-style on their surfboards.

As I watch the beaming Gidget girls show off their stuff, the two Asian women from the Halekulani pool settle into lounge chairs close to mine.

They're talking loudly as they spread their towels on the blue lounge chair cushions.

"My life," says one of the slender Asian women, pausing dramatically, "would have been so different if I'd taken a different path."

I don't mean to listen in, but their voices carry. Glancing over my shoulder, I see they're both in tiny one-piece suits, wearing high heels and gigantic designer sunglasses; but they're oblivious to me, hidden behind their sunglasses, immersed in conversation and contention.

"I had a job in London," the one continues. "I could have ended up in London. Instead I stayed with Jason in Houston while he finished his studies."

"Did you change your last name when you married?" the other asks.

"Yes. To Huhn. It's still that on my green card."

"Huhn," the other one repeats.

Huhn snorts. "Do you know what Huhn means in German? Chicken. It means chicken."

Chicken, I echo silently, turning back to watch Kai help carry his lesson's surfboards into the water. That's

what I am. I'm a big fat chicken. I'm scared to try anything new but scared of never having more.

So instead of running off, leaving the beach for my room
or a spot at the pool, I stay glued to my lounge chair and
watch as Kai gets his girls on their boards and pushes them
out into the water, over the small wave breaking on the shore.

He paddles out behind them, and soon he's in front of
them, a foot on each of their boards to tow them out, his
arms wet, skin bronzed, muscles rippling.

I watch him paddle with his lesson until the three of
them disappear on the horizon.

Suddenly the sky seems so big overhead, heavy with
clouds and jagged places of blue. I feel small in compar-
ison, small and surprisingly fragile. Once I was young
and wanted everything, and then I grew up and settled—
it was settled, wasn't it?—and learned not to look back,
not to ask for more, not to want more because more
didn't come. More didn't exist . . . at least not outside the
imagination.

I sit forward, wrap my arm around my knees, and try
to see where Kai and his lesson have gone on the horizon; but there are too many surfers in the distance, a cluster of bodies and boards. I wish I knew what was more,
anyway.

Is "more" love? Is "more" emotion? Is it peace?
Happiness? Or is more just more of everything?

It's time for my lesson, and I'm terrified. I try to be
nonchalant, making what I hope is witty repartee, but on
the inside I'm so nervous that I feel positively twitchy.
Kai gets me a bright green rash guard, and I tug it on over

my head. It's tight and compresses my boobs but fortunately flares enough at the hips that my stomach isn't on view for everyone. Just my butt.

Speaking of my butt, Kai hands me a bottle of suntan lotion, tells me to apply it to the backs of my legs since they're going to get a lot of sun. I look up at him, eyes narrowing. "You're saying they're white."

He smiles a little. "I'm saying you don't want them burned."

Lotion applied, hair in rubber band, I dab some extra sunblock on my nose before Kai leads me to the row of surfboards in the sand. I know I'm going to get the same land lesson the girls got earlier, and I'm dreading the part where I have to hop up from a kneeling position. Somehow, kneeling and jumping in a bathing suit in front of a man in public seems horribly adult-video-carnival-like.

"Let's do it," I say, gritting my teeth and assuming the position. God, how embarrassing. I look up at him, red faced, smiling desperately, fiercely.

Kai grins. "Okay, paddle, paddle."

I make paddling motions the way he's shown me.

"Okay, I'm going to push you into a wave, now on your knees."

I'm up. Doggy style. Hate this. Really hate this.

"On your feet."

I spring up, arms out at my sides, and hold the pose.

Kai's doing his best not to laugh. I see young girls watching from their beach towels, round bare bottoms tan and gleaming with oil. Aren't they lovely. Aren't I foolish.

"Great," Kai says. "Let's go."

He wraps the leash guard around my left ankle, helps me carry my soft-top board to the water, and holds it while I attempt to slither—no, it's a lurch—on. Kai tells me to slide down on the board, and I squeak down, inch by inch, thinking that none of this feels natural. There is no resonant chord from a previous life. I was not a Polynesian surfer.

We paddle out, which means Kai paddles, towing my board behind his with his toe on mine. I do try to paddle, but it's a long paddle out and my arms are killing me before we're even halfway there. I'm also spending a fair amount of time spluttering when waves hit us. Interestingly, Kai's hair isn't even wet.

But now we're out, before the big lineup but far enough that the waves have some size. Kai's got me facing the beach and the famous Waikiki strip with its beaches and hotels, yet all I can think about is the fact that he's sitting on his board behind me. He must have an amazing view of my giant behind.

Behind the behind. Mortifying.

Worse, I can feel my classy one-piece Miracle suit creeping up, crawling higher on my butt cheeks. I want to tug the suit down to make sure the butt dimples are all covered, but I'm afraid of drawing his attention to an already sensitive area.

He shouts at me to paddle, and I try, but before I can even get to my feet I'm knocked sideways and off.

I drag myself back onto my board, and Kai retrieves me and faces me toward the beach again.

"Get ready to paddle," he says. My stomach heaves. I clench the rails of my board.

"Okay, paddle," he shouts.

I try, not very hard, because I know I'm going to get knocked off my board.

"Paddle harder, Jackie!"

I do.

"On your knees."

I'm on my knees, more or less, as the board tips right and left.

"Up! On your feet!"

I try to rise, but before I'm even halfway up I'm going over and off to the right. The wave crashes over me and catches the board; the board flips up, tugs on my leash, and I'm clawing up to the surface, feeling panicky for air even though I haven't been down long. It's just that it's the ocean, and I've never swum in the ocean that much. Of course, the kids always played on the beach, but not where one couldn't touch bottom, not like this.

Kai's there, holding my board steady while I try to climb on. "What happened?" he asks.

"I lost my balance."

"Keep your foot in the middle of the board. Go from your knees straight up."

He's towing me back to our starting position. My morale is really low. He makes it sound so easy, and for him it is easy, but I'm in over my head. Literally.

We try again. I fall once more, this time to the left.

Kai's getting good at retrieving me. "You've almost got it," he says. "Just relax. Don't stiffen up. Keep your knees bent."

"I don't know, Kai." I'm spluttering from taking a big mouthful of water. "I don't think I can—"

"I do," he says.

I sigh inwardly, thinking evil thoughts. It's very possible I could hate him, but I drag myself back onto my board. He has way too much confidence. Whether it's in me or in him, I don't know.

Kai tows me out again. He reaches for my surfboard, swings it around, and suddenly it's all slow motion.

I see him—wet, skin glistening, sun shining down—and everything looks as it would in a movie with the right lighting and right camera lens. Turquoise water, white-tipped waves, a diamond glazing on Kai, on me, on everything.

For that split second, I feel nothing and everything all at the same time. I hear water rushing and roaring, but it's not just the ocean. It's the sound of life. The sense of destiny. For a moment, life seems to have grown beyond me, becoming far more than I ever thought it was, more than I knew it could be. Life isn't at all what I thought it was, either. Life is grander, more beautiful, more complex, more impossible. Heartbreaking and ravishing, tenacious and fragile, true and false.

And it all hits me in the same amount of time it takes Kai to clasp the front of my board and swing me around so that I face Waikiki and the hotels with their colorful beach umbrellas and parked catamarans and the green velvet mountains behind. Clouds hang low on some of the mountains. In other places, the sky is just enormous blue.

Kai says something to me, and I look at him in this strange dreamworld as I push sticky wet hair from my face. He's smiling, his eyes are smiling, and water clings to his skin, sparkles on his darkly tanned skin, his eyes the exact same shade as the water, his teeth white like the foam.

I could love him, I think, and I know it's not just him, but this whole dream of life, this sense of timelessness and hopefulness, the languid warmth and intense colors of the tropics.

I think I could be happy to be someone else, living somewhere else, making different choices. Living a life I've never lived before.

"Look straight forward," I hear him say, his voice far off in this movie-world set I've stumbled onto. "Start paddling now, Jackie."

Paddling? Oh, yes, paddling. I begin clawing at the water—it's what it feels like, terror and urgency as well as utter bewilderment, because I still haven't a clue what I'm doing in the water on a surfboard in my swimsuit. This is so not me, so not anything I would ever have done.

But Kai either doesn't care or doesn't notice. Instead he's launching me forward, giving the board a hard push, and the wave does the rest, grabbing the board and taking me along. I'm traveling with the wave, and I don't know what to do. I'm moving fast, and this speed and long board and water isn't my world. I am not the kind of woman who surfs. I am not the kind of woman who tries new things. I am not—

"Get up. On your feet, girl," Kai shouts.

I don't move.

"On your feet, Jackie." It's not a request this time. It's an order.

My heart pounds and the water is sloshing and the wave keeps taking me, pulling me, sending me fast to nowhere. Numbly I struggle to my knees and then stagger up.

I am going to fall. I can't get my balance. Wobbling left, wobbling right, I'm about to tip the board over again when suddenly I just stop fighting and stand there. I stand, arms up like a tightrope walker. But it works. I stick. I don't fall.

I go and go, knees bent, body leaning stiffly forward, no grace or style in my stance, but I'm riding a wave. I'm riding a surfboard.

The wave peters out and I drop onto the board with a plop, landing flat before I fall off. Using my right arm, I turn a slow, arduous circle and start paddling back to Kai when he arrives on a wave of his own.

He grins at me as he reaches for my board, holds it steady. "You did it."

"It wasn't pretty."

"You looked great."

"Kai—"

"You looked great."

I'm blushing and beaming and mortified and exhilarated all at the same time. "Thanks."

"I love your style. Big-wave style."

On a little wave. But I smile bigger, warming at the praise. I've done something I never thought I'd do or could do. I've actually surfed.

It's been so long since I felt good about anything, and I spend most of the lesson now anxious to try again and again. We spend another forty minutes out there. I catch a few more waves, biff on more than I catch, but when I am able to hang in there and ride one long wave, I feel victorious. Glorious. Brilliant.

The water's warm, and the waves lap and rock at the surfboard, and it's like being a kid on a floating air mattress. Everything seems so new and interesting.

I feel new and interesting.

Finally it's time to paddle in. Kai has another lesson soon, and we make small talk as he tows me back toward the Sheraton Hotel beach where we did our dry-land lesson.

On the beach, he wraps the leash around the board's skag and carries it to the board rack. I peel off the very tight, very wet rash guard shirt. "Thanks," I say, combing my wet hair back behind my ears. "I can't believe you got me up."

"You had a good time?"

"Yes."

"I told you so." He looks to the beach desk, signals that he's aware his next lesson is waiting, and I exhale in a *whoosh* of disappointment. I'm done. He's moving on.

"Thank you," I repeat, awkward and nervous all over again. I want to ask him what he's doing later, want to get a drink with him after work, want so much but don't know what's appropriate, don't want to chase him but haven't any pride left at the moment, either.

"I better go," he says.

I nod. Smile. "Okay." Then, as he starts to turn away, I blurt, "Are you free for a drink after work?"

Kai stops, turns, and looks back at me but doesn't say anything.

This is embarrassing, and heat rushes to my face. My smile feels as wobbly as my balance on the surfboard, but I have to ask. I know I'll regret it if I don't. "Would you like to have a drink later?"

He still looks at me, a long, assessing glance that's knowing even as it's curious. "You don't want to do that."

"Why not?"

"Because I'm not what you want, girl."

"You don't know that—"

"And I'm not what you need."

I stare at him, irritated as well as puzzled. "You don't know what I need."

"I know what you don't need. You're recently divorced. You're an interior designer, and you have two great kids at home."

"So?"

"So. I'm a surf instructor. This is my life. This is what I do."

"I don't know what that means."

"Yes, you do. It means we're from two different worlds."

This irks me. Of course we're from different worlds. We live in different places, have different incomes, are different ages, but this is also part of the attraction. He's not me, not my world, not anything I've known these past ten, twelve years in Seattle, and it's exactly what I want. What I need. I look at Kai hard, trying to invest the full forty years of experience and wisdom into my expression. "I wasn't born yesterday."

"So you keep saying." He's smiling, though, teasing me. And then his smile fades. "But you're a nice girl, Jacqueline. You don't need me."

I can't figure out why his words are like pouring gasoline on fire. He makes me fight, resist, want whatever it is I'm not supposed to feel, whatever it is I want. And I want . . . *what?* Something. Something. *Anything.*

But not just anything. I want whatever it is he would give me.

And it'd be sex, and I don't even know if it would be good. I don't even know what sex with someone like Kai would be like, because I've grown old in the years of my marriage, I've changed, faded, aged.

I've become what I never thought I'd become, because on the TV shows I saw growing up—and I'm thinking *Partridge Family* and *Brady Bunch* here—women and wives are still perky. Women and wives never grow old or fade or go gray.

God help me, don't let me go that way. . . .

"I want to get a drink with you later, when you're done with work." I look at him, long and level, as cool as a cucumber and so unlike me. "And I'll buy. My treat."

In my hotel room later that afternoon, I don't know what to wear. Honestly, I don't know what to wear. He's young. Cute. Broke. Cool.

But broke. And yes, to paraphrase Kai, a surfer. He's not going to dress up much, is he?

I look at my wardrobe, look at the elegant pieces—mostly black, white, and khaki—hanging in my closet, and I don't even know where to start finding low-key and nonthreatening. Not that he'd need nonthreatening with me. He's probably met so many women, tons and tons of women, that a woman like me—end of her thirties and divorced—doesn't scare him. He, after all, is probably assuming he'll bed me.

I guess I'm assuming he will, too. Otherwise why would I do this? Why would I be here, putting myself through this?

I pull a black linen skirt and black cropped top from the closet and hold it up before me, try to see me the way he'd see me, and I can't. I can't.

I just see a redhead who needs to get her color re-touched, and he probably sees, what . . . vixen? Ha!

I toss the skirt and top onto the bed, strip off my terry-cloth hotel robe, and step into the shower.

Time to shave and shine.

seven

I'm at the bar where we agreed to meet. And it's not the kind of bar I've been to, well, in years. If ever.

It's almost what I'd call a biker bar. Dark, small, reeking of beer, with a handful of men in need of a shave leaning heavily on the counter.

And the men, I imagine, probably reek, too, but that's not kind and I'm just being nervous.

Nervous of what?

Nervous of whom?

Nervous of me.

I walk inside, up another couple of steps, hesitate as every head at the counter turns, stares at me, and I stand there awkwardly. I'm overdressed for the bar. I'm overdressed for everything in life, heavy on wardrobe and style, yet where am I supposed to go?

What am I supposed to do—even if on the outside I look polished, look good?

I turn around to walk out, and as I start for the door, he's standing in it.

Kai.

Dressed.

Dressed remarkably well for a poor surfer. Cool shirt, long shorts, flip-flops, but his dark, sun-streaked hair is combed and he's shaven and he looks . . . amazing.

And then he smiles, white teeth, blue eyes, and the smile burrows inside me, makes me feel. And the more I feel, the more I think I have to feel, the more I need to feel.

"Hey," he says.

I smile, smooth my linen skirt, glad I at least put on a skirt. Makes me feel, if not grown up, then civil. As if all respectable things happen to women in dresses and skirts.

"I . . ." I smile, shake my head, and I'm blushing. This is like a movie, a terrible made-for-TV movie. Older woman falls for younger guy, has a night of incredible sex, and returns home refreshed. Reenergized.

"Didn't think you'd show," Kai says, and as he nears me he leans forward and kisses my cheek.

Lips. Skin. I inhale, smile less steadily. "I wouldn't have canceled."

"This isn't your kind of place."

"You warned me." And he did. In fact, those were his exact words. *It's a dive bar. Someplace you don't go at home, princess.*

Princess. I smile. I'm so not a princess. At least not anymore.

"A beer?" I ask. "Or do you want something else?" I had, after all, promised I'd be buying.

"A beer." He heads to the bar, though. Good man. I'm definitely not as comfortable bellying up to the bar as a man.

Or as he is.

I need to date more. I think of the few dates I've had, and no one interested me, no one has made me want anything. Not to talk, or touch, or get undressed.

And it's the undressing part I seem to miss most about now.

God, there're things I miss about marriage, about being with someone who gets you, loves you, knows what you want, you need.

For years Daniel got that. For years Daniel loved me.

But now is not the time or place. Definitely not the time or place, as Kai's leaning on the bar counter and watching me, that half-smile at his eyes, his expression wiser than any thirty-year-old man's has a right to be. "Beer, or something else, girl?"

Girl.

I know he probably calls every woman "girl," but I like it. Makes me feel good inside. Not just young, but safe. Protected. Although the way he's looking at me right now, I'm not sure he'd protect me. At least not from himself.

He wants me.

Good.

The feeling's mutual. But would I really do anything? Could I really do anything? I'm not even on birth control anymore.

It's then that I realize he's still waiting for me to answer, and I gesture to the barmaid on the other side of the counter. "A beer."

His eyebrow lifts. "Any kind in particular?"

"Um, light. Draft."

He waits for the beer and carries both over to where I still stand in the middle of the dark bar. "Upstairs?" he asks, indicating with his head the narrow staircase in the corner against the wall.

I nod. This is his night, his game. I'm just along for the ride, and it's dangerous but thrilling. Something new is happening in my life.

Something I don't know.

Something I maybe can't control.

It's the devil in me, I think, but this is the moment I've been waiting for, the moment I'd hoped would come ever since Daniel and I made the big decision to split.

Chance. Adventure. Opportunity.

Discovery.

It's even smellier upstairs. I swear, it's like an old frat house party and I'm the only girl invited.

We sit on bar stools at a tall table, and I put down my beer without taking a sip. Kai's already made a serious dent in his.

"So," I say brightly.

He just looks at me.

I take a quick breath, thinking that wasn't the best conversation starter. I'm always chiding Jessie for initiating discussions with, "What's your favorite color?" It wouldn't be so bad if Jessie really cared about your color. But she doesn't. Her question is just her way to force you to talk to her. "You said you grew up in Florida."

He nods, eyes creasing at the corners.

I tip my head. "You don't talk a lot, Kai."

"I'd rather listen to you."

"Did you learn that in How to Woo Women 101?"

His smile broadens. "Nah. I'd just rather listen to you. Look at you. You're beautiful. And it doesn't hurt that I've always had a thing for redheads."

Another quick breath. Easy, girl. That wasn't a declaration of love. It's a compliment, probably designed to get you into bed.

And you've already decided you want to do that, haven't you?

I bite my lip, sure but not sure.

I want to try something new and different, want the whole "no regrets" thing, but sex, wow, sex is kind of scary. I know I'm forty, have had two kids, showed a million nurses and doctors and God and everyone everything I had between my legs when I was delivering my little monsters into the world . . . but still, sex with a young man, sex with a strange young man, sex with a very sexy young man . . .

Not something I've done. Ever.

But something I think I have to do.

Why?

Why? I could very well end up scared or embarrassed, ashamed . . . foolish. And then I could very well have fun.

Or something more adult than fun. Something like . . . pleasure.

"Do you do this often?" I blurt, and he sits even farther back on his stool. Probably not another good conversation starter.

Perhaps Jessie took a page from my book. . . .

"Do you want me to tell you no? That you're the first?"

I bite down hard, jaw grinding. What a male answer. "Obviously I'm not the first."

"So?" His beer is nearly half gone. I've yet to take a sip of mine. So I do. And then another sip. Very small, as I'm not much of a beer drinker.

Kai's watching and grinning. "Wow. That's going after it."

I take another sip, a bigger one this time, just to prove to him that I can handle a beer just fine. But after three sips I look at my glass and see that I haven't made a dent in it. God, I could use a good girly drink about now.

A mango daiquiri would taste so much better and go down far more easily.

Somehow we drink our drinks and make requisite small talk when my brain isn't conversing at all but analyzing the situation and thinking, Sex.

Wondering what sex would be like with Kai. Wondering what sex would be like, period. It's been so long . . . it's been . . . too long. I'm quite sure I wouldn't even know what to do with the various parts. Although strictly speaking, parts are parts, and part P seems to go in part V.

And now we're leaving the bar and walking toward my hotel and Kai keeps looking at me and I just look at him back and we're not saying anything. I don't know what I'm supposed to say even if he wanted to talk.

It's like the now or never point.

We're half a block from the Halekulani and Kai stops walking, faces me. He's got that half-smile that makes everything inside me go crazy and the air catch in my throat, and oh God, I don't know what I'm doing.

What does he see in me? What does he think is so interesting when he looks at me?

Or maybe there's nothing interesting and I'm just a battle to be won.

"Kai—" I start, stop.

He reaches out, pushes hair back from my face.

"What, baby girl?"

Baby girl. It's enough to bring tears to my eyes. Between his touch and his words, I'm falling apart on the inside. It's been so long since anyone made me feel like this. So long since anyone made me want like this.

I exhale slowly, scared to say what I want. What I need. What I fear.

I haven't been with a lot of men. And I've slept with only one person since Daniel and I split, and that one time was hugely pathetically forgettable. He was a nice man—someone I'd known forever—but definitely not lover material. And after being a wife and a mother, I'm a little anxious about my desirability factor.

"You don't have to do anything," Kai says now, and he's stepped back, put his hands in his pockets, and he looks young. Damn young. And I feel like a cradle robber.

I don't know if I can do this . . . I mean, I want to, but can I? Should I? What's a woman to do? "Have you been with a lot of . . . had a lot of . . . you know."

"Know what?"

"Sex."

He laughs. God help me, he laughs, and then he runs a hand through his thick, sun-streaked hair. The shirtsleeve falls back and there's a bicep, and it's big, hard, cut, and I can see the tattoo running around the arm, and it's the sexiest thing I've ever seen.

When did I start lusting after younger men? And when did tattoos turn me on?

I guess since meeting Kai.

"Yeah, you could say I've been with a few women."

"So you're really comfortable with women's bodies?"

He's laughing again, and he's standing with his legs apart. He rocks back on his heels and his shirt opens and his chest is broad and tan and muscles, muscles everywhere.

Christ. What's a woman to do?

"You're comfortable with me?" I manage. It's almost a stammer, and my foolish quotient has just shot to an all-new high.

"Shouldn't I be?"

"Kai—I've had kids."

"Uh-huh."

"And I'm older than you."

"So you keep reminding me."

"That doesn't bother you?"

"Jackie . . . I find you very sexy."

"Why?" Honestly, I'm not digging for compliments, and to Butch at the pool with his big developer business in Vegas and his talks of building casinos and extravagant swimming pools, and the four wives who all got remade by the finest plastic surgeon in Nevada, okay, I could see how I might be attractive to Rich Developer but Superficial Butch, who hasn't been with a nonplastic woman in years. But Kai?

Kai?

"Because you are."

* * *

In the hotel room, I shut the door and look behind me to discover Kai opening the sliding door to the balcony, where he's now standing outside.

"You have a killer view," he says.

I nod and move to stand behind him where a warm wind blows. I lift my face to the wind, letting it pull my hair apart. "It's nice."

"Nice?" Kai shoots me a mocking glance. "This is the best hotel with the best view on the best part of the beach."

He comes to me, saves me from having to make the first move again. And when he kisses me, all thought, all doubt, all insecurity, goes. I don't care about anything or want anything but this. This, right now.

It's been too long since I've been kissed properly, kissed where you feel it all the way on the inside, where you feel wanted—desired—and it's heady, exciting, and calming, too.

Suddenly it all seems right, and I just give in. Let whatever happen.

There is sex and there is love, but this is an incredible combination of sex and love. I know he can't love me— he doesn't even know me—but the way he touches me is the way I want to be touched, and the way his body covers mine in bed is exactly right. I feel amazing. I feel . . . like me. Only good. Better.

I want all of it, all and everything, and everything he'll give me. I don't know why I thought this would be so awkward. It feels so natural, and I'm so comfortable with him. I kiss him as though he were really mine, as though he and I weren't just strangers off a beach, and I give him some of my heart even though it makes no sense. But it just feels right to give him my heart since I'm giving him access to the rest of me.

But nothing lasts forever, not even great lovemaking, and when we finish the room seems very dark and very quiet. Kai seems extra quiet.

My heart squeezes up inside me, and everything feels different. I feel different. I can tell I'm missing a little piece of me. Shouldn't have given him that bit of my heart. Shouldn't have given him anything that would make me feel less. That would make me hurt. I've hurt too much these last two years, and I'm still not my old fighting self quite yet.

He rubs my back once, twice, and then with a pat, pat he's climbing out. Leaving the bed. I'm not sure where he's going, what he's doing, and then I realize he's picking up his clothes. He's getting dressed.

My God. I suck in a breath, reeling a little on the inside. He's leaving. Already. But of course it's already, it's not as if we're a match made in heaven.

I bite my lip. I'd forgotten this part. Forgotten what it was like for a man to roll out of my bed and reach for pants while I just lie there hearing the zipper zip and the belt jingle.

When you're married there's no rolling out of bed into trousers or jeans. There's no zipping of zippers while you're still lying in bed in the dark, all warm body and warm emotions.

Shit.

I'd forgotten this, and all the warmth inside me is rapidly going cold.

Shit.

I feel dangerously close to tears as all hell breaks loose inside me. Be calm, Jack. Be cool. It was just sex, nothing else. But the sex had been good, really, really good, and he'd felt so good near me, with me, and I'd been so comfortable—

"You going to be all right, girl?"

Kai's buttoning his white shirt now, letting the bottom hang out over his shorts.

"Yes."

He straightens the amulet at his neck and then drags a hand through his dark hair. I can't see his face, but I feel the change, the energy fading, leaving. After sex, men get up and go, and women lie in bed and wonder what the hell just happened.

Or at least that was how it used to be for me back in my twenties when I was still dating. Back before I married.

"You've gone quiet," Kai adds, leaning over the table to scoop up his keys.

My chest is so tight, each sound seems so loud. The whisper slide of fabric, the rough zip of a zipper, the scratch of keys on the table.

Why didn't I think ahead to this part?

Why didn't I remember this is how it ends after you'd had sex on a first date?

Shit. The tears are burning my eyes, and I reach up and with a knuckled fist brush one eye and then the other, keeping the tears from falling, showing. It's bad enough that I slept with a younger man. Can't start crying and falling apart like a demented old woman.

But I feel demented. I feel emotional, fearful, fragile. Of course nothing could happen here. Of course this could go nowhere. Island romance, island fling, I chant silently but it doesn't help. Doesn't help at all. Not when everything felt so good and I don't want it, the good, to go. Don't want the energy and warmth to fade.

Kai leans over the bed, cups the back of my head, and kisses me on the forehead. "Be good, girl."

"Okay."

He kisses me on the mouth this time. "Okay." And I hear a smile in his voice as he straightens. And then he leaves.

I sit in the middle of the bed, sheet wrapped tightly around my knees as I watch him walk out and hear the door click—loudly—closed.

Damn.

And the tears fall. I bury my head against my forearm and let the warm skin touch warm skin, trying to find whatever warmth is left. But it's not helping. I feel cold. And empty. And ripped wide open.

Making love had seemed like such a good idea. I'd been so attracted to him, so turned on. But after the itch is satisfied, he goes and I discover I've been kidding myself. I'm not looking just for sex. I want love, true love. Not that it exists, but that doesn't seem to stop me from hoping. Searching. Even in a sexy young surfer named Kai Carson.

And it's not until I'm worn out from crying that I remember. Tomorrow's my birthday. Big fat forty.

The next morning, I don't know what to do with myself. It doesn't feel like my birthday. It doesn't feel remotely festive. I turn on my cell phone. No messages.

What to do? What to do to jump-start my day?

I turn in circles in my hotel room, ridiculously blue and yet restless. What will I do today? I can't face Butch at the pool but can't see going onto the beach. Not if Kai's there, not if he's going to think I'm chasing him. And at this point I would be chasing him, because I want to know what last night was, what it meant, what I'm supposed to think or do or feel now.

I decide to go for a run.

Lacing up my running shoes, I do everything I can not to think or feel, although I can't help realizing this is quite a unique situation for me. It's been so long since I had a proper one-night stand, I'm not sure if I should be shocked by my behavior or proud. I did something out of character, something that will make a good story to remember and tell when I get home. And that's what it'll be, I resolve, a great story to share with Nic, Anne, and Kristine.

Leaving the elevator, I step outside into blue sky and sunshine, the temperatures already high seventies and it's only eight o'clock. With my iPod clipped to my upper arm, I set off and run at a good pace, nervous energy giving me extra kick.

You can't feel bad about last night, I tell myself. Last night was an adventure. You took a risk. You took the road less traveled . . . well, for you, anyway.

I try to focus on the positives. Great sex with a younger man. That should be a confidence builder, right?

But I'm only half-encouraged.

Somehow I'd hoped there'd be . . . more. Looking back at yesterday—last night—I guess I'd hoped there'd be more romance, more tenderness, more excitement.

I keep running.

I'm gone nearly an hour by the time I get back to the hotel.

In my room, the message light on my phone is blinking. Anne, I think, calling to wish me a happy birthday. I strip off my damp running clothes and head for the shower. As I dry off, I retrieve the message. But it's not Anne. It's Kai.

I sink onto the edge of the bed, the phone pressed to my ear, and play his message a second time.

"Hoping you slept good, girl. Wondering what you had planned for today. I've got the day off. Call me if you feel like doing something." He leaves his cell number.

I grab a pen and scribble down his number.

And then stare at it.

And stare at it some more as the icy fearfulness starts to melt from around my heart.

He called.

He called and he wants to see me. He has a day off and he wants to spend it with me.

I smile, bite my lip, and nearly hug the notepad with his phone number. Maybe it's not true love, but it sure makes turning forty a hell of a lot more interesting.

eight

~~~~~~~~~~~~~~~~

Kai picks me up in front of the hotel. He drives a black pickup truck, the windows tinted.

"Where are we going?" I ask, shy as I slide in on the passenger side.

"Where do you want to go?"

My shoulders lift, fall. "I don't know." I don't tell him I'm glad just to be with him, but I am.

"Snorkeling at Shark's Cove." He gestures into the bed of the pickup, where he already has snorkel gear along with a pair of flip-flops and a soggy-looking beach towel.

"Where's Shark's Cove?"

"On the north shore. An hour drive or so." He shoots me a sideways glance. "You up for a drive?"

"Yes."

We head down Kalakaua Avenue, and Kalakaua turns into Diamond Head Road. Kai points out various surf spots and famous beaches as he drives around the south-eastern tip of the island. Hanauma Bay for snorkeling, but it's too crowded to be fun. Makapu'u Point with its blowhole. Sea Life Park, where they filmed scenes for *50*

First Dates. Waimanaolo Bay Beach Park. Kailua. Kaneohe. And so on.

It's gorgeous today, so blue and green and gold. The truck windows are down and the warm wind blows, catching my hair, turning it into a tangled halo of red.

Kai tells me that in the Hawaiian language, there are only eight consonants, five short vowels, and five long vowels. Hawaiian also has no inflection. However, in a large Hawaiian dictionary one can find over 130 different names for types of rain and 160 for types of water.

"Can you speak Hawaiian, then?" I ask, grabbing my hair in one hand to keep it away from my face.

"I only know a few words." He pauses, grins. "Just enough to get me into trouble."

Smiling, I tip my head against the seat and relax. I feel so damn happy to be here right now. So damn glad to be alive. Nothing can happen here in Hawaii, nothing can last, yet the sensation inside me is so warm and buoyant, so full of grace and goodness, that I refuse to look ahead, refuse to think about the end of the day or the flight home. *This* is what I want.

I realize now that I've been really depressed these past few years, and closing my eyes, I let the warm yellow sun cover my face, resting hot and steady on my eyelids. It's warm and breezy, and like a hammock rocking, I'm mellow, so mellow.

I don't want to be depressed anymore. I don't want to suppress all the feelings, don't want to be left with only bad feelings. Life has bad times and down times, but shouldn't it also have joy?

Women should know more joy.

Opening my eyes, I turn and look out toward the ocean curving to the right of the truck, glimpses of blue between elegant palm trees bent out above the coastline.

My friends at home don't seem to have joy. My friends at home seem to be on neutral—getting through—but maybe joy is too much to ask for.

So we don't.

So we settle.

Settling for whatever it is we can squeeze out of marriage and motherhood. Squeezing because we're all so goddamn tired.

Tugging a long gold-and-red strand back from my eyes, I find myself objecting to everything I know about the life I've lived for the past fourteen-plus years.

"You okay?"

Kai's question breaks the lazy stillness, and I look at him, my hand still wound around my hair. The sun plays across his face, his eyes so blue and light against the tanned cheekbones and black lashes, his lashes tipped blond from the sea and sun. So gorgeous. So young. So different from me.

"Yeah," I say, because right now everything is okay.

A half hour later, Kai pulls off the highway onto the shoulder facing the road.

Even though the waves on the north shore get big in winter, it's not a big wave day and Shark's Cove is protected by the dramatic jagged outcroppings of rock and reef. Kai carries our snorkels, masks, and fins to the beach, and I follow, picking my way through the rock and crumbly bright red soil.

In the water, it's as though we've entered a whole new

world. Everything is still and lovely, bright with darting yellow and blue tangs, orange clown fish, striped and spotted puffer fish. Kai touches my arm, points to a giant sea turtle swimming leisurely toward us. I barely move, enthralled by the great turtle, which seems to have wise eyes and a kind smile.

We explore the cove for an hour, swimming with schools of tiny silver fish, before returning to the beach. Kai drags all the equipment back to the truck while I rinse off.

Back in the truck, we stop for lunch at one of the numerous shrimp shacks dotting the roadside. We order plates of garlic and sweet coconut shrimp with fresh Kahuku corn on the cob and eat the shrimp and corn sitting on the tailgate of his truck. It's sunny but not too hot, and I feel very decadent as I lick the garlic sauce from my fingers. "This is so good."

"I'm glad you like it."

"I like everything you've shown me." *And everything I do with you.*

We finish lunch and throw away our plates and cans of cola before continuing toward Haleiwa, with Kai again pointing out landmarks, which in this case is the miles of world-famous surf spots. He leans on the steering wheel, muscles popping in his forearm. "That's Sunset, Pipe, Gas Chambers, Ehukai, Waimea," he says, reeling off name after name of surfers' paradises. "In summer this place is dead. No waves."

I find it hard to believe, as traffic is nasty right now, surfers, media, and fans snarling the one-lane highway for today's surf competition. Loudspeakers, viewing stands, and tents dot the beach to my right. Dozens of young girls in bikinis saunter around as a row of photographers with cameras on tripods snap away and surfers identified by their red, yellow, and blue rash guards make the most of their fifteen minutes in the water.

Eventually we leave the competition behind. Kai tells me that the surf crowd, many from Australia and Brazil, come in for the winter in November and start leaving in March. "The rest of the year, the north shore is peaceful," he adds. "The north shore's the old Hawaii, the quiet Hawaii, where locals and surfers do their own thing."

We follow Kamehameha Highway past pastures and fields until we reach Haleiwa, which took its name from an early mission and was popular at the turn of the century with the opening of the Haleiwa Hotel. The hotel eventually closed and tourism dropped off, and Haleiwa didn't revive until the 1960s, when surfing became popular. Today, art galleries fill many of the historic plantation shops lining the road. The town is old and colorful, and I'm completely charmed.

This is the Hawaii I've always wanted to see, the Hawaii I wasn't sure even existed anymore.

Kai tells me that flashy isn't cool on the north shore. If someone has money on this side of the island, you don't know it. People don't talk about money or throw it around. Simple food, simple drink, simple lifestyle. So different from life in Seattle, I think, so different from the Saabs, Volvos, and luxury SUVs, the expensive but understated clothes, the expensive but understated highlights, the expensive but understated houses that all proclaim one's status in an expensive but understated way.

Life in the Pacific Northwest is good. I'm not trying to criticize it, but I'm just beginning to realize that there might be other ways to live life. To live *my* life.

I've spent the first forty years of my life trying to please others. Could I possibly spend the next forty trying to please me?

Kai pleases me, I think, glancing over at him, glad all over again that I'm spending today with him. When I was younger, I thought birthdays were so special, but my birthdays haven't been special for years. Today, though, I feel special. Today I feel important. Valuable.

Wonderful.

I felt that way last night, too. Sex last night was unbelievable. The sex was so damn good, I vow right now never to have bad sex again. Only hot, super-sexy sex. The kind that makes you shiver on the inside, all eager and excited. Hungry. Demanding.

"You're smiling," Kai says as we carry our frappuccinos back to the truck. The impromptu stop at Starbucks was my idea. I might be 2,600 miles from home, but I still love my coffee.

"Yeah, I am," I answer, sliding into the passenger side as Kai holds my door for me.

"Happy, girl?"

"Mm-hmm."

He shuts the door, goes around to his side, and climbs in, handing me his drink to hold while he starts the truck. "Why are you in such a good mood?"

I shrug, poke my tongue into the mountain of whipped cream on top of my frappuccino. "I'm having fun."

"Good."

He takes back his drink as he backs out of the lot.

"And it's my birthday," I add quickly. He shoots me a quick look, and I nod. "The big four-oh."

Kai brakes. "Today?"

"Today."

"Why didn't you tell me?"

"I am now."

He looks at me long and level before leaning over to kiss me. "Happy birthday, girl."

His kiss is warm, hard, and yet sweet, and everything inside me flips over. "Thanks."

"Anything special you want to do for your birthday?"

My eyes meet his, and I feel bold and fierce and shy all at the same time. "Just you." And then I shiver at the heat I see in his eyes.

"Good girl," he answers, shifting into drive. "Let's go back to the hotel."

We spend two hours in the darkened hotel room, and the sex is even better than last night. I don't know why it works so well, but everything is comfortable, easy, exciting. I'm turned on everywhere, my head as well as my body, and in some ways I feel as if I've known Kai forever, that he's been part of my life forever. As he moves over me again, I'm reminded of him surfing yesterday, of how I'd watch him catch a wave to come retrieve me.

I loved the way he moved on his board through the water and the way the water rushed, the board cutting through the wave, water streaming liquid blue and green. It was beautiful, and he was beautiful, and it was a kind of magic I'd never seen before, a magic that made me look at life differently. That made me want things different. Watching Kai surf made me wonder what it would be like to not be tied to land, or rooted to the earth, but to fly across water . . .

To fly at life.

To not be whoever it is I've become. Eleven years of marriage and two children and a nice big, expensive house. It looks great on paper, but it's damn empty on the inside.

As Kai's body fills mine, I wish I knew how Daniel and I fell out of love, and I want to know how to keep love if I ever fall in love again.

Kai eventually leaves to go home and shower. He's promised to return at seven-thirty to take me to dinner. When he leaves I don't rush into the shower but sink back onto the rumpled sheets of the bed and just lie there, staring at the ceiling, my hands behind my head.

I feel so different.

Happy and yet sad all at the same time. Happy to be here right now. Sad that in the morning I go home.

But home's where I belong. Home is . . . home. Yet somehow the word *home* right now puts a knot in my stomach and a viselike grip around my throat.

I finally force myself to move. After showering, I do my hair and makeup. Forty, huh?

I lean toward the bathroom mirror and inspect my face.

Hazel eyes, okay skin, decent features, great hair. I love my hair, even if I have to touch up the color every three or four weeks. I've kept my hair past my shoulders, and it's thick, the color somewhere between auburn and chestnut. I'm not a natural redhead. I was a boring, non-descript brunette until I tried this shade ten years ago, and I won't go back. In summer I highlight it a little, lighten it up with gold strands, but red gives me confidence. Makes me feel bold. Brave.

But the face staring back at me doesn't look particularly brave tonight. It looks uncertain—excited as well as a little afraid. There's something about one's birthday that makes you want to be claimed. Kept. Cherished.

For the past two years, I've felt anything but cherished. Yet somehow in forty-eight hours Kai's mended something in me, closed a little of the gap where my heart had felt torn.

Divorce tears your heart and your life. Tears it right in two. The before and the after. Daniel and I were together nearly fifteen years when you add the dating years onto the married years. I met him when I was twenty-five, when we were both living and working overseas. I was in Paris. He was in London. I worked with a fashion designer, and he worked for the U.K. office of Microsoft. We thought we were so urban, sophisticated, and cool.

I smile slightly, amused by the twenty-five-year-old me. And then, catching my reflection in the mirror, I see how I've changed. The eyes have creases (crow's-feet—I hate that word!), the eyelids are a little crepey, there are traces of lines near my mouth. It's the me I've always known, just older.

The phone rings. Kai's already here. I dash into clothes, a copper tank and a copper silk skirt with a fringe at the hem that swishes against my legs as I walk. I push gold bangles onto my arm, slick a little gloss over my lips, grab my purse, and go down to the lobby to meet him.

Kai takes me to a little Italian restaurant on the water near Honolulu, and it's quaint and romantic with nets hanging on the walls and ceiling. Strings of lights and starfish and seashells run through the nets. We sit at a table on the patio, the table so small that our knees bump underneath. Tonight Kai's wearing a great black linen shirt, and with his hair slicked back his eyes have never looked more blue. I love his sideburns, and that square jaw of his makes him look like a blue-eyed Elvis Presley. I love his fifties retro style. It's sexy. *He's* sexy.

Kai orders mai tais, and we sit with our drinks and wedges of pineapple and paper umbrellas and talk about anything and everything. Our salad comes and then the entrées of steak and seafood. I share my ahi with Kai, and he shares his filet mignon with me. I can hear music from the small dark bar, and with the twinkly lights and flickering candle on our table, the romance quotient couldn't be any higher.

"Thank you," I say as the singing waitstaff delivers a slice of macadamia-nut ice-cream pie to me with a little pink candle. The waiters leave and I lean forward, kiss Kai. "Thank you so much. You've made this the best birthday ever."

The corner of his mouth lifts, but his expression is guarded as he reaches out to push hair back from my brow. "You should always be happy, Jackie."

"I wish it were that easy."

"It is. Just choose happiness."

* * *

Back in my hotel room, we've left the sliding glass door and blinds open to let in the warm night and pale moonlight. Kai touches my face in the semidarkness; the caress of his fingertips down my cheek is slow and tender, half inspection, half comfort, and I think I've never been touched this way, have never been touched as if I'm so beautiful. But of course, that can't be true.

I'm sure other men used to touch me this way and I just can't remember; but somehow the past is not here, the past isn't even mine, the past can't be reconciled to now, or with the future. For that matter, I don't want to think about the future, can't imagine the future, since I know Kai won't be in it. But somehow Kai seems so important, seems like everything I ever wanted.

His palm covers my cheek, and his thumb strokes across my mouth. Little bits of fire and flame burst within me.

And then he kisses me—or I him? It doesn't matter, only that I want him, want this kiss. Because I remember the last kiss, and the last kiss made everything young again, and beautiful, so beautiful, made my skin soft and my heart strong, my knees weak and my stomach a mass of butterflies ascending. I want this, and his lips cover mine, and there go the butterflies, all Amazon blues and greens, and I might as well be standing in the middle of the Brazilian rain forest as rain and sun compete and the earth is warmth and life is humid. Fragrant. Complete.

I move into his arms, arms that seem to be made just for me. With his arm around my waist, I feel secure. To be held securely again is even sweeter than I remembered, because I know what it's like now to be dropped. To let go.

I don't want to ever let go.

I don't want him to let me go.

But he will, and I will. I have a plane to catch in the morning, just eight hours from now. Eight hours and I'll be heading home, back to the children I love and the square shingle house with the hopeful dormer windows gazing out on a street of upwardly mobile people.

Finally the kiss ends. It had to. Kai looks at me for a long moment, and it's sweet, nearly endless. This is so perfectly Hollywood, and it bites my heart, bites at the place that's already broken and barely stitched together.

I look into his blue eyes and know I don't know him, don't know what I see from what I want him to be. I wonder if I'll ever see him again, and I wonder if I came back, if he'd feel the same.

If *I'd* feel the same.

And looking at him, feeling his hips against mine, his arm still slung around my waist, his hand against my hip, I know I'd feel the same.

This is what I've wanted, even when married.

Someone different, possibly dangerous. A bad-boy rebel, flawed yet great. Someone who is waiting for someone like me.

Someone who has spent his whole life waiting for me.

"I've got to go now," he says. "But I'll be back to take you to the airport in the morning."

My chest seizes, a terrible little intrusion of reality once again. "You can't stay?"

"No. But I'll be back. I'll drive you. Your flight's at nine?"

"Yes."

"I'll pick you up at quarter to seven."

I'm waiting with my bags in front of the hotel at quarter to seven, and Kai's on time. He loads my luggage in the back of his truck and we're off. It's a quiet drive to the airport. I sit close to him in his truck, and he rests his right hand on my leg, my fingers curled into his.

I feel so brave as I stare straight ahead. I can do this. I can go home and get on with my life, taking home with me everything I've learned in the past five days.

I can.

I can.

At the airport he parks next to the curb, and it isn't until he climbs from his truck and lifts my suitcases from the back that I realize how different this is from how I arrived. I arrived in Honolulu and was met by a limousine. I step now from a pickup truck.

Airport police monitor the traffic, motioning drivers on, and I see them watch as Kai sets my suitcases on the pavement.

"Did you have a good time?" he asks, stepping back, hands sliding into his pockets.

I nod, tuck loose hair behind my ear. I haven't flat-ironed it in days. It's thick and wavy and has new sun streaks from the salt and sun. "I did."

"Think you'll go home and be happy?" His gaze meets mine, and his mouth curves, vaguely rueful. "Happier?"

"I think so."

"Good." He suddenly reaches out, smooths another tendril back from my cheek. "Don't settle, Jacqueline. Whatever you do when you get home, don't settle."

"I'll try not to."

"Not good enough."

I want to take his hand. I want to hold it tight, hold on, because I suddenly don't think I'll ever see him again and I can't bear it, can't stand to think someone who was so good to me, someone who made me feel so good about myself, someone who gave me courage to be myself, is about to disappear. And I know it's me leaving, but it doesn't matter that I'm going and he's staying because it's another loss and I'm not ready for another. I was just starting to enjoy feeling so good.

"I better go." I speak quickly, almost sharply, as I reach for the handle on one of my suitcases. "The security line could be long."

He jams his hands deep in his pockets. A small muscle pulls in his jaw.

I can't look at him. I can't look anymore. My eyes burn, and my throat, when I swallow, feels as if I gulped Tabasco sauce. It's hot, and sore, and burns all the way down.

"See you," I say.

His upper lip lifts. "See ya, girl."

And before one more emotion hits, before one more hope or want or need curls inside me, I go, setting off for the airline ticket counter.

I don't turn back, I don't, not until I know I won't be able to see him. That's when I finally turn around, and I'm right. He's gone. His truck is gone.

I stand in the open-air terminal with people pushing past on all sides, and they keep hurrying this way and that, and the policemen in the street blow their whistles, gesturing traffic past.

Life goes on.

Life just goes on.

It's almost ten in Seattle when we land, and it's raining. The airplane windows are splattered with raindrops, and the tarmac glistens in the dark, wet, shiny asphalt stretching in every direction.

It takes over half an hour for the baggage to appear, and by the time I get my luggage and locate my car, it's quarter to eleven.

Eleven-twenty when I reach home.

One by the time I make it to bed.

I can't sleep, not for a long time. I don't know if it's because I'm alone in the cold house. I don't know if it's because in Hawaii it's only ten o'clock or that I still feel as though I'm humming from flying, but I lie in my bed, feel small and alone, and I don't think I can do this divorce thing after all.

It's lonely.

It's scary.

It's so not what I want life to be like after all.

Lying in bed, I hear the rain fall, the quiet steady downpour on the roof, in the trees, against the window, pings bouncing in and out of the gutters. After nearly fifteen years in Seattle, the rain is both a comfort and a friend. I know the sound of rain well, know the fullness it gives a night, the way it ushers in midnight and fades at daybreak. There are mornings when it's still raining as I drive the kids to school, but most mornings we wake to puddles but dry skies.

Snuggling deeper beneath my duvet, I force myself to keep my eyes closed and to think about rain. Not sun. Or the ocean, or the stunningly sweet scent of plumeria, or the cool, gritty feel of sand between my toes.

I'm home, I tell myself. This is where I belong.

nine

There are nearly a dozen voice mail messages waiting for me after I make my coffee in the morning and turn my attention to my desk. The kids won't be home until two forty-five on the school bus, so I sleepily go through the phone calls and return the ones I can.

Half are business calls—requests for appointments, a question on an invoice, a problem from the furniture restorer in downtown Seattle—and then there are calls from friends and my family wishing me a happy birthday, a voice mail from Jessica singing "Happy Birthday" (why didn't Daniel have her call me on my cell?), and the friends wanting to know about my vacation: Did I have a good time? Did I come home with a killer tan? Did I buy anything fun? Did I meet anyone interesting on the trip?

The trip. I smile faintly even as I feel a tug inside, a bittersweet yank of emotion. Yes, I had a good time; and yes, I met someone interesting. Someone who lives very far away. Someone I probably won't ever see again.

I finish listening to the messages and then delete them. For several long minutes, I stare at the phone. I should call Kris and Anne and Nic, but I don't. I don't know what to tell them. Because I don't know what I'm feeling.

I did have fun. *Too* much fun. Maybe I won't tell them about Kai. I take a sip of my coffee. Maybe they don't need to know about him or the romance.

Yet I feel different. I feel better. Better than I have in a long, long time.

But before I can take a second sip of coffee, the phone rings. I recognize the number. Kristine.

"Back in one piece?" Kristine asks as I answer.

I laugh, immediately relax, sink lower in my desk chair. "Yeah. Definitely feel a little jet-lagged, though. It's only six in the morning there now."

"Was it as miserable being on your own as you thought it'd be?"

"Not really." But I wasn't on my own long.

"So what are your plans today?"

"Work. And then meeting the kids' school bus."

"Are you free at noon? We're planning to take you to lunch for your birthday. We figured we'd better do a lunch party now instead of waiting for a free evening."

"I can do lunch."

"Great. The Leschi Café, twelve o'clock."

"You look rested," Anne says enviously as we settle into our corner table overlooking the lake. We drop our purses at our feet, and bright-colored gift bags and wrapped presents are stacked in front of me.

"And happy," Nic adds, leaning forward on her elbows, her chin propped in her hands. "So what happened? Something did."

"I got a tan," I answer, feeling smug and unusually secretive. The whole weekend with Kai still seems so unbelievable—surreal in the best sort of way. These island romances with gorgeous younger men don't really happen, not to real women like me. There are two realities, you know: Hollywood reality and everyone else's reality. What flies in Los Angeles doesn't necessarily fly in Boise, Idaho, or Waco, Texas.

"You keep smiling," Kristine notes dryly, setting aside the menu without even glancing at it. "That's not like you."

"No?" But I am smiling, and I think Kris is right. I haven't smiled in a long, long time. In fact, I can't remember when I last smiled this much. The muscles in my face feel warm, stretchy, and my insides keep fizzing like champagne at New Year's.

"Talk," Anne orders. "Tell us everything. Remember, we're living through you."

My friends are awesome. They love me to death, were incredible this last year while everything came apart and I had to put it back together again, but I know they don't really understand what I'm going through. How can they? They're all still married.

I remember a conversation we had last April when we were out for Nic's fortieth birthday. Everyone went around the table and mentioned what wedding anniversary was coming up next—seventeen years, ten years, fourteen years, eleven years—and when it came to me, I said zero. I was trying to be funny, because I hadn't yet reached my one-year anniversary of being divorced. My friends laughed, but beneath their laughter was tension and confusion. They were uncomfortable, and so was I. I'm one of them. But I'm not.

And they want to live through me. But then they don't.

One of my eyebrows quirks. "I'm not sure you can handle it."

"Oooh, I like a challenge," Kris says. "Let's see what you've got."

Everyone laughs. I shake my head as if to say "You asked for it." "I did meet someone."

"Knew it," Nic pounced.

"And . . . ?" Anne prompts. "Where does he live, what does he do? Will you see him again?"

I picture Kai, and the warm fizzy inside me grows. I'm jet-lagged, wired, and excited all at the same time, and I'm not sure I've got the words to make them understand, to see what I saw, feel what I felt. After all, they know marriage and home, babies and family, and while I knew that once, I'm now alone and wide open, no longer a fortress of wedded stability and security.

"Start with his name," commands Kris, ever logical.

"Kai." I clutch my menu, press the rigid leather edge to my middle. I look from Anne to Nic and then to Kris. "Kai Carson."

"Kai," Nic repeats. "That's an unusual name."

"He's an unusual guy."

"Guy," Anne repeats. "Kai Guy. That sounds promising."

I roll my eyes and grip the menu tighter. "Okay, you want promising? He's thirty. Tattooed. A surfer. *And* we had three days of unbelievable sex. How's that?"

For a moment there's just dead silence, and then Kris starts laughing. "You're serious," she says. I nod. Grinning, Kris stretches a hand across the table to high-five me. "Good for you, Jackie. 'Bout time you had some fun."

My palm smacks hers, and Anne and Nic are smiling, but I see ambiguity in Nic's expression.

"What?" I demand, looking at her.

"Nothing."

"Come on. Say it. I can tell you're not happy about something."

Her lips purse primly. "You had sex with a stranger."

Oh God. "Yes."

"You did use protection, didn't you?"

"Yes."

"Was it good?" Anne is leaning forward. "Really good?"

My smile is back, and it trembles on my lips, exuberant and innocent. I know why people write poems and songs about falling in love, because there's something magical that happens, something all fresh and shiny and new about the beginnings of love, even if this is more infatuation than love. But the hope one feels, the hope *I* feel, is almost unbearable, so big and full, round like a giant balloon or a miniature sun. I wish I could feel this way all the time. For the first time in years, I think I could do anything.

"The sex was great, but it was more than that." I look at them, try to make them understand. "He was great. He was . . ." I drift off, bite my lip. "Amazing. Gorgeous. Smart. Funny. Young." I blush, wrinkle my nose. "But so gorgeous. And he liked me."

"What's not to like, Jack?" Kris counters. "You're beautiful and smart, successful."

"But you should have seen him. He looked . . ." And my voice fades away because it wasn't just his looks, it was the way he was with me and the way he made me feel—especially the way he made me feel about myself—and I didn't think a man could do that, not after the years of criticism from Daniel. Not after the years of criticism from myself. Those few days with Kai made me think things would actually be okay again someday, that my life wasn't over and the adventures were only just beginning. "With him I didn't feel like a mom, or forty, or Daniel's ex-wife. I just felt like me, only better."

"You couldn't get any better," Nic says stoutly.

"I could," I say. "I could be happier." I hesitate. "I will be happier."

"Good." Kris raises her water glass. "Let's drink to that."

During lunch, another group of women are seated at a table near ours. They, too, arrive with gifts and flowers, clearly celebrating a birthday as well. The six women are elegant and stylish, and as they sit and begin talking, we realize they're celebrating a fiftieth birthday.

Kris leans over toward the other table and gets the attention of one of the ladies. "Are you celebrating a birthday today?" she asks.

"Yes, Marsha's fiftieth," the woman answers, and Marsha with her sleek dark hair gives a wave.

"We're celebrating Jackie's fortieth, and if you don't mind, we're wondering what the difference is between forty and fifty."

The women at the fiftieth-birthday table smile, and a silvery blonde leans toward us and drawls, "When you're forty you decide it's time to do what you want to do, even if it means upsetting others. At fifty you do what you want to do, and you don't give a shit what other people think."

The ladies at her table laugh and lift their champagne flutes for an impromptu toast. Nic, Kris, and Anne all turn back to me. "Wow," Kris says, impressed. "Bring on fabulous fifty."

After returning home with my flowers and gifts, I zip out again to buy a small cake and some party plates and napkins so I can have a little birthday celebration with Jessica and William tonight.

I can't wait to see the kids. I've missed them so much, and they'll be home in just half an hour now.

Bundled up, I'm on the street at the bus stop early. It rained in the night, but today is crisp and clear, the sky pale blue against the jutting dark green pine trees. Perched on a neighbor's low stone wall, I leaf through an industry magazine but can't focus. I keep checking my watch, monitoring the passing of minutes. Time seems to be passing so slowly right now. I'm anxious to grab my kids, hug them tight, make them mine again.

The yellow bus eventually arrives, and my kids race off, Jessica practically screaming with delight. William squeezes me until I can't breathe. "Happy birthday, Mom!" he says, and then Jessica is joining in with a chorus of high-pitched, "Happy birthday to you, you live in a zoo, you smell like a monkey—" And I'm sure you know the rest.

We walk back to the house. I am carrying Jessica's

backpack for her as she holds my hand. William is telling me about the Sonics game their dad took them to over the weekend and how Ray Allen scored forty points for his third game in a row. I nod and smile, listening and not listening, so glad to be with them again, glad to see the sun, glad to be alive.

That night after dinner, we read the cards and open the gifts the kids have bought for me—I know the store wrapped the gifts, not Daniel—and then William and Jessica struggle to place forty candles on the small cake I bought.

"We don't need to put all forty candles on," I protest laughingly as the striped candles crowd the pink frosting, tipping this way and that. "We only need a few. The candles are symbolic more than anything."

"But Mom, you're forty," William answers, counting the candles once more to make sure they've got them all.

Finally, cake blazing, we turn off the dining room light. The kids' eyes shine as they sing; their faces glow golden in the candlelight. Love is such a strange thing, grabs you and doesn't let go. Listening to my kids sing "Happy Birthday" to me, I don't think I have ever loved them as much as I do right now. Blond Jessica with her gap between her bottom teeth and William with his handsome face and serious hazel eyes.

They reach the end of the song, and I blow out all the candles before the cake can catch fire.

Dining room light back on, I cut the cake, making sure Jessica and William both have good pieces while I take the first piece I cut, the piece that comes out messy and broken. It's so second nature to take the piece that isn't pretty, that doesn't have all the icing, that I don't even think twice until I take a bite. And then suddenly I look at the beautiful cake and then down at my plate with the mashed top layer and the naked bottom layer, and I don't want this piece. I want a pretty piece. It's my birthday cake. My fortieth birthday cake. Can't I have a good piece on my own birthday?

I cut another slice of cake, this one with a rose, and put it on the plate with all the candles.

"What are you doing?" Jessica asks.

"Getting a better piece of cake," I answer, licking off the frosting on the knife.

"But you had a piece."

"I know, but it's my birthday and I want a rose, too."

Jessica glares at me. "You're supposed to save the roses for us."

I cut into my cake, take a big bite. "Says who?"

And Jessica just looks at me, mouth gaping. I smile around my mouthful of moist cake and gooey icing. I think I'm going to like being forty.

In the morning after the kids have left for school, I go to my desk and check my e-mail and then my voice mail. I'm hoping to find a message from Kai. I want him to call.

I've been back from Hawaii only two days, but in some ways it feels like a week. The contrast between Hawaii and Seattle is so great, almost too great. It was so warm and bright in Hawaii, so full of vivid colors and rushing sounds and fragrant smells. But late January in Seattle is lots of scattered clouds and gray.

And damp.

And cold.

I'm cold. I leave my desk, go downstairs, and make a cup of tea, then stand at the window, looking out at the garden where the rain comes steadily down.

I miss Hawaii.

I miss Kai.

I want to jump on a plane and go back.

I should go back. No reason I can't.

And the rain comes down, steady, so steady, so much steadier than me.

The week passes and I try to catch up on my work, wrapping up one project while bidding on another. But I'm distracted. I keep checking my phone, check voice mail, log on to my computer to check e-mail.

He's not going to call. He enjoyed me while I was there, found me entertaining, diverting, amusing. But I'm gone now, and out of sight is out of mind.

I can't make him want me or remember me. Just as I can't make him call. I'd like to call him, but I don't. I can't. It'd be throwing myself at him, and that smacks of desperation.

I'm feeling desperation.

I'm close to tears as I climb into bed on Friday. It's confusing, the intensity of my feelings. I felt so much there, and now I don't know what to do with all the feelings I woke. Forty is supposed to be calm, but I'm not calm at all.

A day later, my phone buzzes with a text message: "Hope you had a good flight home. Kai."

Kai. *Kai.* Hand shaking, I save the message. But the

moment I've saved the message and put away the phone, I feel the strongest urge to call him. Return a message. Connect with him.

Come on, Jack. Down, girl. Give it some time.

Like how much? An hour? Two hours? Four days? In the end, I wait a day before text messaging him back.

"Was a great trip. Thanx 4 everything."

I push "send" even as I grip the phone, wishing I could say more, wanting to say more, wanting to find out what he's thinking—feeling—if he's missing me at all or thinking about me half as much as I'm thinking about him. I don't let myself call or text message again. The benefit of being forty instead of twenty-five or thirty is that I've finally internalized a measure of self-control.

Hmph. So much for my self-control. Late that night, I sit at my computer and search the Internet for hotel and air deals to Hawaii.

I find the best vacation value at NWA.com, the Northwest Airlines site. I flew Northwest last time to Hawaii—had never flown them before and had a great experience (okay, I was in first class, but still everyone, including the ticket and gate agents, was very friendly), and at NWA.com I can get a three-night, four-day trip with hotel and air for a thousand dollars. A thousand dollars. A lot of money for me right now, but it'd be so worth it to see Kai again. . . .

If he'd even want to see me again . . .

Another day passes and I feel as if I'm losing control.

I want to call Kai. I've been wanting to call him all day—for two days as a matter of fact—but I don't know the protocol for calling sexy young guys.

Here in Madison Park, it's hard for me to think of a thirty-year-old as a man. But Daniel was twenty-nine when we married—obviously at one point I thought twenty-nine or thirty mature for a relationship, but now that I'm the older one, I'm not sure.

I'm not sure about anything.

I study my nails, the ends short, a little chipped, frayed by salt water and nerves. I never chew my nails, but that's what I've been doing all day. Biting my nails and waiting for my surfer to call or text message me back. But in my gut I wonder—worry—that he won't. That he's already moved on, said his good-bye, let go.

I obviously haven't let go, even though what's left of my rational mind is screaming that I should.

What do we even have in common? What would make this work?

We live worlds apart, not just geographically, but socially.

Our lifestyles are completely at odds, and Kai was the one who told me all this. Kai knows we're different.

But he still liked me.

And I very much liked him.

I bite another nail, feel it break between my teeth, and sigh. What am I doing? Not just with Kai, but with my nails? Why am I doing this to my hands? My life?

I'm a control person. I like things tidy. One of the pleasures in being a designer is that I can bring order to chaos. I can organize, improve, impact not just people's homes, but their lives. Since my divorce I've battled to get control over mine . . . yet one visit to Hawaii, one long weekend spent with a sexy younger man, and I'm tied up in knots. I feel like a kid again.

I really, *really* want to call him. I want to hear Kai's voice. I want to remember what it was that I liked about him, remember what made Kai so different from the other surf instructors on the beach.

What would he do if I called him? Would he laugh at me? Would he think I was daring or pathetic? Sexy or lonely? Bold or foolish?

The old guilty Jackie part of me says foolish, but the newer me, the one who loves laughing and playing and just being silly, knows that Kai liked me, so he'd say bold. And sexy.

Especially sexy.

I grin into the palm of my hand, smiling so wide that my cheeks hurt. But even better than the smile is that surge of happiness inside. The feeling of joy and an abundance of hope.

Things will work out. One way or another. Things always work out.

Late the next morning, I climb into my car after a visit to Crowne hardware with a client who didn't have a clue what she wanted and didn't like anything I suggested. This is one of those clients who seem to enjoy rejecting everything, which means endless shopping trips and endless (futile) searches. I know I bill by the hour, but still, I have so many clients and so much to do that *I* need to check things off my to-do list even if my client doesn't.

It's raining as we leave Crowne, and my client zips away in her Lexus sedan as I struggle into my SUV with the client's enormous spec book. Climbing into my seat, I bang my head on the side of the door, squeeze the binder past the steering wheel as I curse the rain, curse my client, who will call me tonight and want to moan about today's limited choices, and curse my new wanderlust—because all I want to do is hop on the first plane out of here. Preferably one heading to Hawaii.

Obviously I can't do that. I have too much work, and William's got a book report due at the end of the week, and I don't think he's even started reading the book.

My cell phone rings as I shut the car door. I dig in my purse and retrieve the phone before the call goes into voice mail. "Hello?"

"What are you wearing?"

My breath catches. *Kai.* "You'd be sadly disappointed."

"Try me."

"A suit, a trench coat, and wet high heels."

"Sounds lovely."

"Mmmm. What are you wearing?"

"Nothing."

His husky laugh sends tingles through me, and I grip the phone tighter. "Nothing?"

"I just woke up."

"What time is it there?"

"Nine o'clock."

"You're not working?"

"It's my day off, and I'm just lying in bed thinking about you."

I grow hot all over, rub a knuckle nervously above my upper lip.

"Had a very sexy dream about you, too."

I can hardly breathe. The heat grows, gathering in my face, making my cheeks hot, my skin burn. "You did." My voice is all but inaudible.

"You were naked."

I close my eyes, run an unsteady hand through my damp hair.

"Riding me," he adds.

I've stopped breathing. I press my forehead to the steering wheel, hear the rain come down on my roof, the windshield, the street, and I'm not in Seattle anymore. I'm not in Hawaii, either. Frankly, I don't know where I am. Who I am. It's unnerving and yet exciting.

Hearing my silence, Kai laughs softly. "Still there?"

"Yes," I whisper.

"Good. For a minute I thought you might have hung up."

"Oh, no."

"So how are you, girl?"

"Good. Great. Work's been busy."

"Is that why you haven't called?"

I lean back in my seat, start the engine. "Was I supposed to call?"

"I hoped you would."

I turn on the windshield wipers, allow the back window to defog. "Why?"

"Why do you think?"

"Because I'm good in bed?"

He laughs some more. "Yes. And because I like you."

And that, I think, settles that. I'm going back to Hawaii. It's just a question of when.

"Tell me I heard you wrong," Anne says with a groan. "Tell me you didn't say you're really going back."

It's one o'clock a day later, and I've met Anne for a quick coffee. But it's not the coffee chat either of us expected. Anne's currently looking at me as if I'm out of my mind, and for a moment I wonder if I am.

No, not for a moment, but for many moments. I've had this same conversation with myself, the worry that I'm rushing into something, that I've no idea what I'm rushing toward.

But I want to go back. I want to see Kai again. "I love Hawaii," I say, voice calm, absolutely even, because there's no way I can let her know about all my self-doubt or Anne will never back off then. Anne's a rock. Beautiful. Smart. Solid in the middle, whereas I'm definitely more flighty, definitely less . . . rocklike, because I refuse to use the word *unstable*. I'm not unstable. I'm just a little less grounded. And almost immediately I think of Diamond Head and Shark's Cove and the red rocky hill we climbed down to reach the beach for snorkeling.

"Hawaii's lovely, but, Jack . . ." Her voice drifts off, and she's staring at me over her cappuccino. "It's *Hawaii*."

"Right."

Anne sighs inwardly, the kind of sigh we all heard growing up when the parents didn't like what we were saying or doing. She doesn't like what I'm saying. Or doing. She hasn't liked anything I've said about Hawaii—or Kai—since I've returned. "It was an island romance," she says now, evenly, matching me tone for tone. She's no dummy. She's a mom, too. Being wives, becoming mothers, has taught us how to deal with unreasonable people.

And that's what makes the greatest impression now.

She thinks I'm being unreasonable.

Why? Because I want romance? Passion? Adventure?

"If I can afford to go, why shouldn't I go back?" I look at her levelly, using economics as my first defense. This is something else husbands and children have taught us. Men respond to the financial picture. Men want to know how much it's going to cost, how much they're going to lose, how much they're going to have to work to earn back capital squandered.

You can almost see it in their eyes as you talk to them. *Ch-ching, ch-ching,* three hours at the office, minus taxes, minus lost investment opportunity, plus disruption of home life, personal inconvenience of possibly having to watch kids or, God forbid, change a diaper himself . . .

"And of course I'd only go when Daniel has the kids. So it's not as if I'm hurting anyone," I conclude, using the kids as my final trump card. Men might respond to the financial picture, but women respond to the relationship picture, with all its emotional ties and entanglements.

Anne doesn't speak. She just stares at the wall.

She thinks I'm wrong.

And her judgment gets my hackles up. I don't have to answer to her. I don't have to answer to anyone anymore.

I'm an adult. A woman. I've been to school, earned a degree, had a career, raised babies, paid bills. Why can't I do what I want? Why do we women feel that we have to answer to one another?

And what's wrong with feeling good? What's wrong with having fun?

"I thought you were going to work full-time again." Anne breaks her pumpkin scone into two pieces and passes half to me. "You said you needed the income—"

"I'm working."

"You said you needed more clients, that you needed to do some advertising, maybe participate in this year's Street of Dreams."

My God. Anne is worse than my mom and my grandmother combined. "I've already made inquiries."

"Jack . . ."

I feel something inside me sink. Strange emotion prickles the back of my eyes. I know what she wants me to say. I know what she wants me to do. I'm forty. I'm supposed to grow up, be mature, do the responsible thing.

"If Kai were older and had a different job, you wouldn't care."

"But he's not older and he doesn't have a different job, and if he showed you such a great time, it means he's probably shown a hundred other women the same great time."

"I don't think he's like that. He treated me really well, made special plans for my birthday—"

"He took you to an Italian restaurant. Big deal."

"It *was* a big deal," I say softly, looking up at her, my hurt cloaked. It's not going to accomplish anything by getting into it with her. She doesn't understand. She's not where I am. She has a husband who comes home to her at night, a family for the weekends, all the usual things I used to know . . . I used to do.

But in the year I've been single, the invitations have declined, the support from others dwindled. It's not that "our group" doesn't care. They have simply returned to what they need to do—their families, their lives, their careers.

And I'm here trying to figure out what I'm supposed to do.

Not just for today, but for the future. For all the days ahead of me, the years of forty and forty-five, fifty, and so on.

If I'm not a wife but a mother, what does that make me?

Maternal? Nurturing? What about sexual?

Kai made me feel sexual. Kai made me feel like a woman for the first time in, oh . . . years.

Years.

"I'm going to go back," I say, and this time it's firm, no argument, nothing tentative in my voice. "I have to."

Anne just looks at me, blue eyes somber, serious, with all the regret and reluctance one watches a fifteen-year-old boy with.

She thinks I'm in trouble.

And you know, I just might be.

ten

fter the kids are settled doing their homework, I head upstairs to my office and call Kai on his cell phone. He picks up before his voice mail comes on. "Hey, girl."

Everything inside me goes warm. I take a quick, nervous breath. He's still a stranger to me, yet he makes me want more.

More him. More me.

"What's going on?" he asks, and I suddenly don't know how to get the words out.

I want to come back . . .

I want to see you . . .

What if Anne's right? What if he is like Adam Sandler's character in *50 First Dates*? What if Kai does have a different woman every week . . . if he didn't like me but just wanted another conquest, another notch on his belt of female scalps? Scalps in bikinis.

"If I came back in a couple weeks, would you want to see me?" I blurt the words fast, not knowing how else to get them out.

"Yes."

There's no hesitation in his voice, yet I squint my eyes, try to imagine him, to see what he's doing right now. All I can see is him sitting on some lounge chair with the new flavor of the week.

My insides cramp. I take a quick breath, hating myself, hating that I'm romantic and foolish and so obviously needy.

Because I do need him. I need to feel again how he made me feel.

Beautiful. Smart. Sexy. Young.

Young.

He didn't care about the stretch marks on my belly, the slope of my breasts courtesy of pregnancy weight gain and subsequent breast-feeding, the dimple dashes on the backs of my thighs, cellulite created by thirty-some years of living, or the creases at my eyes and the deepening lines near my mouth. He never pointed out any of the things I see in the mirror every time I strip naked or step from the shower.

His touch made me feel like new again, shiny gift-wrapped, a gift to be opened.

I've missed that feeling. It's been, well . . . forever . . . since I've felt this way. And thinking back, back to the years when Daniel and I had just met, first started dating, I wonder: Did I feel all shiny and pretty and new then?

I suppose I did, but I don't really remember, because I'd forgotten this feeling, forgotten the butterflies and chemistry, that intense wanting, the way the body craves skin, satisfaction, the way the mind won't forget, much less let go.

I can't let go. "Are you sure? It wouldn't be a problem?"

"No. When are you coming out?" he asks, and his voice goes inside me, fills me, and my pulse leaps. This is so dangerous and so seductive at the same time.

"The kids' winter break from school." I pause. "They'll be with their dad in Palm Springs." And the moment the words are out of my mouth, I feel like a Bad Woman, one of those ladies on the evening television soap operas, *Dallas* meets *Desperate Housewives* twenty years later. But I'm not a Bad Woman. I'm a very average woman except for the fact that I've got my kids in a different house from their father's and I'm having to figure out how to live the rest of my life in a way I never thought I'd live it.

And maybe doing a younger man makes me a Bad Woman, too.

That and the fact that he's sinfully beautiful and shockingly good in bed.

"Just tell me the dates, and if I'm not working, I'll pick you up at the airport," Kai says now, and I suddenly wonder, If little girls grow up to be dissatisfied housewives, what do little boys grow up to be?

"It wouldn't be an inconvenience?" I persist.

He hesitates for a second, and then I hear soft laughter, as if I am infinitely amusing. "No."

"So what happens on the island, stays on the island."

"Mmm-hmm."

"And when I went back to the mainland, that would be it."

"Yeah."

"But now I want to come back and see you, and it's not part of the . . . rules."

Another silence, followed by another soft laugh. "You think too much."

"I know." I feel a hint of panic, fear that I've done this wrong, gone about this all wrong. I shouldn't be chasing some young guy, shouldn't be putting myself out there, open to censure and ridicule.

"Maybe I shouldn't—" I break off, waiting to see if he'll finish the thought for me, indicating his feelings one way or another.

He doesn't. He lets me sit in silence, sit in my desperate need for reassurance. I want him to convince me I should come out.

I must be out of my mind. Having a midlife crisis. Why do I want Kai? Why do I want to do this to myself? I know what he is . . . know what he said he is . . . a beach boy. A player. Trouble.

Trouble. There's that word again.

"I haven't booked my travel yet," I say carelessly, casually, as if careless and casual are what I do best. "But I'll probably be there only a few days. Three, four. And if we can have dinner or drinks, great. But no worries if you can't."

Kai, damn him, laughs that soft little laugh and says, "Sure, girl. Whatever you say."

Daniel isn't so cooperative when he drops off the kids at my house Sunday night. I wait for the kids to go inside before asking him about his travel plans for winter break so I can plan mine.

"I don't know what day we'll fly down," he answers irritably, trying to close his car door on me so he can escape.

I don't let him escape. "But I need to know. I'm try-ing to book an airline ticket myself."

"I don't want to deal with this right now."

"Fine. I'll just drop the kids at your house Saturday the fifteenth on my way to the airport, then."

"Saturday the fifteenth?"

"The first day of their winter holiday. They've got a week off from school."

"I know what winter break is, and I know they've got a week."

"Great. I'll plan on flying out on Saturday, then." I keep my smile friendly. "If you want them after school Friday, I can do that, too."

"I'll look at my calendar—"

"No need to. It's your time to be with the kids." I step back, allow him to shut the door. "Have a good week."

He doesn't move. He looks at me suspiciously. "Where are you going in February?"

"Away."

"Away where?"

It's none of his business, but we were on the same team so long, it's hard to dismiss him. "Back to Hawaii."

He's silent a moment, his face perfectly expression-less, before he barks a laugh. "Are you having a midlife crisis?" It's Daniel's favorite way of talking to me now. I've no brain, no value, nothing of importance anymore. Now that we're divorced, he can talk to me however he likes. Funny, the lack of civilities only reminds me why we're no longer together. Won't be talked to like a dog. Have a good mind.

"No midlife crisis, Daniel."

"So why back to Hawaii?"

I know I don't owe him an answer. I know I don't owe him anything. He's entitled to think what he wants, and I'm free to do what I want. But answering to him, humoring him, is such an ingrained habit. "I like Hawaii."

He makes a face, his expression mocking. "Or your surf instructor."

I stiffen. How does he know? Who told him? And then I realize how the system works. I tell Anne, and Anne tells Phil, and while Phil and Daniel play golf or have steaks at the Metropolitan Grill, they talk shit about me.

Grrrr.

Let them. Hell with them.

"Yeah," I say, beaming up at him. "I had a great time learning to surf."

"You really surfed."

"I really surfed."

"I can't imagine you surfing."

"Well, neither could I, but I surfed three different times and I can't wait to do it again."

"As well as the surfer."

I grit my teeth. "He's a cool guy."

"Heard he's young."

I say nothing.

"You're really reaching, aren't you?"

I still say nothing.

"You know what they say about those guys—"

"Daniel." I look him in the eye. "You're dating Melinda. What's the big deal?"

"Melinda's brilliant. Successful. Ambitious."

"And that makes her superior because . . . ?"

"You're awfully defensive, Jack."

"I don't need you judging me."

"I'm not judging. I just find it funny." He's got that smirking thing going again. "You and your beach boy."

"I'll see you later." I scoop up Jessica's backpack and walk away.

And it hits me as I walk into the house that I'm trapped. Trapped in life, by life, trapped by decisions that seemed so good years ago. Trapped by the me I used to be, trapped by the me I am now, trapped by a future that isn't yet here but teases me endlessly, relentlessly.

To want more. To need more. To crave more with every breath, every thought, every bit of me.

And more right now happens to be in Hawaii.

The weeks pass slowly, but finally winter break approaches and I begin packing for the trip, thinking that for this trip I need more casual stuff and less fancy "cruise wear," as Kai put it. I go shopping downtown, buy a few new swimsuits—two-pieces, something I haven't worn since before the kids were born—as well as fun skirts and tops. Packed, I set my suitcase back in my closet so the kids won't see and then turn my attention to the clothes they'll need for the week in Palm Springs with their dad.

But Thursday after school, when I go to Jessica's room to pack, I find her facedown on her pale pink carpet, her Barbies strewn around her in various states of dress and undress, her head buried in her arm.

"Jess?"

She doesn't lift her head, just turns it slightly. I glimpse tears streaking her cheek, and everything in me squeezes tight. Kneeling next to her, I put my hand on the fragile little-girl bones of her back. "Jessie, what's wrong?"

Again, just that small shake of her head even as her back heaves under the palm of my hand. She's crying, crying hard, and I can't bear it. "Jess, talk to me, baby."

"I can't." Her voice is agonized, strangled.

"Why not?"

"Because."

"Because why?"

Finally she lifts her head and her wet blue eyes find mine and she stares at me helplessly, stares at me as though she's lost all hope."I'm never going to be happy again."

"Why do you say that?"

"Because I have to go to Daddy's tomorrow."

"But you love going to Daddy's."

"But I'll miss you."

"You'll be back soon."

"But then I'll miss Daddy." She sniffles and scrubs at her eyes, but the tears keep falling.

For a moment, I can't speak. I just look at her and I see her face, the heart-shaped face with the stubborn chin and tiny nose, the pink cheeks, and the intensely blue eyes. She has golden-colored hair—from Daniel, not me—yet while she looks angelic she breathes fire, and my fiery angel is positively heartbreaking now. "But you know you'll see Daddy again soon," I whisper huskily, reaching out to touch her cheek and then one of her loose tangled curls.

"But then I'll miss you." She draws a ragged breath, and fresh tears well in her eyes. "I'll never be happy again because I'll always be missing someone. You, and then Daddy, and then you."

Please God, don't make it this hard for them. Don't make them hurt this much.

I inhale, hard, and my fingers tangle in her blond curls. Her hair is so silky, baby fine, like the baby she still is. "It won't always be this difficult." I manage to get the words out without my own voice cracking. "It'll get easier, Jess, I promise."

She shakes her head, pulling away from my touch. "No, it won't. Not if you and Daddy stay divorced."

I just look at her.

"Why do you have to be divorced? Why can't you and Daddy get back together? Why can't you just stop fighting and be a family again?"

"I wish we could—"

"Then do it!" she screams at me, her eyes liquid blue. "Do it now. Do it for me!"

I lift her off the carpet, and despite her brief, initial struggle, I pull her into my arms, where she curls against me, her wet face buried against my chest. In my arms she just sobs, and my heart breaks yet again. My heart, once so sure of itself, is as shattered as my children's.

Life is never what one thinks it's going to be.

I rock Jessica in my arms. "Daddy and I can't get together again, but it's going to be better soon. It's going to be better, I promise."

I drive to the airport so torn. I nearly cried as I dropped the kids off at Daniel's. Jessica clung to me in tears, and William stood stoically at his dad's side after giving me a grown-up hug good-bye. I hate good-byes, especially good-byes with my children.

As I park at the terminal, I know that Jessica is right. If Daniel and I were still together, none of this would be happening. I'd be with him and the children. I'd be making dinner tonight for my kids, sipping a glass of wine in my Palm Springs kitchen as Daniel and the kids floated in the pool outside.

I don't know if Daniel fell in love with another woman or if he just fell out of love with me, but we definitely grew apart—not outwardly, at least not the way one would think, because our friends were all hugely surprised when we announced we'd separated and were planning to file for divorce.

No one seemed to understand how we could take such a drastic step, especially as we both had been such good, devoted parents and clearly loved our children.

We do love our children.

We will always love our children. But we couldn't seem to do it together anymore, not in the same house, not sitting in the same room, when our anger and fights became routine behavior. We didn't talk—we argued. We didn't disagree—we exploded.

Daniel missed the woman he thought he'd married, and I missed the man who thought I'd been beautiful, clever, wonderful.

I didn't think I changed, but somehow becoming settled in a relationship, becoming mother to William and Jessica, made me someone else. Someone apparently less than I'd been before.

Walking through the terminal, pulling my suitcase, I

ask myself if I would have left Daniel over a slipup, a misstep, a simple infidelity. (Is it ever simple, though?) No. No, of course not. But this was more than a mistake on Daniel's part. This was proof that we weren't who we once were, we didn't have what we needed, we couldn't be what we'd hoped to be.

I don't know what Daniel was looking for when he started the affair. More, probably. But that's exactly what I wanted, too. More. And admitting that I wanted more turned out to be the beginning of the end.

On the plane, I close my eyes as the jet taxis down the runway and lifts off.

I always say a little prayer when I fly, always send the kids my love and try to make peace with life. If I could end up divorced, I could end up dead. Grim but true, and airplanes provide great opportunities to face one's mortality.

But we reach cruising altitude without even a bump of turbulence, and the sky above the dark clouds blanketing Seattle is blue and bright, almost dazzling with the intense morning light.

God's country, William used to call the sky at thirty thousand feet. Up here God is always smiling, he'd say, and if I were God, I'd be in a good mood, too, if the sky was always blue.

Once the seat belt sign is turned off, I get up to use the lavatory. On the way back, I catch the eye of one of the businessmen. He lowers his paper to look at me, and his gaze lingers, revealing interest, and I smile a little, a silent hello. It isn't until I'm seated and he reopens his newspaper that I see the wedding band on his left hand.

Bastard.

Maybe in the past if a married man looked at me, smiled at me, I wouldn't have reacted this way, wouldn't have felt so angry and defensive. But now that I know about Daniel's affair (affairs?), the wedding rings on married men glint bright and hard at me.

Was Daniel wearing his wedding ring when he met his first mistress? Did he wear it when they were in bed together? What did he tell her about our marriage?

I take out a book and try to read, but the book doesn't grab me. I try my magazines, and even those—the newest issues of *Oprah, Vanity Fair,* and *Town & Country*— can't hold me. I don't know if it's the rough past few days or my nerves at returning to Hawaii, but the flight feels endless. I fidget, and fidget some more.

I'm as bad as Jessica, I think, going to the back of the airplane yet again to stand in the queue for the bathroom, not that I really need to go. I just can't bear sitting anymore, and we still have two and a half hours to go.

What if this is a mistake, going? What if seeing Kai again is awkward and uncomfortable? What if the sex isn't good? What if all the pleasure was in my imagination?

I step back, allowing more people to squeeze past, my back pressed to another passenger in line. We're human sardines, I think, glancing down at my arm and seeing my Mystic tan, the color a generous golden brown. I like the color. I like me tan, even fake tan.

I'm feeling so different lately, so brave, so young, so headstrong. I'm not sure whether to laugh or cry at this new me. I was never one to take risks like this. I never chased men.

What I do remember is getting pregnant, giving birth, holding my babies for the first time.

I remember how difficult William's birth was and the hours of labor and the talk of wheeling me in for an emergency cesarean if I didn't get him out soon. Then somehow all nine pounds of him was there, his big shoulders wrapped tightly in a blanket, and he was propped in the crook of my arm on the bed because I was so weak that I had no strength left. But I saw him, felt him, looked into his wide, serious eyes, and my world has never been the same. My world has been his, my heart has been his, too.

People tell me children are resilient, that they can heal and recover from almost anything provided they're given time and love. And I tell myself that there are worse things that could happen—death, dismemberment—but those are small comforts while the kids struggle to adjust to a world that isn't Mom and Dad squared. Some kids never have both parents at home, but my kids did. My kids know what they're missing. And I hate that.

Turbulence sends me back to my seat, and we're strapped in for the duration of the flight. Finally we descend, touch ground, and I turn on my cell phone as we file off the plane.

There are half a dozen messages, including two from Kai. The first from him says he's been called into work and can't meet me at the airport after all. The second call is from the beach. He phoned between lessons to see if I'd landed yet.

I take a taxi to my hotel, but I can't check in because it's too early. I wander around the hotel in my slacks and blouse, nervous and exhilarated. My phone rings just as I contemplate going into the hotel restaurant for lunch. It's Kai. "Where are you?" he asks.

"At the hotel. Can't check in until three p.m."

"So get your suit and come on down to the beach."

"But you're working, aren't you?"

"I can still get you a setup."

I so want to see him. "When do you go out on your next lesson?"

"In a half hour, but it's only an hour lesson."

"I'll be there soon."

On the beach, I find Kai just about to begin the land lesson, and yet when he spots me in my suit and sarong, toting my oversize straw bag, he leaves his student to come over and kiss me on the cheek, take my beach bag from me, and walk me to the umbrella and lounge chair.

"I'll see you in an hour or so," he says, patting my butt once before returning to his lesson. I sink onto the lounge's blue padded cushion and feel so much, feel more than I thought I could feel—feelings right now that are more good than bad, feelings that remind me I'm a woman. And human. And that even bad, divorcée me needs love.

I need love.

Swallowing, I reach for the bottle of sunscreen and squeeze a big white dollop in my palm and begin spreading it across my shoulders. I need so much love that it scares me. When did I become starved? Greedy? And does any other woman feel this way?

Kai drops next to me on the lounge chair after his lesson. He's wearing a Billabong hat, sunglasses that hide his eyes, and remnants of white sunblock all over his nose and jaw. Even dusted with salt water, he looks magnificent. He kisses me quickly, and I duck my head, covering my smile, hands knotted in my lap.

"You look beautiful," he says, and I look up at him, a blush spreading across my face. I shake my head once, my heart beating hard, the frantic tempo reminding me of an inexperienced girl with her first real crush.

"How was it out there?" I ask, pulling a strand of hair behind my ear.

"Good."

I nod, fingers locking, unlocking, and suddenly we have run out of things to say. Kai cocks his head, looks at me. "What's wrong?"

I shake my head. There's nothing wrong, but I'm so jittery inside, as if I've had too much coffee and am flooded with caffeine. "I'm just glad to be here."

He smiles, white teeth flashing, and despite his dark glasses I see the creases at the corners of his eyes. Sunburned surfer boy. My heart lurches, and I'm still not sure why I wanted him, picked him, what I saw in a man ten years my junior, a man who is so comfortable in his skin.

Maybe I'd hoped he'd make me feel comfortable in mine.

I suddenly laugh. "What am I doing here, Kai Carson?"

"Having a good time."

My nose crinkles as I smile. "Yeah. That's right."

He leans forward again, kisses me a second time, his sunglasses bumping mine. "It's okay to be happy. You're supposed to have a good time." He stands up, extends a hand to me. "Let's go get something cold to drink before my next lesson."

Later, I watch him paddle out with his final lesson. He's been in the water all day, dragging students on their boards, pushing them into waves, paddling this way and that to retrieve the ones who refuse to paddle themselves.

I relax as he disappears onto the horizon and lean back in my chair. There's a wind and it's warm. The palm trees bend over the edge of the cliff, curving toward the sea, and the wind whips at the fronds, blowing them like a hula girl's grass skirt.

Before I met Kai, I don't think I ever really saw Hawaii. I don't think I saw past the tourists and the hotels and the crowded Waikiki beaches. But since meeting Kai, Hawaii has come to life for me, all green mountains, warm wind, and white-crested waves.

eleven

B y the end of the day, I know he's got to be exhausted. He's given lessons all day and now carried a dozen surfboards downstairs, but he returns to me with an easy smile and a jingle of car keys. "What's your plan?"

"Anything that includes you."

He laughs, jingles his keys again. "Good girl."

It does sound like a great line, I think as we walk away, but he knows I mean it. I'm back here in Hawaii because of him.

We head to Chuck's above Duke's for dinner, and as we pass through Duke's patio, I spot Santa Claus dancing on the steps to the live band now playing. Well, at least he looks like a tan Santa Claus in a loud tropical print shirt. Santa's hopping from one foot to the other, and I point him out to Kai as we pass.

"Kris Kringle," Kai says, and I grin, because that's exactly what I was thinking.

We sit down and take our menus, and I haven't been this happy or this relaxed since, well . . . when I was last here.

Sitting on the balcony of Chuck's, I can see a red-and-yellow catamaran come in and surfers pass carrying their boards. Every night around six the breeze picks up, and tonight is no exception. The breeze is warm, and it flickers our votive candle and makes the torches lining Duke's patio below leap.

Hawaii is so amazing. It's like being in a foreign country, some place far away. I try to remember why Daniel and I stopped coming to Hawaii. Didn't we have fun here? Didn't we play?

And then I remember. Palm Springs. We bought the desert vacation house and locked ourselves into regular scheduled Palm Springs trips.

We should never have bought the vacation house. We should never have allowed ourselves to get into such a rut. Maybe making everything routine was the kiss of death. Maybe everything became so comfortable and familiar that we bored ourselves. Took the good things for granted. Took each other for granted.

As the waitress takes our order and leaves, Kai looks at me. "Jackie Laurens, Seattle designer, mother of two. What are you doing with me?"

"I don't know."

He laughs, pulls off his sunglasses. "I think you're just trying to escape your real world."

"Escape?"

"Girl, we live in different worlds. Have different values. I don't like money. You do. I can't stand being around fake people—"

"My friends aren't fake."

"I get the feeling your friends don't like me."

My mouth opens, closes. I'm not sure what to say. I finally manage to string some words together. "It's not that they dislike you . . ."

"But they don't approve. Surfer Kai's a beach bum. Surfer Kai's not good enough for you. Surfer Kai might be taking advantage of you. Am I right?"

I look down, at the table with the placemats and little votive candle. "Have you heard this before?"

"I come from a world like yours. My family's a lot like your friends. Wealthy. Successful. They've got it made."

"But . . . ?"

"I don't think they're happy. They've got to work like dogs to pay the bills, pay for that three-car garage, that big house on the beach, the private tuition for their kids. They're always working, but do they ever see their families? How much time do they really have with their kids?" His jaw juts. "How much time did you and your husband spend with your kids?"

"We spent a lot." I hesitate. "Yes, Daniel traveled for his job, but when he was home he was always doing something with the kids, coaching their sports, taking them places. He was a great dad."

"Was he a great husband?"

"Initially."

"What happened?"

"I don't know. I wish I did."

"How can you not know?"

"People grow—change—over time. Goals change. Personalities change. I guess we changed, and we didn't grow in the same direction."

"That sounds like a cop-out."

"Have you ever been in a long-term relationship?"

Kai reaches for his water. "Six years."

Six years. A lot longer than I expected. "Did you ever live together?"

"Nearly all six years."

"Were you ever unfaithful?"

He's not wearing his sunglasses, but his blue eyes reveal nothing, his expression just as blank. "Why?"

"I'm curious."

"Was your husband unfaithful?"

"Yes."

Kai tips back his chair. "How did you find out?"

"E-mail." I smooth the napkin flat on my lap. When I found all the e-mails, Daniel was livid. He wanted to know what I was doing going through his computer, searching his things, and I told him I didn't know. His computer was on. His Outlook program open.

"You went on his computer?" Kai asks.

I nod. I honestly didn't think I'd find anything. I knew Daniel and I had had problems, but it didn't cross my mind that he'd cheat. True, we didn't have much of a sex life anymore, but he was so tired all the time and his travel schedule was truly grueling, and when he was home he was coaching William's baseball team or Jessica's soccer team. Daniel loved the kids, that much was certain.

The part where he loved me . . . less certain. But an *affair*?

Daniel still says Melinda wasn't his mistress, just a good friend, and perhaps she was just his good friend, but she was getting attention from him that I wasn't.

Our waitress approaches with our beer. Kai thanks

her and waits for her to leave. "Did you confront him?" he asks me.

I can still remember how terrifyingly cold I felt when I first discovered his relationship with Melinda back then. Everything in me went numb. "Eventually." I hate talking about this. It's been two years, but it still makes me feel sick inside. "Once I calmed down. At first I didn't know what to do, what to think. I was so upset."

"What did he say when you confronted him?"

I shrug. "That he didn't love her, he loved me. That Melinda had blown their friendship into something more than it was, into more than it'd ever be."

"So you divorced?"

"No. I forgave him and we moved on."

"But you're divorced now."

I say nothing, just look out at the water where the setting sun has turned the surface a sparkling bronze.

I know now I didn't move on. All I did was shut down.

Shut down, shut off, shut away inside myself so only the external Jackie remained—smooth, glossy, polished interior designer turned corporate wife.

Eleven years. Two kids (never mind the two miscarriages). The vacation house in Palm Springs. The annual ski trip to Vail, even though I don't ski. But the kids do—thank God—and Daniel does.

Daniel.

I take a swift sip of my beer and blink back tears that I don't want to shed. I don't want to think about Daniel. I'm on vacation. I'm here to see Kai.

"Did he want to work it out?" Kai persists.

I shake my head, uncomfortable now. Daniel was the

one who filed for divorce, but he said it was because I wanted it, because I hadn't ever forgiven him and he couldn't spend his whole life punished for a mistake he regretted.

"No. Yes. I don't know."

Thankfully, our entrées arrive and the subject is dropped. But even as I eat, I find myself reliving this past year. During the first few months after the divorce, friends were always asking me if there were any warning signs before the marriage ended.

Jackie, is there anything you can tell us? Any way to predict real trouble?

I'd tell them this: *Don't sweep problems under the living room area rug. Don't let everything problematic go unspoken, don't let it pile up there, because it's going to eventually trip you. And you're going to be really hurt when you fall.*

And the other thing that's even more important: *Don't ever say something—even in anger—that you don't mean. Because one day when you shout impulsively, "I hate this! I can't do this! I want out," you just might get your wish.*

We spend the next couple of days in a comfortable routine, where Kai works and I sit with a book on a lounge chair and we visit between lessons. On the second day, I go buy lunch so it's waiting for him when he gets out of the water. Kai's extremely appreciative, and his pleasure warms me. I'd been nervous about returning, but being back here is perfect. This visit is everything I wanted and more.

But as Kai finishes his lunch, I feel a flutter of fear. I can't let myself be this happy here. This isn't real life, not my real life. He's right. It's just an escape. An amusement park for adults, much as Disneyland is a paradise for children.

Kai leans back on the lounge chair. He's been watching me. "You think too much."

I am, of course, thinking too much. And feeling too much. I know in days I'll go home and Hawaii will become again just a distant memory.

I don't want it to be a distant memory. I don't want it to ever end.

"Just enjoy the moment," he says. "Enjoy it for what it is."

I look at him, see how relaxed he is, how tan and fit and beautiful with youth and ease in his eyes, with strength and a lazy acceptance of who he is. What he is. How he is.

He doesn't try too hard. He doesn't have to. Women and opportunity just come to him, both tumbling into his lap, desperate to be taken, desperate to be experienced. It's so easy for him. He doesn't have to wish or want or need.

Not like me.

Not like me, who wants and needs everything. Who wants a man to love her more than he's ever loved anyone or anything.

Not like me, who has been good for certain things, the dutiful things, but not for the fragile, the delicate, the intangible.

To be loved for one's laugh, to be cherished for a

smile. To be looked at as though I were good again, rare and special. Because when I first met my husband fifteen years ago, that's how he looked at me, and back then it seemed as if he'd never stop looking.

He stopped looking.

"I will miss you," I say finally, knowing I have to say something, knowing that Kai is still watching me, waiting for me to speak. The sun plays down on the top of his dark head, lingering over muscles that corporate men of forty-something don't have, those little lines and cuts in the traps and deltoids, the biceps shaped, curved, connected to the triceps.

"Everything ends eventually, girl."

"I know." But I don't know, or at least I don't want to know, don't want to believe it. And maybe that's my problem: my inability to accept what is true.

Maybe this is why I'm divorced and my friends aren't.

I don't agree with the way we humans function. I don't want to be human, mortal, if men biologically need a million women; and women get married and then bored of sex; and children battle, are difficult to raise, and then leave home and never look back.

Who made up this life, anyway? Who designed people to be so hurtful and lonely and alone?

"But it's not over," Kai says now, reaching for me and pulling me against his chest. His arm circles me, holds me firmly, holds me so I don't feel so small or fearful. He leans down and presses a kiss to my temple, murmurs, "You're still here and I'm still here. So, Jackie, relax. Let go. Just try to enjoy it."

Later, after Kai leaves, I slip on a hotel robe and go

outside to sit on my balcony. This time my hotel view is of Waikiki's city lights and the distant hulking shape of Diamond Head. Curling up in my chair, I think about what Kai said and realize he's right.

I have to learn to let go to be happy. But there's so much I'll have to let go of—the past, my hurt, my fears, my guilt, my control freak tendencies. The list is over-whelming. Maybe the secret is taking it one step at a time.

No, maybe the secret is not thinking about everything all at one time. Maybe I need blinders. Something to limit my view, something that lets me see only what's in front of me and that's it. Because what's in front of me right now is good.

What's in front of me is great.

Hawaii. Kai. Sex. Fun.

I really should enjoy this, because things at home are different. I'm in paradise. It's okay to savor paradise.

I vow to change. Right now, right here. I'm going to really start living and stop worrying, stop fearing, stop all the bad, negative mantras. I'm going to be positive. I'm going to feel good. Here. But also at home. I want to feel good at home.

I want to feel good, period.

The next morning, I wake up to rain. Kai calls me soon after to say that the beach desks will be closed and all surf lessons have been canceled.

"What do the tourists do when it rains here?" I ask.

"Go to the Ala Moana Mall. Go shopping."

My nose wrinkles. "I don't want to do that."

"What do you want to do?"

"See you."

He laughs appreciatively. "And?"

"Get naked."

He laughs even more softly. "I like the way your mind works."

"I'm glad."

"I want to get naked with you, so maybe we should split the day up. Get naked, show you some more of Hawaii, and then get naked again."

I'm smiling. "Carson, I think we've got a plan."

Kai's plan for showing me more of Hawaii means we go hiking. In the rain.

Within fifteen minutes of setting out, we're drenched, but it's a warm rain, and the mud squishes under our shoes as a sticky iron red. We're laughing ourselves silly as we splish and splash our way up the mountain. Kai and I are sharing fantasies—what we'd like to do with the other and describing the scenario.

Kai wants me to dress up as a schoolgirl, and I want him to be a cowboy. I'll wear a short plaid skirt, knee-high socks, and my hair in braids, while I put him in leather chaps minus the pants.

Kai's horrified. "That's disgusting. Crotchless leather pants?"

"They're chaps."

"I feel dirty."

Giggling, I nearly tumble over a rock. "You'd look great."

"I need a shower."

"It's my fantasy." A big fat wet drop lands squarely on my forehead. I knock it off. "And speaking of fantasies, isn't wanting to get naked with a schoolgirl kind of . . . kinky?"

"You'd look great in a little pleated skirt."

"I have a daughter that wears pleated skirts."

"I'm not interested in your daughter."

"I'd feel like a freak."

"How do you think I'd feel in crotchless leather pants?"

"Fabulous."

He stops walking and turns to face me, and I walk smack into the middle of his chest. He's taken off his wet shirt and tucked it into the back of his shorts and I lean against his warm, bare chest. "You're fabulous," I say, my voice dropping as I press closer.

His body is hard. He's hard. I'm just as turned on, and one kiss leads to another and pretty soon we're ducking behind a fallen tree and getting busy.

The tree bark is rough, the rain is warm, and Kai is amazing. I feel amazing.

I feel younger than I have in fifteen years.

Of course, nothing lasts forever. Not even six idyllic days in paradise. Vacation's over and I'm back home again, even more crabby and jet-lagged than last time.

Nic calls Monday after the kids have returned to school, asking if I've time to meet her for lunch. I don't know that I should go for lunch, but I don't want to be alone. We agree to meet at Cactus at eleven-thirty.

We're so busy talking that we take half an hour just to order. Nic's a former Catholic school teacher and is in the process of starting her own photography business. She doesn't have an official studio, shoots mostly kids— black-and-white candids in parks and their own home.

She's finding it's taking a lot of time and not necessarily paying a lot in financial dividends. "I like the work, though. It's interesting, and it keeps me busy. I was getting so bored staying home."

"Why didn't you go back to teaching?" I ask.

"I wanted to have more freedom and flexibility than teaching would have given me. I wanted to work when the kids were in school and then be home when they were home."

"That's how my business started."

"And now you work . . . ?"

"All the time."

"That's because of your divorce."

She says it so bluntly that the air catches in my throat. I look at her closely, trying to figure out exactly what she meant. "I'm working a lot because my business has really grown."

"But you don't need your income, do you? Daniel pretty much took care of you, didn't he?"

"He was generous with the kids, and he made sure the kids had a roof over their heads. But I have to work. I can't pay my bills without having a job."

"Maybe you guys could still reconcile."

"*Nic.*" I rub my scalp near the elastic holding my ponytail, close my eyes. "We weren't happy. We were fighting all the time. It wasn't good for the kids."

"People aren't always happy, Jack. But lots of people stay married."

This is exactly why I don't have lunch with Nicolette more often. She makes me crazy. She's a great person—serious, hardworking, spiritual—but she's also stubborn and opinionated and tends to see things as black or white. "Are *you* happy?"

She glances up from her menu, her dark brown eyebrows pulling. She wears her dark hair short, cropped, pixielike. On anyone else it'd look severe, but she has such delicate features that she can pull it off. "As happy as I can be."

"Is that a yes, I'm happy, or a no, I'm not?"

"I don't really believe in happy."

I flash back to Hawaii and the hike and the lovemaking and the rain. It was such a wonderful day. Everything felt so good. I loved that feeling. I want more of that feeling. "How can you not believe in happy?"

"What is happy, anyway? Is it cheerful? Is it exuberant? Is it a sense of well-being and good fortune?" Nic closes her menu and pushes it away. "The question shouldn't be, Am I happy? but rather, Does my life have meaning? And yes, my life has meaning. I've created two children, and loving them, caring for them, and helping prepare them for life gives my life purpose."

"So you don't think happy is a valid emotion for adults?"

"I think it's valid. I have moments of great happiness. Watching Ben learn to ride his bike. Taking the kids to Cannon Beach and chasing them in the surf. Going to a Saturday matinee movie. Those are all happy things, and I feel happy doing them. But it's not realistic to feel happy all the time."

"It's not?"

She lifts her hands, counts off on her fingers. "There are bills. Doctor's appointments. School admission tests. Taxes. And that's not even including the hard-core stuff like cancer, accidents, death."

"And is that what we're supposed to teach our kids?" I find it impossible to hide my dismay. I don't want my kids to know this stuff. Not yet.

Nic blows out air, ruffling her wispy dark bangs. "But life isn't always happy, so better we teach them how to find a deeper joy in life. How to be at peace."

"You make it sound as though we need to teach our kids to settle, to not want so much—"

"Yes."

I don't know how to answer her because I think it's wrong to limit our children's dreams, narrow their vision, color and darken their optimism. I understand the need to prepare children for reality, but Nic seems to be suggesting that happiness isn't attainable and children are better resigned to life than to be disappointed by loss or failure.

I think of the way I've lived my life and the way I'd want Jessica to live hers, and I don't want her to be like me. I don't want her to play it safe. I don't want her to hang back, not take risks because she's afraid to risk or fail. Pain is part of life. Making mistakes is, too.

I know I've made mistakes, but I'm determined to learn from them and do better.

Live better.

Live happier.

* * *

I reach into my purse for my cell phone as I leave Cactus an hour later. I call Kai, but when his voice mail picks up, I don't leave a message.

Kai calls me back as I'm making the kids dinner. "How's your day?" he asks.

"Okay."

"Doesn't sound okay."

I'm amazed at how well he can read me already. I put the lid on the spaghetti sauce and turn the heat down on the burner, reducing it to a simmer. "Are you happy?" I ask him, leaning against the counter, pot holder still on my hand.

"Yes."

I rub my forehead with the stiff cotton pot holder, the thick quilting rough against my skin. "Why?"

"Why am I happy?"

"Yes."

I can hear the faint hiss of air over the phone. He's either sighing or exhaling. "I like my life."

"Is that it?"

"I like what I do."

"You don't make a lot of money."

"I don't need a lot of money."

"You can't travel the world."

"Why do I need to travel when I live in paradise?"

I smile reluctantly. "People would argue you that point."

"But I'm not those people, and I don't care to know those people. I make my own decisions. I don't let other people make up my mind for me." He pauses. "Not like you do."

"I don't."

"You do. You're a nice person. You want to be liked by everyone. You want people to approve of you. While I could care less if anyone likes me, much less approves of me. I'm living my life the way I want to live it, and that makes me happy."

The water has come to a boil, and I reach for the bag of noodles. "I wish you were here tonight. We're having spaghetti."

"I wish I were there, too. I'm starving."

"Great. Come on over."

"I'm on the next plane."

I smile, wedge the phone between my shoulder and ear, and dump the dry pasta into the boiling water, stirring the spaghetti noodles to make sure they don't clump. "Kai."

"Yes, girl."

I hear the smile in his voice, and a lump fills my throat. How can he be ten years younger than me? He makes me feel safe. Protected. "I wish I were more like you."

He laughs softly. "You're perfect just the way you are."

"I'm serious."

"So am I. Now finish cooking dinner and feed your kids. I'll talk to you soon."

I don't want him to hang up. I don't want him to disappear into his world and leave me in mine.

But he's not disappearing, I tell myself, and I'm going to see him again. Soon.

* * *

Anne and I meet that weekend for a cup of coffee. Daniel has the kids for a company party, and Philip's watching theirs. This is supposed to be a cozy chat, but the mood is anything but cozy at the moment.

I've just told her I'm going back to Hawaii again, and she isn't handling the news well.

"How are you even going to get used to being single if you're always running away?" Anne demands, not even trying to hide her impatience.

"I'm not running away."

"You are."

"Anne, the guy I'm dating lives in Hawaii. I'm going to see him. Okay?"

"No. Meet guys here, Jack. Date *here*. This is where you belong. Not in Hawaii."

"I love Hawaii."

"You love having sex."

"Maybe."

"But you can't keep flying twenty-six hundred miles to get laid. It's absurd and fiscally irresponsible."

"Not if it's a great lay," I joke, trying to lighten the mood.

Anne leans across the table, a thick wave of blond hair falling in her eyes. "Jack, be serious. This is serious. You can't keep doing this, can't keep running over there anytime you feel lonely. You're supposed to date here, make friends here. This is where you live. This is where you need to settle down."

"I'm settled—"

"*You're not.* You don't even look at men here, and you're on the phone with Mr. Hawaii all the time. It's not right—"

"Why not?"

"Because it's not real, and it's not good for you."

"I'm happy."

"Cocaine can make you happy, but that doesn't mean it's good for you."

I growl in the back of my throat. Carefully I lift my decaf latte, sip, and sip again. I'm so close to firing something back at her that will hurt, and I don't want to hurt her, don't want to be an ungrateful friend, but she's got to ease up. I'm not in the mood to be lectured. In fact, I don't think I'm ever going to be in the mood to be lectured again.

"What do you have against Kai?" I ask as soon as I'm certain I've got my temper in check. "You haven't met him. You don't know him. You can't judge him."

"I'm not judging him—"

"No, you're judging me."

"I'm not, honestly, Jack, I'm not. It's just that we never see you anymore. You're always on a plane, heading off, having this little romantic escapade, and it doesn't make sense. It's not helping you get on with your life."

"But I'm getting on with my life. I'm dating—"

"You're not dating. You're having sex."

My jaw drops. I snap it closed. "Maybe I'd see more of you if you didn't nag me so much."

"Nag?"

"Yes. You're always on me, criticizing, poking, commenting. It's as if you don't want me happy. Why? Why can't I be happy? Is it because no one we know is? Because everyone feels angry? Stuck?"

"We're not unhappy, and we're not stuck."

"Then why is it every time we girls get together we always talk about how impossible our husbands are, how frazzled we are, how much a struggle life is? How come that's all we talk about, Annie? Why don't we ever talk about how happy everyone is? Hmmm?"

"Because the happiness you're talking about is infatuation. It's escapism. It's vacation romance. An island fling."

My jaw hardens. That was another jab at Kai. Another jab at me. God, women can be brutal. "Maybe this thing with Kai isn't a fling. Maybe it's not an infatuation, either."

"Jack."

"What if I loved him?"

"Jack."

Abruptly I stand, contemplate grabbing my purse, but I don't move. Instead I cross my arms and stare down at her defiantly. And I am defiant. I'm furiously defiant. No one has the right to tell me how to live, what to do, the decisions I should make. No one. Not even my best friends.

Anne sighs and, realizing we're crossing into murky waters, draws a deep breath. She ruffles her thick streaked blond hair so that it tumbles around her face, but there are lines at her eyes, deep lines at her mouth. She's feeling the strain, too.

"What do you really know about him, Jackie?" she asks quietly, one hand outstretched. "Have you been to his home? Do you know his work history? Is he financially solvent? Can he keep a job? Has he been to school? Had any trouble with the law?"

I say nothing because I don't really know any of those things, just what I've seen. What I've felt.

Anne holds my gaze. "He could be violent."

"No."

"Married."

I don't say anything because I suppose he could be violent. And he could be married. Or he could have a girlfriend and I just don't know. I wouldn't know. Because she's right. I've never been to his place. I know he went to college, but I don't know if he graduated. I don't know exactly how long he's worked as a surf instructor or if he's bounced from job to job. I don't know. And yes, there are things I'd like to know, things I maybe should know before I go falling in love with him—and maybe this isn't even love but infatuation. But it's so intense and so sexy that I'm not ready to give it up or move on. Move on? Move on to what?

"Madison Park is hard," I say quietly. "I'm lonely here. I feel trapped sometimes in my house, in the affluence and conservatism. I don't feel as if I belong anymore, not the way I once did."

"You just have to keep meeting people, making new friends—"

"Divorced friends," I interrupt bitterly.

"You *are* divorced."

"But that doesn't mean I want to make new friends."

"They'd at least be free to go out with you when Daniel has the kids. They'd know what it's like to be single again, understand what you're going through."

Whereas Anne doesn't. Even if she wanted to. And sometimes I get the feeling she doesn't want to. She doesn't want the stress my divorce has introduced, or the change. After all, it wasn't just my world that changed. It was all my friends' lives, too.

It's quiet now, and neither of us talks. I can hardly look at Anne, my temper is so hot. Inside I seethe, but I am afraid to say a word, afraid to let this get bigger, more confrontational, than it already is.

After a minute has passed, Anne speaks again. "I just worry about you."

"Well, *don't.* I'm an adult. A woman. I know what I'm doing."

Anne's silence tells me she doesn't agree. "I just think," she says slowly, quietly, "that you deserve better."

twelve

t home, I'm so annoyed that I pour a glass of red
wine and fill the bathtub with hot, hot water and
dump in a huge scoop of soothing bath salts.
After stripping off my clothes, I slide into the water, sub-
merging until everything but my nose is covered.

Anne's just trying to be my friend. Anne's trying to be
supportive. But Anne's making me crazy.

I *know* I'm not being practical. I *know* Seattle is my
home. But I also know that the happiest ten days I've had
in the last year have been the ten days I spent in Hawaii.

I force myself to take a deep breath and exhale slowly. I
do this three more times, try to clear my head, clear the tension, but I'm really struggling to find inner calm right now.

Why can't I go back? Who says I have to be practical?
Who says I can't just have fun?

"Everyone says so," I mutter grumpily, using my foot
to turn the faucet back on to add more hot water. Especially my good pal Anne.

I wish I could pick up my wineglass with my foot.

I wish I could kick Anne with my foot. *Jack, that's not
nice.* No, but the thought makes me feel good.

I sink even lower, hold my breath, and just float beneath the surface.

Anne says I deserve more. Anne and the rest of my friends say I need someone who will be everything I hope for, someone who will appreciate everything I am.

That sounds fabulous, it really does, but is that *real*? Will I ever meet someone who will think I'm as wonderful as my friends think? And even if it's possible, does life really work out that way? Because honestly, I've lived long enough to know we don't always get what we deserve. We don't always get the good we should.

I come up for air, push my wet hair from my face, and reach for my wineglass. One sip, and another. It's good wine. One more sip before lying back down to float some more.

Life isn't poured in equal cups for everyone. Some people get more and some get less. Some get it hot and some have it cold. Some get drowned by the generosity while others thirst, hungering for more. Some are happy with their portions while others are never filled, never content, never able to say, "Good, I've had enough. I'm satisfied."

I fall into that last group. It is true. These past few years, I was never quite satisfied. I was always hoping for just a little bit more, for another generous measure.

And now that I'm single, I'm even more demanding. I feel like getting a megaphone and standing on the steps of my kids' school shouting, "Bring it on. Pour it out. More. I want more!"

My friends do not talk like this. I doubt they even think like this. I've heard them mentioning more, but they do it in that good, mature way that speaks of acceptance. They've all reconciled themselves to the life they have, the life they live.

As Anne said a few weeks back, some days you're happy, some days you're not. But in the end this is what you get. This is marriage and maturity, this is motherhood, and this is how it's always going to be.

And I, who used to think the same and talk the same, have broken rank.

I used to be like Anne, used to be like my other friends. But the divorce changed me. I'm not a caterpillar in a little cocoon anymore. I've broken out. If I follow the analogy, I'm a butterfly now.

But what I don't understand is how in the hell did my caterpillar body become that of a butterfly? How did that fuzzy thick green body become long and slender with wings?

And even if I don't understand how the caterpillar metamorphosed, the fact is, I am different now. I've got these big wings. But no one wants me to fly.

Anne calls the next morning to apologize for coming down on me so hard, but I missed her call because of client appointments. Her voice mail apology is comforting, but I don't need the pressure from her or the others. Right now I'm stretched damn thin.

And while I'm grateful my career is doing so well, the workload is threatening to suffocate me. I don't want or need another serious conversation about me, my life, my choices, or my new affinity for Hawaii. I appreciate that my friends want to look out for me. (We're just *protect-*

ing you, Jackie.) But if I'd wanted "protection," I would have stayed married.

Which is to say, if I'd wanted people to boss me around, I'd still be a wife.

My to-do list is a problem, though.

It's getting out of hand. For the next week, I work far too many hours every day. I'm up early to run numbers and write invoices, stay up late to sketch designs and get my drawings completed. During the day when the kids are in school, I'm booked solid, scheduled so tightly that I'm practically meeting clients every hour on the hour. And I still can't get everything done.

We're out of groceries. The kids need to see the dentist. I'm increasingly late for the afternoon carpools. My color needs to be touched up (badly). The laundry is piled a mile high on the laundry room floor. William's got another book report due and I don't think he even read the book.

I need help. What I need, I think, isn't a husband, but a wife. A wife to run the errands, make sure we have fresh milk and meat and produce. A wife to get the laundry caught up while overseeing the homework. A wife to book my hair appointment and leave a little note on my desk letting me know where and when. Yes. That's exactly what I want, but if my dating a younger man in Hawaii caused quite a stir, can you imagine how folks would react to my taking a wife? (I'm imagining a mail-order bride. Russian, maybe, just for shock effect.)

Kristine swings by Friday afternoon at four-thirty with a couple of six-by-eight fabric swatches.

"What are you doing in my neck of the woods?" I ask

as we head to the kitchen, where she lays the fabric samples on my kitchen counter.

"Andrew had a play date with a little boy down the street. The mom called me, said the nanny was having car problems and could I bring her son home." Kris makes a face. "Sure. Let me just ask my nanny."

"I didn't know you had a nanny," I say, offering her a Diet Coke.

Kristine passes on the soda. "I don't. I've just been using a U of W student a couple afternoons a week. But have you ever noticed how many moms around here have full-time help? And what do these moms do all day while their nannies raise their children? I know Meredith doesn't work. She's always at Starbucks. Or the club," she says, referring to the Seattle Tennis Club.

"She does do volunteer work—"

"She doesn't."

"I think she does. She's co-chair for the school auction. Last year they raised nearly half a million dollars. Apparently Meredith is the school's savior."

"That's even more disgusting."

"You're in a worse mood than I am. What's wrong?"

Kris sighs, rubs her forehead. "Doug's leaving for Germany on Sunday. He'll be gone for another week. He's just gone so much lately. It's hard. Hard on me, hard on the kids."

"Let's get together next week for dinner. Bring the kids here, or I'll take my kids there. It'd be fun. I get lonely in the evenings and would love some adult company."

"What night? We've speech therapy late on Monday

and Thursday, Wednesday is karate, Friday's free . . . or
maybe not. I invited some moms from my Peps group
over. Would Tuesday work?"

"Tuesday's the night we have ballet and basketball—
or is it baseball now?—I can never keep the sports
straight."

"So there's no free night next week."

"Pretty pathetic, huh?" I lean on the counter and pull
the burgundy fabric swatches toward me. "These are pretty.
I like the quilting in this one, and the thin darker stripe in
this one. What are you thinking of doing with them?"

"Covering the couch and ottoman in our new addition."

"But the ottoman was just upholstered."

"I don't like it. It's too light, too summery. Now that
they've begun staining the beams, I can see that the colors are all wrong."

"I like them," I say, handing back the fabric. "But I'd
have to see everything together. You've bought some new
furniture since I was last there."

"Come over with the kids."

I laugh. "When?"

Kris grimaces. "That's the problem, isn't it?"

But the conversation with Kris gives me an idea. I
don't need a wife, but a nanny—an afternoon baby-
sitter—sounds wonderful.

I call Kris later that evening, and she gives me the
name of a baby-sitter she uses, a college student in a
sorority at the University of Washington. Kris says she's
sure her baby-sitter knows other girls who'd like part-
time work.

I talk to Kris's sitter and follow up with her roommate,

and thirty minutes later I've got child care for after school. The kids aren't thrilled with the prospect of a baby-sitter, but I assure them she's young and pretty (what sorority girl isn't?) and a lot more fun than I am.

But on Saturday when Daniel and I meet at William's basketball game—many of the other parents giving us a conspicuously wide berth—Daniel has plenty to say about my hiring a baby-sitter without discussing it with him first.

I try to remind myself that Daniel wants what's best for the kids, but it's hard to keep that uppermost in mind when he lectures me as though I'm some punk kid. I shouldn't have hired her without a face-to-face meeting. I should have gotten a list of references (I did) and then called each of them to follow up (I didn't). I should have checked out her driving record, made sure she had insurance (I did ask about insurance, and she said she was covered), and inquired about her car.

As Daniel talks, I have to move aside repeatedly to let people pass and find myself wishing his girlfriend were here. When Melinda's around, Daniel doesn't speak to me—which is actually more comfortable all the way around.

"Lisa's great, Daniel. I really like her, the kids like her. She's already sat for us twice, and not only did she make sure they got their homework done, she even arranged a play date for Jessica yesterday."

"But have you sat down with her and talked to her about your expectations? Did you cover things like limiting TV and GameCube? Did you talk to her about their diet and how we're concerned about William's weight?"

The basketball court is loud, echoing with the dribbling of balls and referee whistles. I have to raise my voice to be heard. "No, I haven't sat down with her yet, but we talked, and we'll continue to talk. She's only been with us two afternoons."

"I just don't want her giving them crap. They eat enough crap as it is."

"I don't feed them crap."

He doesn't look at me; instead he focuses on a point just past my shoulder. "No fast food, no fries, no cheeseburgers, no chicken nuggets."

The buzzer sounds. The game's about to start. "Daniel, *I* cook dinner."

"I don't want her to cop out, do the lazy thing."

"She won't be taking them to Wendy's or McDonald's, okay?"

"I want to meet her. Cover the rules with her myself."

He's concerned that the sitter will just feed William more crap.

"She's not going to feed them crap," I say wearily, hating that we've come to this and knowing we're just going downhill from here, knowing we're back to the anger, the verbal sparring, the seething discontent. It's a he-says, she-says, and no one is going to win. "And she's only at my house part-time, just two to three hours a day, Monday through Friday."

"Why? So you can go back to see your boy toy?"

I stiffen, ignore the jab at Kai, because this isn't about Kai, it's about me. Daniel hates that he can't control me anymore. "Because *I* need the help. I can't get everything done—"

"You would if you used your time better. Didn't run around so much. Didn't meet your friends for lunch all the time."

"Do you help organize Melinda's schedule, too? Or does she already do everything perfectly?" The game has started, and we're missing William play just to fight. How pathetic is that?

"You're not a businesswoman, Jackie."

Not a businesswoman? I'm a damn successful businesswoman. Maybe not a venture capitalist like Daniel, and maybe I don't bring in the income he does, but I'm smart and creative, and I'm making a name for myself.

I step closer, drop my voice, jab my finger toward the ground. "You don't know the first thing about me, Daniel," I hiss, oblivious to anyone and everything but the bitterness between us. "Just because you were married to me doesn't mean you knew me or under-stood me."

"Vice versa! You were so involved with the kids and your little decorating projects, you didn't have a clue what I needed. You didn't even know I was there."

"Not know you were there? How could I not? You wanted dinner every night at seven regardless of how much I had to do or what carpools I had to drive. You had dry-cleaning runs for me, laundry to fold, banking errands. I wasn't your wife. I was your goddamn assistant."

"And not a very good one."

I walk away then. I should have walked away sooner. Legs shaking, I climb into the wooden stands, sink slowly onto the nearest bleacher, and fight tears.

I hate him. I hate him so much. I hate what he's done to me, to us, to the memory of us. I hate that he's so superior and righteous and I'm so wrong. I hate that he's turned me into this angry, brittle woman. I hate that he's taken the love I felt and broken it into pieces, mashing it beneath his heel on his way out.

Because he can say what he wants to say, but I did love him.

I did.

I loved him so much that I gave him my heart and my mind, my body and my life. I wanted him to be the father of my kids. I wanted him to grow old with me and be with me through thick and thin. I wanted the American dream, and he was part of it.

William's team wins, and Daniel takes the kids after the game for a celebratory dinner. He calls later to say they're going to stay the night. "We're going to go see the new Disney movie!" Jessica shouts into the phone.

"Great." I'll just sit home. Alone.

But after they hang up, I know I can't be alone tonight. I'm feeling caged, trapped. Isolated. It's probably just the intense workweek, and the fights with Daniel don't help.

I get on the phone, call Anne to see what she's doing tonight, but they have concert tickets with another couple. It's Nic's gourmet dinner club tonight. Kris and her husband have Sonics tickets.

It's not until I hang up that I realize Anne's right about one thing. On a Saturday night, I need different friends. I need single friends, and at my age, single friends are all divorcées.

My God. I draw a deep breath and hold it. I'm going to have to make new friends.

Kai calls me the next morning before the kids are dropped off. I'm sitting in the middle of my bed, leafing through the most recent issues of *Architectural Digest* and *Veranda* while having a second cup of coffee.

"What are the Laurenses doing?" he asks. "Heading to church, or going to brunch at the country club?"

I flip *AD* closed and roll over onto my back. I lift a foot, examine my toenails. I need a pedicure. "The kids are with their dad, and I'm looking at magazines in bed."

"You should be going to brunch. You're a country club brunch girl."

"I'm not."

"Do you have shoes that match your suits?"

"Yes. . . ."

"Case closed."

"Anne says I need to make new friends." I cross one arm over my chest, hold the phone more tightly. "She says I need to make divorced friends."

"Which one is Anne?"

"The one who was supposed to go to Hawaii with me but couldn't because her husband got sick."

"Oh, that's right. The yokel couldn't be left alone because he had a flu bug."

"He's not a yokel. He's a doctor."

"Even worse. A doctor who can't be left alone with a flu bug. Give me a break."

"He didn't think he could manage the kids."

"He can cut into people but not take care of his own kids?"

I'm laughing despite myself. "It's not that simple."

"Of course it is. He was being a big baby and you know it. And this is the friend who tells you that *you* need to make new friends?"

"She thinks I need divorced friends."

"Why?"

"Because they'll understand what I'm going through and have more free time."

"That's horrible."

I reach for the magazine that's poking my back and push it away. "I don't think she meant it to hurt me. But it did."

"So what did you do last night?"

"Watched an HBO movie."

He's silent for a moment, and I'm not sure what he's thinking. I wait for him to speak, but when he doesn't I break the silence. "Kai?"

"Hmmm."

"You're not upset with me, are you?"

"No, girl."

"But . . . ?"

He hesitates. "Maybe your friend's right. Maybe it's time you met people there. Dated more there. I don't want you sad or feeling lonely."

"That's part of life, though, you know?"

"You're too special to be sad or lonely, Jackie. Promise me you'll start meeting people, going out on dates."

I laugh incredulously. "You want me to date?"

"I want you to have a great life."

"I don't want to date."

"And I don't want you spending the next year watching HBO movies alone."

I don't answer, and the silence stretches. Slowly I sit up, leave my bed to go open the window blind in my room. Sun peeks through thin layers of cloud. "But I like you, Kai," I finally say.

"And I like you. A lot. Which is why I want you to meet someone who can take care of you. Make your life better."

"But I don't want a man to take care of me! I've had a man take care of me, and it didn't make my life better." No, I don't need taking care of. And I don't need a man to provide for me. That's why I have a job. "All I want from a man is great company. That's all I need."

"I guess you're in luck."

The week passes, and the new college girl, Lisa, is working out really well. Those two and a half extra hours every afternoon enable me to get a lot more done, see more clients, and even do some grocery shopping and hit the gym. The kids like Lisa, and she's even helping cover some of the carpool runs for me, especially the ungodly Tuesday and Thursday days where both kids have activities at the exact same time.

But despite my schedule—or because of it—I welcome the calls from Kai. He checks in several times a week, and every call leaves me smiling. There's just something about him that makes me feel good. Hopeful. Optimistic.

"I want to come back," I tell him one night as I drive, racing down Montlake Boulevard to pick up Jessica from ballet. "I miss Hawaii a lot."

"You do."

"Yeah. And you just a little bit."

He laughs. "Come back."

"I wish I could."

"You'll have another vacation someday."

"Someday sounds too far away."

"I'm not going anywhere."

"So even if I don't come out for months, you'll still be glad to see me when I do?"

"Yes."

"Even in six months?"

"Yes."

"A year?"

"Yes."

"You won't have a girlfriend by then?" I ask suspiciously.

"Oh, I'll have several, but I'll still make time for you."

"That's terrible."

"Yeah, but you like it."

I hang up, retrieve Jessica from ballet, and creep our way back along Montlake to get William from his first baseball practice of the season. As I sit trying not to fume with traffic, I don't think I can wait six months to see Kai again. I don't think I can wait even three.

I miss him. I really miss him.

For dinner, I take the kids to Bing's Bodacious Burgers. The place is funky and relaxed, a favorite for lots of families after sporting events. The kids get their burgers, and I get the Gorgonzola chicken salad on a ciabatta roll.

While we eat, I continue to play with the idea of returning to Hawaii soon. Realistically, when could I go? There's a three-day weekend later this month, and then next month in April, there's Easter. I'm supposed to have the kids for Easter. Could I take them to Hawaii with me for their spring break?

I look at the kids as they munch their fries. No, I can't take them with me to Hawaii. It's too soon for them to meet Kai or even know about him. I like Kai, and I love spending time with him, but I'm not sure he's ready for a woman with kids.

Maybe I'll just go one of the weekends Daniel has the kids. He can keep them an extra night or two. I've already got Lisa in the afternoons. It's not as if he can't come to my house and pick up the kids from Lisa once he's done working.

I book the ticket and hotel and don't tell anyone. I'm not leaving for a couple of weeks. It's no one's business where I go or when.

Less than a week before I leave, I go see Michelle, my hairdresser, for a cut. My color's good, just had that done, but I could use a trim.

I've been seeing Michelle for nearly ten years. She's the one who made me a redhead, and I'd go anywhere she worked. I'm such a fan that gradually over the years all my friends have begun going to her, and thankfully, she doesn't make us all look the same. Nic's hair has gotten shorter, darker. Mine is long and red. Anne's is just above her shoulders and different shades of honey cut in thick, choppy waves. Kristine's hair is the one that always changes. I don't think she knows if she wants to be a serious brunette or a more playful blonde.

"You've got some spa appointments, too, today,"

Michelle says, wrapping the drape around my shoulders and attaching the Velcro at the back.

"Thought I'd get everything done at once."

"Including that Brazilian wax."

My cheeks get hot and I cross my legs, suddenly fidgety. "Thought I'd try it once."

"Yeah?" She puts her hands on my shoulders. "All that hair going-going-gone?"

I close my eyes, not really wanting to think about all that hair going-going-gone, but Kai says that's what the girls do in Hawaii. Totally bare down there.

I take a breath, open my eyes. "You've had Brazilians—"

"I haven't."

"Come on. You work in a salon/spa."

"I do my own grooming."

"You wax yourself?"

"I don't let anyone touch me down there."

I think it's funny we have these intimate conversations with our hairdresser, but this relationship has evolved over ten years. Michelle isn't just my hairdresser, she's my image maker. My confidence builder. My guru for self-esteem. Michelle makes it possible for me to look like other women—compete with other women. Because God knows it is often about status, and since my divorce I've lost a great deal of status. I need whatever help I can get.

"When do you leave for Hawaii?"

Michelle has shampooed me and is now combing my hair straight in preparation to start cutting. I look up at her from beneath wet hair. "How do you know I'm going to Hawaii?"

"You're not getting the Brazilian for yourself."

"Maybe it's not for Hawaii."

"Anne says it's Hawaii."

Oh. Great. "When was Anne here?"

"Yesterday."

I sigh as Michelle begins lifting layers and trimming the ends. "She needs to mind her own business. She's become obsessed with me going to Hawaii."

"She's just worried about you."

I listen to the *snip, snip* of Michelle's scissors. "Why is she worried? What is she worried I'm going to do? Run away to Hawaii and never come back? Abandon my kids, sell my house, behave irresponsibly?"

"She doesn't want you taken advantage of."

I grab the arms of my chair and squeeze. For Pete's sake! *I'm* the one going there. *I'm* the one chasing him. *I'm* the one who's older and wiser. Why is it him taking advantage of me? Why can't I be taking advantage of him? "Maybe I want a relationship like this. Maybe I want danger. Trouble. Change."

Michelle holds a long strand of wet hair between her fingers. "You want me to cut your hair off?"

"No!" I glare at her. "I just want a chance to do my own thing."

Michelle finishes the cut and then blow-dries my hair straight, going over it with a flat iron to make sure it's glossy smooth. As she peels off my cape, she pats my shoulder. "Your aesthetician is waiting to give you your Brazilian. Go do your own thing."

I go to the aesthetician, and there's not a lot I can say about the Brazilian other than, Holy Mother of God.

Valera contentedly rips the hair off my privates in efficient strips, and with each brutal yank the pain gets worse until I'm close to screaming. *Girls wear it bare here.* Great, Kai. Get a local girl.

Valera tells me to turn over onto my stomach.

"My stomach?" I squeak.

"You've got to take it all off."

"All off where?"

"Everywhere."

And then I understand. "I don't have hair there."

She gives the pot of hot wax a stir. "Oh, yes, you do."

Slowly I turn onto my stomach and look helplessly, desperately, at the door. As Valera goes for the butt cheeks with her hot wax, I think I could just possibly kill Kai.

thirteen

The eyebrows (and other things) are waxed. The hair looks great. I've gone for another Mystic spray-on tan. My bags are packed. I leave day after tomorrow.

I've never told my friends the exact day I'm heading to Hawaii. They must know it's soon, though. I've noticed a coolness this week, but I'm ignoring the tension. This isn't about them, it's about me. And I can't wait to get on the plane.

While I haven't given my friends my trip specifics, I have discussed the details with Daniel. I had to tell him, as I had to make arrangements for the kids.

Daniel made the discussion as difficult as possible, sighing irritably before cutting me off midsentence. "Just put all the info in an e-mail," he said unkindly, and hung up on me.

I'm being punished. Again.

Fine. Punish me. But I'm not going to apologize for liking someone who likes me back. And Kai does like me. I can see it in the blue heat of his eyes, the set of his jaw, the long, slow way he has of looking at me, a sexy, hungry assessment that makes me think of dinner and dessert all at the same time. And I want to be dinner and dessert. In fact, I want to cook the dinner and serve dessert. I want to feed him the meal myself.

Sex at twenty is so different from sex at forty. All that talk about women coming into their own and peaking in their thirties—it's true. Maybe not all women have this sexual revolution, but I have, and Kai is clearly the beneficiary. Thank God he's still young enough to do. And do. And do . . .

Thinking about doing, I book a manicure/pedicure. I can't wait until I leave on Thursday. I love going to Hawaii. And I don't have to stay home just because no one else approves.

No one else approves.

Just one day later, my friends stage what can only be called an intervention.

Anne has rallied the troops, and they've trapped me at Nic's house tonight, cornered me to talk some sense into me.

But they don't know, they can't seem to understand, that I'm not like them anymore. And I'll never be like them again. At least not while I'm single.

And something else that they can't, or won't, understand is that I'm relieved to be single. Looking back, I see how unhappy I was.

It never crossed my mind that I'd feel trapped with Daniel. I never imagined in my wildest dreams we'd not only fall out of love, but would come to resent each other the way we do. Looking back now, I wonder if we were ever compatible, or was it just novelty? Newness?

Like what's happened these past few months with Kai?

Novelty, newness, new. The new eventually becomes old. Novelty becomes ordinary. And then what?

What?

There is a pause in the conversation, the former buzz and hum silent. I look up, aware that everyone is looking at me. Waiting.

"You're not going to keep going back . . . are you?" Nic's leaning forward, hands folded in her lap, and she's like the Kristen Davis character in *Sex and the City*—so good and earnest, so determined to remain good and earnest. It hits me yet again that in the divorce I divorced goodness and earnestness along with Daniel. I divorced the pretense that I was anything but me . . . that I'd want anything but happiness. Happiness for me. Happiness for the kids.

"Why not?" I ask, trying not to fidget even as I try to disguise how I object to the intrusive quality of the questions. Is it really any of their business? Why should it matter to them if I go or don't go? How will it impact my friendship with them?

My arms are folded across my chest as I sit back in the tall wing chair in Nic's living room. She inherited the chairs from her grandmother, and they're every bit as conservative as I imagine her grandmother used to be. "I like Hawaii."

"But that's not why you go." Nic has become a bulldog, eerily similar to Anne when Anne has a burr in her tail.

"You go," Nic continues as if I cannot follow her, can't put this together, "because of Kai."

"Mmmm." It's the most I can commit to. I'm irritated and fast becoming angry. If my friends don't see enough of me lately, maybe it's because I don't find their company as enjoyable as I used to. We're adults. Friends. Equals. But lately the balance of power seems to have shifted.

As the three of them sit looking at me, my frustration grows. "I'm happy there," I say defensively.

"But what about the kids?" Nic persists, and I suck in air through my teeth, hold it in the back of my throat. It's that or scream, because that pocket of air is keeping the scream of vexation from getting out. Nic's delicate brunette beauty is so deceptive. She's slender, small boned, high cheekbones, wide brown eyes—and tenacious.

And it hits me that she's more like Anne than I ever thought.

More like Kris.

They're all so . . . strong. So fixed and *opinionated*.

Is this how I used to be, back before life as I knew it ended, forcing me to become someone else?

Did I used to be so confident? Confident to the point of smugness? I don't remember ever seeing myself that way, but somehow I think I must have been. It was part of our bond as women, as friends. We are wives and mothers. First. Last. Always.

"The kids are fine." I force my fingers open, flexing them straight. "We still have rough days, but things are definitely better and better."

"That's good." Kris reaches for the open bottle of wine and tops everyone's glass. "I wish I could say that. The boys are driving me mad." She hesitates, toys with the stem of her glass. "They're testing Marc next week." She hesitates yet again. "They think he may have the same learning disabilities as Andrew."

There's a moment of silence on our part as we digest this. "Learning disabilities" sounds pretty nonthreatening compared with the reality Kris lives with. Her five-and-a-half-year-old has therapy nearly every day of the week in an effort to get him ready for kindergarten next year. In an effort to keep him from a future of special education. No woman wants her child segregated, exiled to classrooms of only "special needs" kids. It'd be one thing if special education were really special, but unfortunately in Washington it seems to be a place where anyone who doesn't fit in the mainstream gets dumped.

Dumped into a world of behavioral problems, disabilities, and low expectations.

It's not the future any mother wants for her child.

"I don't know what I'll do if he has the same issues." Kris's voice is quiet, calm, but it's that very calmness that makes us aware of her panic, her desperation. She is calm because she is hoping her calm—that control—will curry favor with the gods.

"What makes you think Marc has the same issues?" Anne asks gently.

"He's been kicked out of his preschool."

Anne's jaw drops in outrage, but Nic, the former teacher, cocks her head, ready to problem-solve. "He's acting out, then?"

"He doesn't sit still, doesn't follow directions, doesn't line up with the other kids, won't hold hands with his buddy when they walk to the playground." Kris draws a breath. "This is how it started with Andrew."

I picture my Jessica, still hell on wheels, a child who gets her card at school pulled to yellow at least once every couple of weeks. "Marc's a great kid."

"And he's only three," Anne chimes in.

"Four," Kris corrects quietly. "Almost five."

We're silent again, each thinking. What is it about motherhood that takes all our unfulfilled dreams and transfers them onto our children?

The intervention ends with a whimper, not a bang. After we get off on a tangent discussing Kristine's problem, and then everyone else's worries about their kids, they never get back around to me and my Hawaii misbehavior.

I'm grateful for getting off topic, too. I don't think my friends realize how dangerously close they're coming to alienating me.

I've had a long, hard year, and my friends are supposed to be on my side. They're *my* friends, and maybe they don't approve of the choices I'm making but this is *my* life, and I'm the one who has to live it—win, lose, or draw. They've got their own lives, and they get to control those.

End of story.

But the next day, it's another story. That night, I'm rummaging through my stationery drawer where I keep greeting cards and birthday cards, trying to find a "thinking of you" card for Kristine, when I come across a photo of Jessica as a baby.

It's a photo of Jessica as a toddler with her daddy, and

something inside my chest pinches, a hot, tight heat that goes all the way through me.

In the photo it's summer, and Jessica is nearly sixteen months. She's standing on her toes, trying to get close to her daddy, who is outside sitting in a patio chair. Her head's tipped back, her bright blue gaze fixed on his face. Her expression's rapt, with that intense devotion babies have for their parents.

My chest grows hot. It burns on the inside, burns to look at her looking at him with such eyes of love. His expression is male, more guarded, but I know Daniel, and he adores her just as much. In essence, despite the years between them, the difference in gender and time, his expression, his devotion, is the same.

The love affair we have with our children. The passion we have for our offspring. It's as if you're given the chance to do life over again, finally given that opportunity to benefit from all the lessons learned and mistakes made.

And that brings to mind life, which seems to be an endless series of beginnings and endings. I remember Kai's statement that nothing lasts forever, that eventually everything ends, and for the first time this doesn't sound bad. I can see a definite upside to endings. Yes, the marriage to Daniel is over, but so is the negativity. The trapped, frustrated Jackie gets to have new beginnings and a new outlook. I can try new approaches to life, learn new tricks, develop a new attitude.

Endings can also be good things.

It's Wednesday, and I leave for Hawaii tomorrow. I can't wait, absolutely can't wait to grab my suitcase and jump on that plane, but I have last-minute work to do as well as a meeting on the Eastside in the home of potential new clients.

I run errands during the day, returning fabric samples, picking up new swatches, ordering a custom sofa, checking on curtains that are weeks late what with the client's party next weekend.

My favorite client, the one who can never make up her mind about anything, calls and leaves a long message on my voice mail, complaining about the lack of progress on her remodel and how she's been billed hours and hours and yet she has no kitchen to speak of, no fixtures ordered, no cabinet finishes selected, nothing firm.

I sit in my car at the traffic light and listen to her unhappy rambling voice mail and feel my anger grow.

I've had it with unhappy people. I feel as though I'm surrounded by unhappy people who are determined to be unhappy. It's as if being unhappy makes them happy.

Like my client, Liz. Liz is incredibly wealthy, extremely beautiful, married to a handsome, successful husband, and she has nothing to do all day but shop and volunteer at her kids' school—which is great. Except nothing pleasant ever comes out of Liz's mouth. She's always grumbling, always complaining, always blaming everyone else for her unhappiness, and I don't need this anymore.

I don't want this anymore.

I don't have to work with people who make me miserable. I'm my own boss. I should start acting like my own boss. I should start making smarter decisions for myself.

Starting with getting rid of Liz and then working only with clients I enjoy. Setting limits with others. Not allowing my friends, or Daniel, to boss me around. Trusting my judgment and doing what I feel is right.

And suddenly my anger melts. That big knot of tension inside my chest starts to dissolve. I can breathe.

I can see a future where I'm making decisions and taking control, and I feel better about myself. I feel better about the world.

I'm going to be an adult. And yes, I know. It's about time.

I get my kids squared away with sports and ballet and dinner before heading over the 520 bridge to the Eastside.

I don't know very much about these prospective clients other than that the woman, Sarah, seemed absolutely desperate to meet at their home in Medina tonight. I didn't want to meet tonight, I've still got last-minute packing and organizing to do, but Sarah practically begged me, and she sounded so teary and desperate that I couldn't say no. Apparently her husband travels almost constantly but is home tonight, a rare occurrence, and she wants me to meet him.

It takes me all of ten seconds to realize the husband isn't interested in meeting me. Once we're seated in the living room, he sits with his glass of wine, looking bored and/or exhausted while Sarah unrolls the house plans for their new home to be built on Lake Washington.

The home is beautiful. Seven-thousand-plus square feet. Three-car garage. Master suite with spa and sauna, plus his-and-her walk-in closets. A complete fitness room with French doors and balcony. A media room. A game room. A wine cellar. Their kids have grown and left. It's just the two of them. And he's always gone.

"It's going to be gorgeous," I tell Sarah even as she keeps looking at her husband, Henry, as if trying to catch him in a moment of enthusiasm. But he never once shows a hint of excitement or pleasure in the home being built.

He's letting her build the house because he doesn't know what else to do with her.

She's building the house because she's lonely as hell.

And this is exactly what I can't and won't do anymore. Sarah's a lovely, lonely fifty-year-old woman, but building a seven-thousand-square-foot home won't make her happy, and paying for an expensive lakefront home won't make Henry a better husband.

While I know I could do a good job with the house, I'm not interested enough to spend the next year on a project with the couple. I honestly can't bear Sarah's loneliness or his apathy. I don't want to feel her loneliness or his apathy. I've felt enough loneliness and apathy of my own.

There are other ways to live, other ways to relate, and I'm going to find them.

As I drive back over 520 to Madison Park, I look at the indigo sky glittering with stars and the bright lights of Seattle's skyline. I can see the outline of the Space Needle and the lights of Montlake Bridge and Husky Stadium. Even though I've lived in Seattle nearly fifteen years now, I never get tired of the view. I love the way jagged peaks rush toward the sky, framing low pewter lakes and lavender bodies of water. The mountains here are everywhere—the Cascades, the Olympic Range, Mt. Baker, Mt. Rainier. I love the white ferries that cross the Sound. Love how the city has sprung up between the lakes and the Sound.

Living in Seattle has given me confidence, and in this past year I've grown even stronger. Sometimes I'm intimidated by this new, powerful me. The me who refuses to settle for second best, the me who won't take a number and wait in line anymore, the me who insists on happiness, not acceptance.

This new me reminds me of Jessica as a toddler. At two, the moment Jessica realized she could assert herself, she did. Her discovery, that she could walk away from me—run from me, argue with me—filled her with power and pleasure. As well as fear.

It doesn't take long for the omnipotent two-year-old to transform into the terrified toddler. So much freedom! So much independence! So much *danger.*

I feel like Jessica now. I feel as though I'm still just a child and I've somehow failed to mature. I'm forty, yet I feel fourteen.

Make that three going on four.

Does anyone else ever feel like a faker? Does anyone else ever feel like a pretend grown-up, someone who's masquerading as her mother or the nice woman next door?

I sometimes suspect we spend a fortune on hair and clothes because it makes us look the part even if we don't quite know how to feel it on the inside. You know, dress for success and you'll get the job. Put on the right face, say the right words, and you're an adult.

But I realize now I haven't been an adult, not a real

one. I react, not act. I make decisions on the defensive. My emotions aren't controlled. My thoughts aren't controlled, either. And tragically, there's no mother here anymore to tell me what to do, no parent to demand I behave.

That's why I'm the adult now. Even without the right outfit, hairstyle, and makeup.

At home I pay Lisa, and after she leaves I lock up and head upstairs, turning off lights on the way.

I check on Jessica, who is asleep on top of her comforter, her stuffed animals strewn about her. I slide her beneath her covers, dim her night-light, and then head to William's room.

William's bedroom door is ajar, and the closet light is on. I step into his room to check on him. He's sitting on the floor of his walk-in closet next to an acrylic storage box containing his thousands and thousands of baseball and football cards. This is his favorite thing to do late at night when he can't sleep, and he's never been a great sleeper. Late to bed, early to rise, engrossed in his world of sports and his fear of unlikability. He may be a sports nut, but he's the most likable kid I know. No one tries harder, no one cares more, and if William weren't my kid, I'd still want to know him. "Hey," I say, pushing his closet door wider to squeeze myself in. "You're supposed to be in bed."

He looks up, light brown hair tousled. "I couldn't sleep."

"You didn't even try."

"I did. I just wasn't tired."

"William, you've got swimming and basketball tomorrow. You've got to sleep."

He scratches his forehead, cheeks flushed from his industrious labor inside his closet. "I'll skip school."

"No, you won't."

"I don't like it."

"You do great in school."

He shrugs, and I see the fabric of his pajama shirt strain at his shoulders. It's also pulled taut across his middle, but I know he'll grow into his body, as he's built just like his father. Someday he'll be six feet two like Daniel, broad of shoulder and hopefully confident, too. Hopefully.

"Mom?"

"What, baby?"

His head ducks as he sorts another couple of cards, stacking some, spreading others in tidy piles before him. "Nicole called me fatso at school today." His size 16 shoulders hunch, my baby who wears size 16 shirts and 16 pants. My baby with the heart of gold. He looks up at me now, a hint of tears in his gray green eyes. "Am I fat?"

I love this boy more than life itself. "No, honey."

"But Nicole said—"

"She's wrong. You're not fat. You're big right now, husky big, but it's how your body grows."

His fist reaches up to knock tears from the corners of his eyes. "Do girls like husky boys?"

My heart catches at moments like these, it just falters and flutters, and I feel ripples of pain everywhere. Growing up is so hard. I'd never want to be a child again. "Husky girls do, William."

William's head rears back and his eyes blaze and he's the spitting image of Daniel. Furious, fiery, handsome. *"Mom!"*

I wink. "I'm teasing. Of course girls like husky guys, husky guys have lots of muscles."

"But pretty girls?"

"William, don't worry about the girls. You're almost ten and too young to get married right now, but when it's time, you'll have all the girls you could ever want."

The flush in his cheeks deepens. "Really?"

And looking at him, cross-legged with his box of cards amid his cleats and flip-flops, I know he'll grow up and go. Grow up and become a man with a home of his own, and in the end all I have are these years, precious and few.

Right now I try to remember it all, if such a thing is possible. I try to remember the way his jammies stretch and strain, how his hand clutches the hundred cards and the lone dirty, mud-crusted cleat next to his bare foot.

He's gorgeous because he's mine, but he won't be mine for long. Our children become part of the world so fast, and it's our job to prepare them, transition them, our job to love them and gracefully step back and let them go. . . .

"I love you, William Gerald Laurens."

He uses his stack of cards to push the hair back from his brow. "I love you, Mom."

I stand there another moment before I shake my head, knowing I will never be prepared for the day both my children leave, knowing I'm still not comfortable on those long weekends when Daniel has the kids and I try desperately to fill my time, those four and five days, until they come home again. "Go to bed soon," I say finally.

"Okay, Mom."

He's not even paying me any attention, lost in his statistics and scores. "I mean it, William."

"I know."

Smiling wryly, knowing that he has me beaten, I leave him to his sorting and take myself to bed.

fourteen

Kai greets me at the airport with a flower lei and a kiss. "Welcome home, girl," he says, placing the lei around my neck before kissing me.

I kiss him back, crushing the flowers. He smells good. Feels good. Makes me feel like the most gorgeous woman alive, and I hug him harder, tighter. There's this delicious happiness inside me as I climb into his truck. I've got five days ahead of me, five days of fun and sun and gorgeous, sexy Kai.

As Kai pulls from the parking lot, I can't help wishing Hawaii were home. There's no pressure here, no guilt, no anger. I love the warmth, the sultry climate, the water, the waves. I could get used to this laid-back surfer mentality.

With my design background, I could work anywhere. I could build a business here, make new clients, network with other industry professionals.

I could have more time outside with my kids. Buy a beach house. Keep my beach boy.

Glancing at Kai, I smile a little, wondering what it would be like to live with him.

Unlike Daniel, he wouldn't have a closet full of

thousand-dollar suits, handmade Egyptian cotton shirts, rows of silk ties. No five-hundred-dollar shoes. No late-night meetings. No last-minute business trips away . . . trips that end up lasting two weeks, first in Chicago, then in London, and finally in Hong Kong.

Kai takes my hand. "You're quiet."

"Just thinking."

"About what?"

"Nothing." But then he looks at me and his eyebrows lift, and I start laughing. "Okay, everything."

His fingers squeeze mine. "Regretting you came?"

"No. Not at all." I look at him, his profile chiseled, great brow, great cheekbones, great jaw. He's even got great eyelashes. "If I didn't come, I think I'd explode. Things are so hectic at home right now. Work's crazy."

"And I hardly work at all," he drawls.

I squeeze his fingers back. "I'm not comparing careers. You have your work, I have mine."

"You don't really feel that way."

"I really do. I like you. I like your life. It's cool."

He gives me a long look. "You're sure?"

"Positive."

He drags me toward him on the seat. "So what else is going on, girl?"

When he calls me "girl" I see that happy younger woman inside me, the one who's dying to break free, see the light of day. The one who wants to laugh and play at home, not just here. "My friends have been pretty brutal lately." I grimace, remembering the intervention. "They don't approve of my coming here. They think I should stay home, be like them. But I can't be like them. Not anymore."

"Why not?"

For a moment I can't answer, feeling that old shadow of frustration and resistance. Sometimes I don't know why I can't be like them, and other times I only know I don't want to be like them. "My world, the one I have in Seattle, revolves around couples. Families. Weekends in Madison Park are made for couples . . . families. As a single person, I don't do what the rest of my friends do. I don't get invited to the concerts, the dinners. Movies."

Kai shoots me a narrowed glance. "I don't understand."

"It's a world designed for two. Like Noah's Ark, everybody files on in twos. If you're not two, you don't get an invite." I see his expression, and he's still perplexed.

Turning on the seat, I face him squarely, his hand still linked with mine. "Hawaii's different. That's one of the reasons I like coming here so much. Hawaii's culture isn't about status, prestige, social significance. It's more open. Free-spirited."

"Individualistic," he adds, and he's pretty much summed it up.

"You, and Hawaii, give me freedom I don't get at home. Here I can try things, do things, risk things I couldn't get away with in Seattle. Here I can be anybody I want to be."

His hand squeezes mine. He has such a lovely hand to hold, lightly calloused on the palm, but strong, tan, and warm. "Who do you want to be, girl?"

"Me." Happy. Free.

He lifts my hand to his mouth, kisses it. "Then be

yourself. Because you're pretty damn special, Jackie Laurens."

For a moment I don't speak. I'm too filled with warmth and gratitude. Somehow—and I don't know how—Kai made me realize I was important. He made me see that I've nothing to feel guilty about. If I've done my best, I've done my best, and that's all I can do.

"I'm glad I met you, Kai." My voice is thickening up, emotion neither of us needs. But somehow coming to Hawaii, getting close to Kai, splits me open, makes me feel, and the feelings, even the sharp bittersweet ones, are good.

"I'll always be here for you."

He merges onto the freeway, and I get my first glimpse of Diamond Head and the blue, blue water. "You say that now."

"I mean it."

I blink back the salty sting of tears and grab my hair to keep it from blowing in my face. "So a year from now?" I tease.

"I'll be here for you."

My eyebrows arch. "Five years from now?"

"You just call me."

I laugh and scoot close to him, then prop my feet on his truck's black dash. "You're too good to me."

"Everyone should always be good to you."

I snuggle closer, my hip pressed to his, my hand on his knee. "Can we just drive and drive? Keep going forever?"

He laughs softly. I feel his rib cage shift against mine. "It's an island, girl. We're going to be making lots of circles."

I giggle, seeing us going around and around, forever and ever. "That's okay. With you it'd be fun."

"I love your laugh," he says, glancing down at me.

"And I love that you can make me laugh." At home I know I don't laugh, at least not very much. "Everyone at home is more serious," I say.

"Maybe people where you live take themselves too seriously."

I think about this and remember Kristine and how she struggles with her boys, and Nic, who hasn't prepared her kids for the realities of life. "But maybe we have to be. We've got to make sure our kids do well in school, so they can score high on the SATs, so they can get into a good university, so they can have a good career—"

"So they can what? Make a lot of money someday? Meet someone similar, and marry, and have kids and accumulate status and more wealth? Then they put their kids into private schools, where their children are pressured to excel, and get great grades and high SAT scores." He lets go of my hand and drags a hand through his dark hair. "What are people doing, Jackie? What is it all about? What's it all for?"

He looks at me, and his expression is hard, mistrustful. I just look at him, uncertain what to say.

"I know that world, girl," Kai adds after a moment. "It's why I left the mainland. Don't want it, don't believe it. Not going to sell my soul for capitalism, consumerism. Money is the root of all evil—"

"No." I stop him. "Not money, Kai. Greed. We have to have money. We have to be able to live, eat, pay the basic bills. But how much money? Maybe that's the question."

"We don't need much, we really don't, Jackie. The world tells us we do. Everyone's competing, trying to be better or best. And let's face it, you wouldn't live where you live if you didn't enjoy your standard of living. I've looked at your area on the Internet. You can't buy a house for less than a million dollars—"

"My kids have always lived there. It's where their friends are—"

"It's where *you* like to live."

"My friends are there, yes."

He sees the anger in my eyes, and he laughs. His hand settles on my thigh and strokes down to my knee. "I'm not criticizing you or your world, girl. I'm just saying, you've chosen to live there. It's expensive to live there. Enjoy it. And if you don't enjoy it, find something you like better."

The next morning, Kai's teaching in Waikiki in front of the Outrigger Hotel and he's got me a beach setup. He takes my beach bag and carries it to the lounge chair beneath one of the blue umbrellas.

"You'll be all right here?" he asks, straightening my sunglasses on my nose.

"Yes."

"Need anything?"

"No."

"I'll see you in an hour."

He's already leaving, but I stop him. "Kai." He stops, turns to look at me. "Why do you have to live so far from me? Why can't you live in Seattle or Bellevue?"

"Because I wouldn't be a surf god and you'd quickly get bored with me."

"That's ridiculous!"

He gives me a cynical look. "Are you sure?"

I fall silent. I'm not sure. Sometimes I don't know if it's Hawaii I love or Kai. "You might like Seattle."

He moves back toward me, reaches into my tote bag for my sunscreen and squirts a big white circle in his hand. "We talked about this already. I don't leave the rock."

I watch as he covers his face, rubbing it in before applying a second white layer to his nose. "If this can't go anywhere with us, why am I here?"

"You're here," he answers, wiping his hands on the back of his red board shorts, "because you want an adventure."

I have the most blissful day. In the late afternoon, waiting for Kai to finish his final surf lesson, I just sit on the lounge chair gazing out at the endless horizon of ocean.

Not far from me, a sea turtle pops his head up. The kids on the beach all stop and stare. I haven't seen any sea turtles for ages, and I feel as though everything is suddenly right in the world.

All day today I've felt this way. Good. Calm. Content. I'm noticing color, too, like how yellow the underside of the palm fronds are. They're more yellow than green, and other colors blast at me, the shocking red T-shirt on a little boy, the orange tube top on the sunburned teenage girl, the turquoise goggles on the man walking into the ocean to swim.

Has color always been so strong? So determined? So bold?

Color never seemed like this before, even though I've worked with color professionally for years. I just don't ever remember it jumping out at me like this, and I'd think it was hallucinogenic drugs, but I've taken nothing. I'm not even drinking a piña colada or Tropical Itch. I wonder what it is that would make the world tip and slide, tilting color like a liquid rainbow, painting everything the deepest, brightest hue.

I'm smiling at an elderly Japanese man walking along the beach, stooped and pigeon-toed in his tight, wet, too small purple Speedo when it suddenly hits me. All this color, all this life. It's joy. It's hope. It's peace.

I've got me back again.

I wait on the Outrigger Hotel's steps for Kai to finish putting away the surfboards. The guys at the beach desk are closing up shop, too, taking down the umbrellas, stacking the lounge chairs, carefully counting and locking up the Maui Jim sunglasses.

The routine is always the same, and it's comforting. I'm a stranger here, but life on the island has its own rhythm, much like life on the mainland.

The guys at the beach desk need to sell their suntan lotion and sunglasses, dependent on the commission. The beach boys—surf instructors like Kai—give lessons and hope there'll be a tip. No one makes a lot of money. Everyone must be an ambassador of aloha.

The surf instructors say the things tourists want to hear. They pose for the photos, standing next to sunburned smiling women and kids, hands up in the "hang loose" sign with the massive soft-top surfboard between. They clap out-of-shape men on the back, tell them they're riding waves now.

A cluster of girls in bikinis and little skirts are waiting for Kai when he comes back up from the hotel's basement. He knows several of them, kisses them, and they stand around him, talking excitedly. He smiles, listening, and then reaches out to one of the girls, catches her straw beach bag before it falls, and adjusts it on her shoulder.

The same thing he does for me.

My heart kind of falters. The touch means nothing. He's not interested in the girls. He knows I'm sitting here in the shade, watching. But still.

Still.

I'm forty. They're twenty-something. Maybe right now I'm relatively unlined, but how long can this last? How long can I compete with much younger women?

"How does this end?" I ask Kai later, turning onto my stomach to kiss his chest, right above his heart. I wish I were a bigger part of his heart, wish that really great sex meant eternal happiness and not just a temporary release. Because I don't want just a temporary release. I still want true love and romance.

True love.

Kai takes a strand of my hair, twirls it around his finger, gives it a little tug. "Does it matter how it ends?"

"Yes. I want it to end happy."

The corner of his mouth lifts. "Are you happy now?"

"Yes." Well, happy and just a little sad, because I don't feel this way at home. I don't have anyone who touches me like this at home or is willing to spend all afternoon with me in bed. I don't have anyone who grabs me and pulls me into the shower or rolls me under him in the sand or kisses the side of my neck or calls me "girl."

Or calls me, period.

Kai pulls me down on his chest and kisses the side of my neck. "Then if you're happy now, that's all you need."

But it's not all I need. I need more. I need forever. I have to have forever. Don't I?

I touch Kai's mouth with mine; his lips feel cool, his breath is warm. I shiver, and the kiss deepens and continues to deepen, and I feel so much. I hate thinking that what I feel now—good, young, beautiful—isn't going to last, that it won't last. But maybe that's life. Maybe that's reality.

I hate reality.

"Kai," I whisper, and he lets me go. I lift my head to look into his eyes, and even in the shadowy light of my darkened hotel room, they're still blue, endless blue, forever blue. Daniel's eyes had once been the deepest, sexiest brown. I wonder how long—if I had that long with Kai—it would take for the love/lust to go, the desire to fade. How long would it be before we irritated each other or one of us would tire of the other?

How long before I didn't think his eyes were endless blue or he'd begin to notice all the wrinkles in my face he insists he doesn't see?

"So when I go home this time, I'm supposed to just forget you?" I say, running my palm along his jaw, savoring the feel of his beard. He needs to shave, but I like it rough, sharp, like it that I feel something when his skin touches mine.

"Your life is there, baby girl."

My life.

My life.

Tears almost prick my eyes. My life is in Madison Park. My house is there. The kids are there. My work with my clients is there. And it's where Anne and Kris and Nicolette live. They're wonderful friends, and I can't imagine not having them, knowing them, seeing them for our coffees and our talks.

So why do I feel this way? Why does my heart feel pulled in two directions?

Kai's just a man, I tell myself, looking down into his beautiful face, seeing the jaw with the hint of beard, the curve of his cheekbones, the long, dense lashes at his eyes, black lashes that frame those blue eyes that I can't stop looking into.

He's just a man.

There are lots of men.

And there's no such thing as soul mates, anyway.

Love never lasts. Love is an illusion. Love is about sex, and sex isn't that important . . . not compared to the important things like truth and kindness, friendship and trust.

That's what my girlfriends give me and my children need.

That's why I live in Seattle and keep my kids near their father.

That's why I come to Hawaii for sex.

And if that's how I feel, why do tears fill my eyes now? Why does everything inside me constrict?

Kai reaches for my hand and holds it, holds it tight in his. "You're thinking too much again," he says, and I nod.

He's right.

He's right about a lot of things.

This was only ever a vacation romance, nothing permanent, just a holiday fantasy.

But when he lifts his head to kiss me, I can't stop kissing him. And then he's rolling us both over and he's on top of me and we're making love again and this time it's fierce and intense, stormy. Even half an hour later, when we've both found what we need, the stormclouds are there, inside me.

If I thought going home last time was hard, it's going to kill me this time. How do you just leave happiness, and your heart, behind?

Today's my last full day here. Tomorrow I fly home. Of course, I'll be back—I know that much, how could I stay away?—but still, it won't be for a while, at least a month or more.

I vow not to think about leaving. At least not today, not when Kai's working on the north shore. I've never been with him to the surf school on the north shore and happily hitch a ride to work with him.

He's teaching at the Turtlebay Resort, and I sit at a table at the pool bar, making business calls on my cell phone and organizing various client projects.

After work, Kai tells me a bunch of the boys are having a bonfire on the beach and wants to know if I'd like to join them.

We go to a north shore beach where there's already a bonfire and little hibachi grills and cases of beer. I'm reminded of college parties, the kinds of parties where it's not about atmosphere or quality wine, but just about getting together, hanging out.

Kai introduces me around. A few faces are familiar, fellow surf instructors from Waikiki, while others are friends from the north shore. There's Marco, a professional surfer from Brazil; Michael, an artist and surfer from New York who supplements his income with his painting and personalizing surfboards; then Cole, the surfer from Florida who has his own video production company, filming tourists on vacation as they take their first surf lessons; and someone named Patrick, a blond helicopter pilot with a little dog for a co-pilot.

Later a Jeep pulls up with more people, two guys and a girl. Kai tells me the guys are brothers and the younger one, John, just returned from the pro surf circuit.

"Is he good?" I ask, watching John go around and shake hands surfer style, which is somewhere between a high five and arm wrestling.

"Yeah, considering he's only just turned twenty-one."

Twenty-one. Wow. It's an odd realization that I'm socializing with twenty-year-olds now. At home, women wouldn't do this. At home, women socialize with women who are just like them.

I didn't know this rule existed, but after eleven years of marriage and living where I do, I can pretty much sum up friendship this way: If you're married, your friends are married. If you have kids, your married friends have kids. If you and your husband make a certain amount of money, your friends have the same level of affluence. If they belong to the country club, you do. If they vacation in Jackson Hole or Santa Barbara, you should. If they attend fund-raisers and ask you to join them, even if the tickets are five hundred a plate, you do.

Keeping up with the Joneses.

Letting the Joneses run your life . . .

"Do you want to leave? Go back to town?" Kai asks, correctly reading my ambivalence.

"I don't know."

"Something's bothering you. Ever since John arrived you've looked miserable."

I am uncomfortable. I feel like I did that first day I walked past Duke's in Waikiki and saw all the young, beautiful people drinking together on the patio. The girls in their bikinis had tan, flat tummies, and the guys were shirtless, muscular, and comfortable in their skin.

"I just don't think I belong here," I whisper, taking his hand. "I feel so . . . old . . . again."

"You're not old."

"Kai, I could be John's *mother.*"

"Actually, you're older than his mother. His mother is only thirty-nine."

He laughs as I groan. "Tell me you're joking."

"Nope, but Jackie, you don't look like his mother, so you can relax."

Oh, my God. I'm on a beach, partying with a guy who has a mother younger than me? I might as well be arrested and sent to jail.

"You're sure you don't want to go?" Kai persists. "We can now, before they throw our burgers on."

"No. Let's stay. It's not every day I can eat hot dogs and hamburgers on the beach with teenage boys."

Kai laughs, smacks my ass, and heads to the surf where the Jet Ski waits.

I watch as he climbs on and zips out. Twenty-year-olds, I repeat. Partying with twenty-year-olds.

At home, twenty-year-olds take care of my kids. Twenty-year-olds ask me for advice. Twenty-year-olds read my fashion magazines and keep me informed of the latest trends and celebrity gossip. I like my twenty-year-old baby-sitters. I like the college girls with their hip clothes and pierced navels and hidden tattoos. I love their stories about concerts and clubbing and long-distance boyfriends at other universities.

The girls are great. They're smart and pretty, successful and funny. So what exactly is my problem with hanging out with twenty-year-olds here? Like I'm doing something taboo? Or, as my German grandmother would say, verboten?

A little later, John approaches and offers me a beer.

"Thanks, I'm good," I say, showing him my beer. "I'm still working on this one." I don't bother to add that it's the same beer I've had since arriving. I'm having a hard time sliding into fun mode, and the beer isn't going down easily.

Young John stands next to me on the edge of the beach where I'm watching Kai ride the Jet Ski. "You're here with Kai?"

"Yes." I shade my eyes to see up into John's face. His hair is that surfer blond and his eyes a light honey brown. He's tan and lanky tall, but cut, muscular. My baby-sitters would really love him.

"Kai's a good guy," John says.

"I think so."

"How long have you two been hanging out?"

Hanging out being Hawaii-speak for dating, I suppose. "A couple months." I see John's expression and add hastily, "I live on the mainland. I just see Kai when I'm here."

"Cool." He crosses his arms over his chest, flexing pec muscles. "Kai said you design houses."

"I'm an interior designer."

"So you decorate houses?"

"Sometimes I help with paint and fabric, and sometimes I reconfigure the interior of an entire house."

"That's cool."

"Yeah."

"So how old are you?"

My stomach falls, one of those dazzling maneuvers that leaves me antsy and breathless all in one fell swoop. What do I tell him? That I'm forty and old enough to be his mother? That I'm actually *older* than his mother? "Do you know how old Kai is?" I ask instead, deliberately stalling until I see where this is going.

"Um, twenty-eight?"

"I think that's pretty close."

"So you're twenty-eight, too?"

"Yeah." I cross my fingers behind my back.

"I know it's not cool to ask a lady's age. I was just curious."

"It's all right."

"So how'd you meet Kai? Was he your surf instructor?"

"Pretty much."

Kai climbs off the Jet Ski and walks toward us. He's

naked save for his board shorts, and he has that slow, lazy smile that always makes me think of sex.

Kai slides his arm around me and gives John a look I can't quite decipher. "Are you hitting on my girl?"

"You don't want me to?" John says, happy to get into it.

"Not if you value your life," Kai answers, and I can't tell if they're joking because Kai suddenly seems very hard, very male, very aggressive.

"He's not hitting on me," I say brightly between clenched teeth. "We were just discussing my career"—I take a breath, drop my voice—"and my *age.*"

Kai laughs and John walks away, heading for the Jet Ski.

I turn to Kai and whisper against his chest, "He thinks I'm twenty-eight."

"I told you that you look young."

"Kai, he's twenty years younger than me. He could be my son."

"Don't tell him that. He thinks you're pretty sexy. And if I hadn't come to rescue you, he'd be making some moves right now."

I groan. "You're joking."

"No. You're hot, Jackie. Guys want you."

"Even young ones?"

He laughs and pats my butt again. "Especially young ones."

After dinner, they build the bonfire even bigger. A few more girls arrive, and one of them pulls out a joint. The joint starts getting passed around.

Some pass it on without smoking, others take a hit;

but before the joint can be passed to me, Kai stands and takes my hand. "Let's go."

He lifts a hand in farewell and walks me to his truck.

"You don't smoke?" I ask.

"I just had enough, that's all." He leans toward me, kisses my cheek. "Besides, this is our last night. I'd rather be alone with you than with a bunch of the boys. I can see them anytime. I only get to see you every now and then."

We get back to Kai's truck, and as he starts to drive, I pull my purse out from beneath the bench seat and automatically check my cell phone to see if I've had any messages since I left my purse in the car for the bonfire.

Six new voice mails.

Six voice mails in less than three hours.

I scan the list of missed calls, and it's not good.

Daniel.

Daniel.

Daniel.

Lisa.

Daniel.

Lisa.

Something's happened at home. I know it, know before I've even played the first message. Daniel never calls me, and he'd call that many times only if something had happened to one of the kids.

fifteen

~~~~~~~~~

What's wrong, girl?"

Kai's voice sounds far away to me, adrenaline making it hard for me to swallow, hear, think, feel. "Seven calls. Nearly all from Daniel."

Kai's already driving, but he pulls over. "Do you want to call before we lose reception?"

I look up and realize he's right. We'll lose reception around the next curve. As soon as we reach Waimea, the coverage ends. Don't know why, don't want to know why, just need to reach Daniel and find out what's happened.

I call him without checking my messages. He answers immediately.

"Where the hell have you been?"

"What's happened?" I ask.

"I've been calling you for the past three hours."

"I didn't have my phone with me."

"What's the point of having a cell phone if you don't carry it with you?"

I close my eyes, fight panic. "What's happened?"

"There's been an accident."

I knew it. "The kids?"

"Lisa was driving. William's fine. Jessica's in surgery now."

Surgery. My baby. "How serious?"

"She's stable. Mainly broken bones. Possible concussion."

Oh God. "And Lisa?"

"She's shaken up, but otherwise fine."

Good. "And William? He's really okay?"

"William wasn't in the car. Lisa was on her way to pick him up when the accident happened."

"What did happen?"

"A car ran the stop sign. They were broadsided."

I can see it in my head, see it in slow motion, Lisa in her Jeep, Jessica in the backseat. I can see the impact, feel the crunch, the hit, I can see the Jeep spin out of control into the way of oncoming traffic.

"Jessica wasn't wearing a seat belt," Daniel says flatly.

"She always does," I say, and I'm numb on the inside. I can't believe this has happened. . . .

"She wasn't today. Not with Lisa."

I hear the bitterness in his voice, the bitterness and blame. He doesn't think I should have ever hired Lisa. Doesn't think I should have left the kids. Doesn't think I should be in Hawaii with a young surfer.

A heavy lump fills my throat, the same kind of lump that's in my chest, making it hard to breathe. The guilt's intense.

I need to be there. I should be there. What am I doing here?

I wipe away a tear before it can fall. "Will you call me as soon as she's out of surgery?"

"Are you coming home?" His voice bites with sarcasm.

I battle rage. *Of course* I'm coming home. "Tell the kids I love them and I'm on the first flight out of here."

I hang up, clasp my phone between my hands. For a moment there's only silence, and I know Kai's looking at me, waiting for me to say something. But I can't. I can't find any words because they're all jumbled—anger, fear, guilt, shame.

"It's your little girl?" Kai asks.

I nod and then look at him, tears filling my eyes. "She wasn't wearing a seat belt."

"It's not your fault, Jackie."

"I should have been there," I whisper, and he looks at me for a long moment before starting the truck and heading for Waikiki.

I pack as I make phone calls to Northwest Airlines to see if I can get on a flight home tonight, but there's nothing leaving before tomorrow at one p.m., and I don't get into Seattle until ten. I'd be showing up at the hospital at midnight tomorrow, and I can't wait another twenty-four, forty-eight hours to see my daughter. I've got to go now. I don't care where I have to fly to—a red-eye into Los Angeles and then a morning flight to Sea-Tac, or into Las Vegas and then San Francisco and Seattle. Just get me on a plane.

I call Hawaiian. Same thing.

Kai's uncomfortable with my pacing, so he leaves to drop his time card in the mail slot at the Hans Hedemann

Surf Shop. After he's gone, I head to the hotel's business center and get online to see if Expedia can give me any other flight options.

At Expedia, I start inputting all possible flight combinations. Finally, I find a red-eye flight out of Honolulu tonight, arriving in San Francisco, where I'll hop on a plane to Portland and from Portland to Seattle. It means thirteen hours of flying and two connections, but at least I can be with Jessica by noon tomorrow.

I purchase the ticket, print my e-ticket boarding pass, and return to my room.

Kai arrives back at the hotel just as I finish packing. I tell him I've got a ticket and am leaving in two hours.

He offers to take me to the airport, but I tell him it's not necessary. "I know you've got things you need to do, groceries to buy, bills to pay. Take care of your stuff. I'll be fine."

"I don't mind, girl."

I know he doesn't mind, but I also know that this is it. I won't be coming back.

I can't do this anymore, can't keep returning or trying to make something happen where nothing can happen.

Kai's been correct all along. He said we were from different places, and he's right. I'm from a place called home. Family. Responsibility.

Kai's from the island, and he's about living the good life, which means no responsibility, no commitments, no pressure, nothing to take away from the surf and sun and fun.

Fun. I feel my insides pinch. I'd like to have fun—I've

been trying to have fun—but at what cost? At what cost to my children?

"I think I'll just take a cab."

His jaw's hard. "Why spend the extra thirty bucks?"

Because I'm going to hate saying good-bye to you. Because if I say good-bye fast, maybe it won't hurt as much. If I say good-bye now, maybe I won't know what I'm losing.

"You know I'm not good with good-byes." I look at him long, knowing that this is it, knowing that even if I want to be a kid, I can't, knowing that even if I haven't had enough time to play, it's over. Childhood can't last forever. I have to suck it up, do what needs to be done. "You know I get emotional. It's better this way."

I try to smile, but my face is frozen and my heart is just as frozen. I have to be hard, cold, fixed. I have to do what's right. I'm too old for Kai. Too old for Hawaii.

"Besides, you need to go get your rest before you work tomorrow. You're not as young as you used to be."

He doesn't smile. His blue eyes have turned glacier cold. He knows I'm shutting him out, knows it's all ending here and there's nothing he can do, nothing to say, no way to make my guilt and anger go away.

And I am angry. I'm so angry. I'm angry at the baby-sitter for getting into an accident, and angry at Daniel for breaking the news so cruelly, and angry at me for not making the marriage with Daniel work and the divorce easier for the kids. I'm angry that the kids had to be hurt in the first place, that we failed to provide them with a safe harbor, a home that was a refuge against the world's pain. Instead, adults brought the pain home.

Maybe it's too late for recriminations like this, but it's how I feel, and it's hard to ever see myself as separate from my role as Mom. Because I know this: No matter how successful I become in life, no matter how much money I make or prestige I earn, it won't matter at all if my children grow up and can't find peace, satisfaction, happiness. Nothing I will ever accomplish will be as important as getting my kids through life, and maybe that's why I struggle.

I know this. I believe this. But that didn't make marriage easier, and it didn't keep us together.

"You want me to just leave now?" Kai asks, arms crossed. The distance is already there between us.

"The bell captain can help me with my luggage."

Kai looks at me, and it's almost as if we're strangers. There's this emptiness and coolness, and I don't want it. I want *him*. I really dig this guy, but he doesn't leave the island and I live on the mainland and I can't keep coming back and forth. It's not practical. Not feasible. I don't have the time, the energy, or the money.

If there were a way this could work, if he could meet me partway . . . But this relationship will always be on me. I'll be responsible for getting here and making the time and arranging the child care. And I can't take on responsibility for one more thing. I'm too tired. Too stressed. Too hurt.

The ice around my heart hardens, tightens, and it feels so thick and cold and unforgiving, and I hate it. I hate that I feel so much here with Kai, how I've loved these visits and each and every day spent with him, hate that I can want someone this much and can't make it work.

Hate that it's going to end this way.

Hate that I can't find the words to say what I'd like to say.

But how would words change anything, anyway? How would telling him that I dig him, want him, just possibly might love him, help to change our jobs, our ages, our backgrounds, our incomes?

He's not going to move to Seattle and become a stepdad to my children. And I'm not going to move to Hawaii and become a surfer's girlfriend.

"I'm out of here, then," Kai says.

I feel a cracking in the ice, I feel heat behind the terrible cold. Tears nearly fill my eyes, but I won't let them. Won't. I won't let him see how hard this is for me. I'm an adult, must behave like an adult. Despite everything. "Okay."

Kai can't even look at me. "Let me know how she is."

"I will." My voice breaks despite my best effort.

"She's going to be fine, Jackie."

I nod. "I'll just feel better when I get there, when I can see her." The heat grows, and I'm starting to crack, melt, control precarious. "I miss her. Miss William, too."

"Soon, girl."

I nod, once, a jerky nod, and he's gone. Like that. No hug. No last touch. Nothing.

I hear the hotel door close, and the tears start falling. I can't let him just go like this, I can't let him think I don't care. I race to the door, look down the hall, but he's not at the elevator. He's gone.

It's done.

I won't cry. Crying won't solve anything. I lift the phone, call the bell desk, ask for help.

The bellman chatters away as I stand next to my bags. "Going home?"

"Yes."

"Did you have a nice stay?"

"Yes."

"Where do you live?"

"Seattle."

"Beautiful place. My sister and her kids live there. I go see them every couple of years."

I nod, hold my breath as we take the elevator down together, hold my breath to keep from making a sound.

No one ever said that life would be fair, but I honestly didn't think it'd hurt this much at my age. I thought once I left my teen years behind, once I grew up and got a job and started a family, all the bad stuff would be behind me. No more zits, no more baby fat, no more uncertainty. Somehow I'd thought that growing up meant life would get easier.

The flight leaves Honolulu at eleven. We're to land in San Francisco at five in the morning—three o'clock Hawaii time—then I change planes, catch the flight to Portland and then on to Seattle.

I can't sleep.

I tried to call Daniel for updates, but he's not answering his phone and not returning my calls.

He'd call me if it were serious, I remind myself. *He'd call if she were in danger.*

The knowledge is small comfort. I'm her mom. I'm in agony not knowing all the facts, the details. I can see Jessica in my mind, and she's so small still, all feisty blue eyes and indifferent blond curls. She's a monster and a beauty, a joy and a terror, and she and her brother own my heart, own it in ways no man will ever know. It's not the love of a lover, but the love of a warrior. My children must come first. My children must be safe. My children are everything to me. And yet where are they? Not with me.

My eyes burn, but they don't water. They just burn and burn like my guilty conscience and conflicted heart. Here I've been in paradise, playing, flirting, making love, while my children are thousands of miles away . . . with one now hurt.

Hurt. Jessica hurt. And a little voice inside my head tortures me, asking if this accident is somehow my fault.

Daniel is the first person I see when I reach the hospital. He's standing in the hallway outside Jessica's room, pacing and talking on his cell phone, despite cell phones not being permitted in the hospital. He looks up as I approach and abruptly ends his call, pocketing his phone.

"I thought you were jumping on the next plane," he says by way of greeting.

"I did."

He makes a point of glancing at his watch. It's almost noon.

"I took a red-eye into SFO—"

"She's been asking for you constantly."

I bite back my temper. I want to lash out, want to rage, want to hurt him the way he just continues to hurt me. But it'd serve no purpose, it'd heal no wounds. There might be a momentary sense of justice, but the victory would be short-lived. He will always be in my life. As long as the kids are young and must go back and forth between us, I will have to speak to him, interact with him. I have to keep it civil even if it kills me. "I'll stay with her the rest of the day."

"What about William?" he asks, hands on his hips, every bit the parent. Even with me.

"Lisa's picking him up."

"Lisa's not working for us anymore."

"I've already talked to her today—"

"I don't want her around my kids."

"Be reasonable."

"I am. How can I trust her? Jessica wasn't even in her booster seat or wearing a seat belt."

"Lisa feels terrible."

"As she should. She was stupid, and her stupidity nearly cost us our child."

"Jessica's going to be fine, and I'm not going to hang a guilt trip on a twenty-year-old college student!"

"She's not taking care of my kids."

I take a step toward him, drop my voice. "You don't get to make the call on this one—"

"Watch me."

"Then get a lawyer, Daniel, because I have custody of the children."

"Maybe you shouldn't."

"What does that mean?"

"It means maybe you're not a fit parent." His brown eyes hold mine. "Maybe you're more interested in chasing after your boy toy than being a mother."

"I'm a great mother."

"You're an absent mother!"

"And what about you, Daniel? What about you being on the road for three weeks every month?"

"That's business."

"Is it? How do we know? Maybe you've got a girl-friend out of state, another mistress—"

"You're such a bitch."

I pull back, shaking. Tears blaze in my eyes, and I'm so angry that I could take a swing at him, I really could.

"You've never let me forget," he hisses. "*One* mistake, Jackie, *one* mistake and you throw our lives, our marriage, our children's future, away."

"We weren't happy. *You* weren't happy."

"No, *you* weren't. The rest of us were just fine."

Fine. We're back to fine, but what the hell does "fine" mean, anyway? But this isn't the time or the place. I just want to see Jessica now. I want to be with my daughter. "I'm going to check on Jessica. I'll be here the rest of the day." And without a glance back, I enter her room and let the door close behind me.

Despite the cast on her leg and arm and a big purple bruise on her forehead, Jessica's looking remarkably good. She's talkative and bubbly and rather giddily points out all her flower and balloon bouquets. Jessica's ballet class has sent balloons, and Anne and Philip and their kids sent flowers—daisies in a cute white painted basket. There's a massive stuffed elephant with an even bigger "Get Well" Mylar balloon tied to its gray trunk from Daniel's parents and a dozen long-stemmed pink roses from Daniel. Even William got her something—a jar of jelly bears with a Ty Beanie Babies giraffe.

"What did you bring me, Mom?" Jessica asks, scooting back in her bed.

"Myself."

"Are you *serious*?"

Isn't she the spoiled princess? I lean over, kiss her forehead. "I've a few gifts I picked up in Hawaii, but they're down in the car. Do you want me to go get them?"

Jessica beams. "Yes, please!"

Although Jessica looks to be doing well, her doctor wants to keep her one more day for observation. Daniel comes by that evening with William, bringing bags of McDonald's Happy Meals. (Isn't it ironic that he can buy them crap but I can't?) While the kids and Daniel have dinner together in Jessica's hospital room, I sneak home, shower, change clothes, get Jessica's favorite blanket, and grab some books to read to her.

Daniel and William leave once I return to the hospital, and I pull my chair close to her bed to read to her. She's big into picture books right now and has a whole stack of favorites that I brought from home. *Detective LaRue, Walter the Farting Dog, Skippyjon Jones.* We're rereading *Skippyjon Jones in the Dog House* now, laughing at the antics of the naughty Siamese kitten who thinks he's a Chihuahua.

William will tolerate me reading some picture books, but for the most part he's moved on. I miss the nights we used to read our books together, looking at the pictures, admiring favorite illustrations, enjoying the clever writing. I love picture books. Adults don't get books full of bright, colorful pictures. Adults have to grow up.

"Mommy, I'm worried about you."

We'd been looking at the picture of Skippyjon Jones coloring on the wall, creating "his finest piece of artwork ever," and this seems to come from nowhere.

I lower the book to better see Jess. "Worried, why?"

"I'm worried you're settling."

"Settling?" How does she even know what settling means?

Her blue gaze is somber. "You want this person in Hawaii to be your boyfriend, but he's your first boyfriend since you and Daddy divorced, and maybe he's wrong. Maybe he's not smart enough. Or nice enough. Maybe he will hurt you."

I'm shocked. Completely taken aback. "How would he hurt me?"

"Maybe he doesn't love you, and then you will be sad, and your heart will get broken."

"My heart's not going to get broken."

Her lips purse. "It could happen."

Where has she heard this? Because this isn't coming from Jessica. Jessica knew nothing about Kai. Obviously someone's been talking . . . but who? And why? Although I actually know the why. It's the who I'm most concerned with right now. Jessica looks up into my eyes. "Maybe you shouldn't go to Hawaii anymore. Maybe you should just stay home with us."

I manage a small tight smile, fighting back the thickness in my throat. I feel betrayed. Betrayed by those close to me. This has to have come from Daniel, these have to be Daniel's words. I can't imagine him saying these things to a five-year-old, but maybe he did to someone else. Still, the damage has been done.

"Jessica, Mommy's a big girl. Mommy's smart. Mommy won't let anything bad happen to her, or to you. I love you and William most in the world, and I will always protect you."

She stares at me a long moment, her eyes the blue of cornflowers, light on the edges and darker blue toward the center. "But who will protect you?" Her small fingers curl around mine. She's holding my hand so hard, I can feel the pads of her fingertips pinch. "Daddy used to protect you. You always said he did."

Undone, I say nothing.

"You said the bad guys wouldn't hurt us because Daddy was there, that Daddy would scare off the bad guys and everything would be fine."

I'm going to cry, and I don't want to cry. I don't want to fall apart here, now. I haven't slept for the past forty hours, and I'm exhausted from the worry and guilt and regrets. "I'll scare the bad guys away."

"How? You don't have a gun."

"I don't need a gun."

"Will you use a knife?"

I laugh, thank God, then sniffle. I lean toward the counter for a tissue from the box by her bedside. "I don't need a knife. I'll protect you with love. Because my love is bigger than fear and hate, and my love is stronger than the strongest man."

Jessica just stares at me, and then little by little, the corner of her mouth lifts, revealing her missing bottom tooth. "You could be SuperMom and on your cape there will be hearts everywhere."

"And lips," I say, leaning forward to cover her cheek and neck with noisy kisses. "SuperMom with hearts and lips."

Jessica giggles and tries to wiggle away and then changes her tactic and wraps her good arm around my neck instead. She pushes her face against mine. "When the car hit Lisa's car, I was scared. I wanted you here."

The burning lump is back in my throat, burning all through my heart and chest. "I wanted to be here, too."

"But you weren't."

"No."

Her arm tightens. "Mom?"

"What, honey?"

"Are you going back to Hawaii?"

I see the beautiful beaches of Waikiki and the palm trees curving tall across white sand, smell the sweet plumeria, and feel the pounding of my running shoes on Diamond Head Drive. I loved Hawaii. And Hawaii loved me. "No, baby. I'm staying home."

I can feel her snuggle closer, feel the lift of her lips as she smiles contentedly. "Good."

sixteen

Jessica's released the next day, and Daniel insists on being the one to drive her home. I'm left to collect all the flowers and balloons and stuff them into my car. I know William would help me if he were around, but he's in school.

Daniel drives Jessica while I follow in my car. He drives to my house, carries her into the family room, and gets her settled in the bed I made for her on the sofa. As Daniel covers her with the comforter from her bed and tucks her favorite stuffed animal under her arm, I fill the tables around her with her flowers and balloons.

After Daniel leaves, I make us lunch—grilled cheese, Jess's favorite, with sliced Fuji apples—before putting on an old VHS tape of *Mulan*. She's seen *Mulan* a hundred times now, but she never seems to tire of it.

I'm fast-forwarding through the previews on the tape when I hear my cell phone ring. Could it be Kai? My heart jumps a little, and I count the rings before my voice mail picks up.

What if it *was* Kai calling?

And even if it was, what would we say?

I force myself to put thoughts of Kai out of mind and concentrate on *Mulan* and Jessica. I'm home where I should be. I need to be a good mom now. Focus on what's important. My children. My family.

The next morning, I wake early to go check on Jessica. I tiptoe into the family room and see she's still sleeping. Quietly I make coffee before retrieving the paper outside. I read in the living room, and when I hit the weather page, my eye goes automatically to the far corner of the Pacific where the Hawaiian Islands would be.

Kai.

I should call him, let him know Jessica is okay. But I'm afraid if I call, I won't ever be able to hang up. I'm afraid I'll start crying, afraid I'll say something clingy and needy.

Better not call. Better move on. Better just get this sad phase over with, because I had to know somewhere deep inside me, in the small place I don't like to go, that it was always going to end like this.

I had to know it wasn't ever going to work out.

Where could Kai and I really go with this relationship, anyway?

How were we going to exist off the beach, inside timber and drywall? He's a water person, and I'm a woman who grew up in arid conditions. I know water as in faucets, not waterfalls; dammed lakes, not oceans.

Don't think about him. I get up, top off my coffee. I'm not going to call him or text message. Won't write or miss him. Won't. Must erase all thoughts of Kai and his

warm chest, his sea-drenched skin, and his aquamarine
eyes.

Jessica's driving me crazy. She's been home a week
now, and she's up and hobbling around with her cast on
her right leg and the cast on her left arm. She's never gotten as much attention as she has this past week, and it's
just ruining her, turning her into an even bigger pain.

Thank God she goes back to school tomorrow. I don't
think I could handle another day with little miss princess.

I drive Jessica to school the next morning, since she
still has the leg cast, exhaling with relief as I turn my car
around and drive back home. Jessica's back in school.
It's early May. Summer's just around the corner. Everything's going to be okay.

But I don't feel okay.

I still miss Kai, and I don't know how I can miss him
this much. I hardly know him. We had what? A total of
fifteen days together?

How do you fall in love with a man in fifteen days?

I park in my garage, turn off the engine.

Let it go, Jack.

Accept the facts, Jack.

The garage door slams behind me as I enter the house,
and on my way to the kitchen I see the laundry room.
Mountains of dirty clothes. How is it possible that there
are that many dirty towels and clothes again? Didn't I
just do five loads the day before yesterday?

Bending over, I begin sorting the colors and the whites
and making new piles. I come across William's white
grass-stained baseball pants and drop them in the load for

bleach, but not before I come across his jock strap with the cup still in it. Wrinkling my nose, I pull out the cup, toss the cup into the sink, and add the jock strap to the whites.

After starting the load of whites, I stand over the washer until it's time to add bleach. The water's hot, and it steams up at me.

Maybe surf instructors don't make a lot of money, but they don't wear a lot of clothes.

At least with Kai I wouldn't have to do a lot of laundry.

Then I leave the laundry room for the kitchen, where all the breakfast dishes are still waiting for me.

A couple of days later, I bump into Nic at Paule Attar in Madison Park. She's just leaving as I'm arriving.

"Welcome home, stranger," Nic says, giving me a hug.

"Thanks." I step back, admire her hair. "Looks good."

"Michelle."

"I'm just going to see her now." I suddenly remember Nic dropped off dinner for us last week, a dinner to help us get by when Jessica was hurt. "By the way, thank you so much for dinner. I left a voice mail for you—"

"I got it. I've just been busy. My sister's in town, and she has a baby. It's a zoo at my house." Nic retrieves her sunglasses from her purse. "Is Jessica doing better?"

"Much. Yesterday was her first day back at school. Thank goodness. I'm behind on work again, but I also needed my color done." Nic would understand this. Appointments with Michelle are hard to come by. Michelle's booked solid weeks in advance. "Where are you going now?"

"Home and then to University Village. My sister's dying to go shopping, and it's a pretty day."

"Sounds like fun."

Nic blows me a kiss. "Talk soon."

In the salon, I sit in Michelle's chair as she mixes my color. "How was Hawaii?"

"How do you know I went to Hawaii?"

"You were in here getting your hair cut just before you went."

I'd forgotten. And I didn't just get my hair cut, I got an eyebrow wax and that ungodly, unbearable Brazilian. Now that Kai and I are finished, I guess that's one thing I won't have to do again. "It was good."

Michelle's dark arched eyebrow lifts higher. "Just good? Last time you were here you were really excited. You'd bought new clothes, were getting your first Brazilian—"

"Don't remind me. The Brazilian was *embarrassing*. I felt bad that Valera had to move all those girl parts around, but she says she does it all the time."

Michelle begins to brush the color on my scalp. "So when are you going back to Hawaii?"

I lean forward, reach for the stack of magazines on the counter of her station. "I'm not."

She pauses, brush in midair. "No?"

I just shake my head, open the copy of *W* magazine. It's an old issue. I read it last month, but I pretend to be interested now.

Michelle hesitates, but when she sees I'm done

talking she silently applies the rest of the color. But as she finishes up, she peels off her gloves, drops them on her tray, and says, "Did he have a girlfriend?"

I know we're still talking about Kai. I knew Michelle wasn't done, either. "No."

"A wife. Kids. What?"

I look up and meet her gaze in the mirror. "Jessica was in an accident while I was gone."

"Is she okay?"

"Broken arm, broken leg, concussion."

"No way."

"I couldn't get back quickly. I had to catch three different flights, fly all night. It was horrible. I felt so horrible."

"But why does that mean you can't go back to Hawaii anymore?"

I shrug.

"You liked Hawaii," she persists. "You were having fun with your surfer guy."

"I'm forty, Michelle. I'm a mom—"

"Yeah, I'm a mom, too, but it doesn't mean we're dead."

"You're not even thirty."

"So?"

I just shake my head. "I can't hurt the kids. I just can't be that selfish."

"And you being happy is selfish?"

There's no answer. My eyes burn and my throat burns, and I return my attention to my magazine. It's either that or cry.

We don't always get everything we want. We don't always get what we want or need, don't always get the guy, the love, or the happy ending. But that's life.

Kai doesn't call. And I don't call him. It's over, we both know it's over, no point in dragging this out.

But the bad, sad, empty feeling inside me doesn't go away. One day becomes two days, two days become a week, and every day I feel worse, not better.

The ending with Kai reminds me of the ending with Daniel and the ending with the boyfriend I had before Daniel. Endings are just that, endings, and they never get any easier.

You'd think, though, after your heart has been batted about a few times, you'd know how to pick up all the pieces, dust them off, put them under your arm, and walk away quickly, albeit with dignity. But it never quite happens that way. The heart has this terrible, horrible, impossible ability to keep hoping.

To keep believing.

Goddamn heart with its goddamn optimism.

I wish for once my heart would pack up, move on. Get a good job as a lighthouse keeper on a rocky inlet and leave hope and love to those who can handle the ups and downs better.

I do not handle ups and downs well at all.

I am still, at forty, too romantic, too emotional, too sensitive, too intense. I am still slightly breathless and eager about this experiment called life, and it's aggravating, it really is. Especially now that I am back to hurt, back to lonely, back to crying in my pillow and the crook of my arm when no one is looking.

I fell hard for Kai, I don't know how else to put it. I just fell for him, but now it's over and I've got to pick myself up off the ground and continue on.

With dignity.

Dignity.

I smile even as tears fill my eyes. There's nothing dignified about loss, nothing dignified about the realization that I'm now just another woman on the beach to Kai, another flavor. Women come and go, and he won't have any problem meeting a beautiful new woman to divert his attention. I'm the one who will find it hard to replace Kai. Hundreds of women looking for a good time go to Waikiki. Not many sexy surfers hang out in Madison Park or downtown Seattle.

There's no one I can talk to about the hurt, either, not unless I pay a counselor or therapist. My friends never approved of the relationship and are glad it's over. Daniel wanted the relationship to fail, finding the idea of me with someone young and sexy and noncorporate laughable. *Laughable.* But the hurt isn't laughable; neither is the ending of my whatever it was with Kai.

Maybe that's what makes this ending so hard. If only those visits with Kai had felt more like a fling. If only I'd been more in control of my feelings. You know, been lighter, calmer, more confident and able to enjoy the very hot, sexy sex as just . . . well, hot, sexy sex. But no, I couldn't do that, had to make the sex emotional, ladening it with nuances and meaning, subtleties I'm certain no man intends. After all, men are men, and women are women, and most men don't cherish us the way we want to be cherished.

I wanted to be cherished.

For a blip in time, Kai made me feel cherished, too. He made me feel like the most amazing woman in the world. And I wanted that. Still want it. The only problem is, I didn't want it just on holiday, on some tropical island. I want it here at home, too. I want it every day with a man who is interested in long term, not just five days of island fun.

I'm still struggling with the jet lag nearly three weeks later, finding it hard to wake up in the morning and exhausted in the middle of the day.

I'm crabby, crampy, and I feel extremely PMS-y. That's the one thing I've noticed most since turning forty—I have a lot more cramps and backaches than I used to in my thirties. "Menopause," I grunt to myself, popping Motrin as I get close to my period, hoping it'll help with the aches and sensitive boobs. But what's supposed to be day one of my period comes and goes and nothing. Day two the same. Day three and still nothing.

I'm usually disgustingly regular, and I'm alarmed.

It's my age, I tell myself. Stress. Stress can throw things off, and since the divorce I've been late. A day late.

Not three.

But I don't feel pregnant. Nothing in me says pregnant. I'm just crabby and tired and sad and missing Kai.

Damn. I don't want to miss Kai.

I don't want to be pregnant, either.

I'm sure I'm not pregnant.

I'll wait another day. I'm sure my period will come.

* * *

Cooking dinner that night, I'm beyond jittery, I'm nearly climbing the walls with worry. I should have just gone and bought a test kit. Why put myself through this? The kit would have put me out of my misery.

Or locked me in it.

Because what if I was pregnant? What would I do? What would everyone say?

I look at the kids, who are clearing the table and jabbing each other with elbows as they try to pass through the doorway, each one refusing to let the other by, and it's impossible. Me, having a baby, is impossible.

I couldn't cope. I'd be poor and stressed and out of my mind and—

No.

No way. No baby. There's no baby. I'm not pregnant.

I'm pregnant.

It's the next morning, the kids are at school, and I'm sitting in the stall of the drugstore's employees-only bathroom, staring at the home pregnancy test stick.

Two pink lines. That's not good. That means pregnant.

Maybe I'm reading it wrong.

I pick up the box, study the side with the little color illustrations and the captions beneath the drawings. I read every word, everything, brain freaking. This isn't real. How could it be real? We had protected sex. Always. In the beginning, always. But the last visit . . . ?

I squeeze my eyes shut, remembering that one time we didn't, that night in my hotel room when things got heated and intense and we just did it. Went for it. Went for each other.

The bathroom door opens and shuts, and I see wide black pants and sensible black shoes on the other side of the bathroom stall, waiting for me to come out. But I don't move. I can't.

I almost hear my eighth-grade health and science teacher tonelessly drilling into our junior high brains, "It only takes one time. Just one little mistake . . ."

I should have known better. I do know better. I'm forty, for heaven's sake.

Call Kai. I want to call Kai. I should call him and . . . what? What do I tell him? *Kai, I'm pregnant.* And then he says, what? *Girl, I'm on my way.*

I'll move to Seattle and marry you, and we'll raise the baby together.

The lady on the other side of the stall door clears her throat. Her sensible black shoes shuffle.

I've got to get off the toilet. Leave. Go.

Awkwardly I rise and stuff the First Response box with the foil pouch, the used test kit, and the paper insert explaining how to read the test in the receptacle hanging on the wall before exiting the stall.

We pass each other as she heads into the stall, and I think I've successfully managed to avoid eye contact until I'm at the sink to wash my hands. As I look into the mirror, I see the lady staring back at me.

She's an employee of the drugstore, is wearing the store apron, and her expression is neither friendly nor cold. It's just . . . indifferent. I'm just some woman using the employee bathroom. She doesn't know that I've just learned I'm pregnant. She doesn't know that my world has just changed forever. Again.

* * *

I'm supposed to have coffee with Anne at ten, and I debate calling to cancel because I'm in no condition to talk about the you-know; yet while I can't talk about it, I also don't want to be alone.

We meet at the Starbucks closest to our house, and Anne's already in line. "The usual?" she asks, about to place our order.

"Yes—no." I can't have a double-shot latte if I'm pregnant. I already had a cup of coffee at home.

Anne's forehead wrinkles. "No?"

"The mint tea."

Anne gives me a perplexed look before ordering the tea and her caramel macchiato. She knows I don't like tea, not even the green tea that's full of antioxidants and supposed to keep us young forever.

Together we sit down. She drinks. I don't even touch my tea. I'm sick on the inside. And numb. Can't think. Can't focus on anything.

"How's Jessica doing?" Anne asks.

"Good." I look up, brighten. "The casts aren't slowing her down a bit."

"Not surprised. She's a pistol."

"Isn't she?"

"How are you?"

I shuffle my feet beneath the round table. "Good."

"Liar." Anne tucks hair behind her ear and gives me her you-can't-bullshit-a-bullshitter look. "You look like hell. What's up?"

I miss Kai. I'm pregnant with his baby. And I'm trapped here in Seattle. Tears fill my eyes; I bite my lower lip ruthlessly. I'm not going to cry, I'm not. "I'm just tired. Working too hard."

"You haven't had much time alone since—" She breaks off, and her eyes lock with mine. I know she was going to say Hawaii, but she doesn't. Instead she pauses, then nimbly substitutes, "Jessica's accident."

I manage a tight smile. I feel as though I'm going to throw up. Am I really pregnant? Could that test be wrong? There are false positives. It's happened.

"When do the kids go to Daniel's next?" she continues.

"This next weekend."

"That'll be good for you."

I look down, the table a blur, and hurriedly wipe tears. If I'm really pregnant, that means I'm going to be a mother again. That means there's a baby on the way, a baby growing inside of me right now, a baby with a different father from William and Jessica's, a baby with a thirty-year-old surf instructor for a father.

Jesus.

"Jackie."

I jerk my head up. Anne's looking at me with worry and love. "You can't blame yourself for the accident," she says softly. "You're not to blame, no matter what Daniel says."

"I know."

"But do you believe it?"

I lift the tea, smell the pungent herbal mint aroma. How can anyone think this is tasty? I put the cup back down. "If it was your child, would you feel guilty?"

The corner of Anne's mouth lifts. "Yes."

"But I know. You don't use sitters. You're always with them."

"Philip doesn't like to spend the money."

"That's not why you don't use sitters. You don't think it's good for the kids."

"But I don't have to work," she says almost apologetically. "Not like you."

Not like me, I echo silently, on the verge of bursting into hysterical tears. Not like me, who is pregnant and divorced and very much alone.

Not like me, who fell in love with a younger man so unacceptable that he isn't even mentioned by my friends.

And maybe this is what pushes me over the edge. Anne knows I'm sad. She knows why I'm sad. She knows I'm missing Kai like hell, and she won't talk about it. She'll sit there and say she cares, she'll sit there and make conversation, but she won't let me say what I need to say most.

And if I can't talk about Kai, how do I talk about being pregnant?

If he's unacceptable, what about his baby?

I'm wild on the inside, wild and scared and cornered like a caged animal. I can't sit here and make polite conversation one more minute. Can't pretend I'm okay. Can't pretend anything.

I stumble to my feet, make excuses about appointments and work to do before the kids finish school, and dash to my car.

Pulling out of the parking lot, I run a wild hand through my hair, once, twice, and catch a glimpse of myself in the rearview mirror. I look nearly as crazy as I feel.

Pregnant.

I'm *pregnant.* Jackie Laurens, forty, single, and pregnant.

What the hell am I going to do?

I go through on autopilot the rest of the day, meeting a client at the Design Center before swinging by the marble importer, where I pick up some samples from slabs in stock to take to another client in Laurelhurst.

Because Lisa has a paper to write, I'm back at the kids' school at two forty-five and listen to them bicker the entire drive home while I mindlessly grip the steering wheel.

There's going to be another child. Another baby Laurens, but the baby won't be a Laurens, as that's Daniel's name. What would the baby be, then? Whiting, my maiden name, or Carson, Kai's last name?

I laugh and the sound is strangled, and I feel hopeless, helpless. I can hardly keep my head above water now, how on earth will I manage with a newborn? How will I do it all on my own?

William mutters something unintelligible in the backseat and Jessica shouts, and suddenly they're both hitting each other. Howling. Screaming. I swerve over, pull onto the shoulder of the road, and fling myself around. "What is the matter with you two?"

"William hit me."

"Jessica bit me."

"He started it."

"She wouldn't leave me alone."

"I—"

"Stop it! For God's sake, *stop it*!" I scream above their raised voices, shouting so loud that it throbs in my chest, hurts my throat, stuns them into silence. "Stop it right now!" Then my voice breaks and silence fills the car and I see their shocked faces in the rearview mirror.

I lay my forehead against the steering wheel and shudder with tears that I don't let fall. How can I have another child when I can't even manage the two I have?

When I can barely keep my company going? When my customers call and call and leave frustrated messages that nothing is moving as fast as they'd like?

When Daniel doesn't speak to me and my friends barely see me and I feel so sad again, so lonely and alone?

I didn't feel lonely with Kai. I didn't feel bad with Kai. I felt good and strong and funny and beautiful, but he's not real, Hawaii's not real. It was just an escape, a fantasy 2,600 miles away, and I can't escape. Can't run away. Must face my responsibilities, must be a grown-up, must see an OB and find out when the due date would be. . . .

At home, the kids settle quietly at the kitchen counter to do their homework, and I make them a snack. While both do their math, I go upstairs to my office and call and make an appointment with Dr. Montgomery, the doctor who delivered both Jessica and William and whom I haven't seen in years, since I can get my annual exam from a nurse practitioner.

The receptionist is able to get me in to see Dr. Montgomery a week from today. A week later I pee into a cup, get a blood draw, and then wait for the doctor to visit me in my paper gown in the examination room.

"Jacqueline!" says Dr. Montgomery, entering the room with a great smile. "How are you? How are the boys?"

"Girl and boy," I correct, although Jessica could be a boy. She's certainly a take-no-prisoners kind of girl.

"I should know that," he corrects himself with a laugh.

"You shouldn't have to remember. You've delivered thousands of babies in the past few years."

"Yes, but you and Daniel make beautiful babies."

I nod and smile, my lips feeling tight over dry teeth.

"How is Daniel?" the doctor continues, flipping through my chart.

"Good."

"I didn't think he wanted another baby."

My lips stretch tighter, and my throat feels like sandpaper. "We're divorced."

"I'm sorry."

"It's been about sixteen months. Two years. Something like that."

"I'm sorry."

"Things happen."

"So . . . ?" The doctor looks up at me, thinning salt-and-pepper hair flopping on his tan forehead. I know the doctor has a place in Aspen and is an avid skier. Jessica was induced so I wouldn't risk going into delivery when Dr. Montgomery was away with his family on winter break.

"I'm single, and . . . pregnant." I manage a tremulous laugh. "At least, the home pregnancy kit said I was pregnant, and I haven't had my period yet."

"How late?"

"Almost two weeks now."

He shifts a small circle on his clipboard. "December thirty-first."

"December thirty-first," I repeat dumbly, although I know exactly what he's telling me. My baby's due date. Kai's baby's due date.

"But it could be a Christmas baby, knowing your tendency to deliver early," the doctor adds, and scribbles something in my chart before looking up at me. "There are risks in your forties, Jacqueline—"

"I know."

"The baby's father?"

"Not in the picture."

The doctor looks at me long and hard. "You can terminate the pregnancy. No one would know."

But I'd know. I grab the paper gown and press it against my thighs, feel the air against my exposed back and bottom. "I'm keeping the baby."

"You have a couple weeks if you change your mind."

"I won't."

He smiles a small, kind smile, but I'm numb inside, and his smile bounces off me.

"I recommend an amnio, Jacqueline. I know you didn't have one with the first two pregnancies, but at your age—"

"I understand." I cut him off, not needing to hear more about my age. I'm forty, not fifty, not sixty, and it pains me more than a little to have my fertility called into question.

Dr. Montgomery is talking again, reminding me to take my prenatal vitamins and schedule a checkup a month from now and other basic things I used to know. I just sit there nodding and tugging on the edges of my gown, desperate to get dressed and out of the office and on my way home. I don't even know why I'm here. It's not as if he and his staff can do anything for me now. I'm pregnant, I knew I was pregnant. It's just a matter now of waiting seven or eight months.

seventeen

n my car on the way home, I think and then don't
think. It's overwhelming; there's no other way to put
it. What's happening . . . what's going to happen . . .
it'll change everything. Nothing will ever be the same.
William and Jessica will go to their dad's, and the baby
and I will be home alone together. The baby and I . . .

Suddenly I hear Dr. Montgomery's voice asking if
I'm going to keep the baby or if I want to terminate the
pregnancy. I feel squeamish all over again. Guilty and
squeamish.

I have thought about getting an abortion. Of course I
have. But even as I tried to imagine having a baby on my
own, I tried to imagine driving to an office and letting
someone take the baby from me, and I couldn't do it.
Couldn't let it happen.

It was hard conceiving Jessica—two and a half
years of trying and two miscarriages before she came
along—and to think now, just when I never thought
I'd have another child, I'm pregnant. Of course I'm
panicking, but an abortion?

But what about the kids I already have? What about my family? What would another baby do to them?

I don't know. Maybe once I could have said that having a baby would be good for them, but they've been through so many changes already, had the proverbial rug yanked from beneath their feet. What will they think— feel—when I tell them I'm pregnant and having a baby and there's no daddy?

I'm in my driveway, and I turn off the motor, and just sit there. Finally I think about the one person I haven't let myself think about.

Kai.

I have to tell him, don't I?

And I can see him, all bronzed and blue eyed, tattoos inked over bulging biceps and dark hair slicked back from the perfect brow and cheekbones and jaw chiseled for a *GQ* model instead of a laid-back surfer from Florida.

What will Kai say when I tell him? What will he do? *Think?*

I can't imagine he'd want me to keep the baby, and if I do, I can't imagine he'd want to be part of the baby's life. And then how will that be when Jessica and William are spoiled rotten by Daniel and child number three is always left home, left behind?

My God, what have I gotten myself into?

I bite my lip, bite hard, force myself to see this as it really is, not as I'd like it to be.

Which room will be the nursery? (My office.)

How will this affect my business? (I'll need a real nanny again—and God, professional nannies cost a fortune.)

How will this affect me personally? Beyond the whole body thing—God, I'm going to get big and fat soon—I'm going to feel sick and get queasy and barf. I'm going to have headaches and backaches and body aches and leg pain and weird dreams. Food cravings and mood swings and fresh stretch marks and possibly—although I pray not—hemorrhoids. I never got hemorrhoids or varicose veins with William or Jessica, but I'm not thirty-three anymore.

If I should ever want to date again, what man will be interested in a woman who has three kids, two by her ex-husband and one by some man she barely knew on a Hawaiian island?

How to explain to future men that I'm really not all that reckless and impulsive, that I'm not a risk and dating me isn't asking for disaster, although, come to think of it, what man—never married and without significant baggage of his own—will want to take on a forty-year-old woman with three children under the age of ten? What man would want to raise two other men's children?

My stomach churns. I don't like thinking this way, but I can't be naive, can't just blithely assume that everything is going to be okay. For example, financially—Daniel can help provide for his two, but what about surfer baby? Will surfer baby be able to attend summer camp, get his or her teeth fixed, go to college?

Will surfer baby hate watching his or her older brother and sister travel the world with their dad while he or she sits home with me?

I'm jarred by the sharp rap of knuckles on my window. Opening my door, I see William standing there in his baseball uniform. "Mom, where have you been? The game started an hour ago."

Game? Today? "The game's Thursday, William—"

"*Today's* Thursday." He's near tears, and his expression is tight, his jaw set. "Dad's in San Jose, and he even called to make sure I wouldn't miss the game. But you weren't here and you didn't answer your phone and I couldn't get anybody else."

"Where's Lisa?"

"Taking Jessica to Brownies." He climbs into the backseat. "Can we just go? If we don't hurry, the game will be over by the time we get there."

William's not far off: There's just an inning left. The coach puts him in with one out, but the next play is a double play, and like that, the game is over.

His team loses, and William clutches his bag of chips and Gatorade provided by this week's snack mom as we drive home. He says nothing, doesn't eat, just sits next to me in the passenger seat, staring out the window.

"Where were you?" William finally blurts, hostility rolling off him in waves.

I shoot him a side glance. "Why?"

His shoulders shrug and he gives me a look hard enough, sharp enough, to cut. "Dad says you have a boyfriend. Were you with him?"

My heart sinks. "No."

"But you do have a boyfriend?"

God, Daniel, you're a piece of work. "No."

"Dad says you do in Hawaii."

"I'm not in Hawaii, am I? I'm right here, in my car, feeling horrible because I made you miss your game."

My throat aches, and I clutch the steering wheel. "I'm sorry, William. I'm sorry about the game. And your dad—" I break off, hold my breath, fighting for calm, fighting for the right tone.

I can't bad-mouth Daniel to the kids, but these are my children, too, and it's not fair of him to poison them against me. This is not a competition. Not war.

"But you *are* dating," William persists sullenly.

"I had a few dates here in Seattle before Christmas, but it was just coffee, nothing more." I signal, turn, and soon we're passing the Arboretum.

"So where were you today, then?"

"The doctor's."

William turns to look at me, his expression uncertain. "Are you sick?"

"No."

"Because if you're sick—"

"Baby, I'm fine."

He hesitates and then nods, and we drive the rest of the way home in silence. It's dark by the time we reach the house, and Lisa and Jessica are in the kitchen eating Goldfish crackers, string cheese, and sliced apples. "Hey," Lisa says, sliding off a bar stool. "I didn't know what you'd planned for dinner, but Jess was hungry."

"It's okay." I fish for my checkbook, cut her a check for the week's work, and let her say good-bye to the kids before I face them. And for the first time in a long time, I haven't anything to say.

Finally I draw a breath. "Finish your homework. I'll start dinner. Is spaghetti okay?"

Jessica starts to protest, but William elbows her and

she yelps but then concedes. "Fine," she says grumpily, thumping her cast on the counter. "As long as we can have garlic bread, too."

The weeks pass, and I've become nauseated as hell. I'm sipping water and munching saltines in secret and am completely off coffee. I know it's only a matter of time before my friends notice, especially Anne, who knows my addiction to caffeine. I wonder when I'm going to tell my friends what's going on with me.

When I throw up in the bathroom during Jessica's end-of-year dance recital, I know it's time to tell them.

I'm a mess. I can hardly keep a mouthful down, and I'm angry as all hell. I'd forgotten how the first trimester makes me feel out of control. I remember meeting women who said they loved being pregnant, and I never understood it then and can't understand it now.

My bad moods are scaring even me. I need help. Support. Encouragement. Forgiveness. *Something.*

After the dance recital, I muster my courage and call Kristine, Nic, and Anne, inviting them over tomorrow for a girls'-night-only dinner at my place. Daniel has the kids tomorrow, and I figure it's as good a time as any to break the news. I'm tempted to book a table at the Madison Park Café, a favorite restaurant of ours, but realize a French bistro could be dangerous. I might throw up, and on hearing the news, one (or more) of my friends might scream.

Late the next afternoon, Kristine calls. "I'm not sure I can make it tonight," she says breathlessly. "I've got a meeting—"

"Skip it," I interrupt, leaning across my kitchen's golden granite counter to stretch out an arm to keep William from punching his sister for her calling him a dumb-butt just now. "This is important. You don't want to hear this secondhand."

"You're not moving to Hawaii, are you?" Kris asks, deadpan.

"Not yet, no."

"You're getting married."

I glare at the kids to try to keep them in check. "No, not that. But I am making my famous Oriental chicken salad and I've got a bottle of wine in the fridge."

"So what's going on?"

"Come at six-thirty and you'll find out."

"What about your kids?"

"Daniel's got them." Quickly I cover the phone's mouthpiece to shush Jessica, who is making ape noises to rattle William.

"I heard he and his girlfriend broke up."

I'm surprised. I hadn't heard anything about it. Not from him (why should he tell me?) and not from the kids. "I didn't know."

"I guess she wanted more of a commitment from him, and he thought it was all moving too fast."

From the corner of my eye, I see Jessica swing her foot up under the kitchen counter to connect with William's shin. He shouts, and I'm frantically snapping my fingers at Jessie and pointing fiercely at William, a jab-jab of my finger in his direction to make him release his sister's throat and sit down again. "I'm sure Daniel doesn't want to lose any more of his assets to a woman."

"But Melinda's successful."

"She's twenty-nine."

"And?"

"Come on, Kris. You were a lawyer, too. At what point did you stop practicing law?" I don't even need Kristine to answer this one, I know the answer already. When Kris got married and had her first baby, she stopped working to stay home with Andrew.

Kris falls quiet. "You think she wants kids?"

"She's twenty-nine. And a woman."

Hip against the counter, phone pressed to my ear, I watch Jessie lean toward William, stick out her tongue, and hold back her nose, revealing two stretched nostrils. Lovely. My children are so well behaved.

William goes quiet and red, the quiet before a storm, and I know I have to get off the phone before there's bloodshed. "So you're coming tonight?"

Kris sighs. "I'll be there."

"Good."

"Do you want me to bring anything? Appetizer? Dessert?"

"Just yourself."

After getting off the phone, I cross my arms and stare down my nose at the kids, giving both a severe look. "What was that about?"

Jessie and William settle into their seats and smile at me angelically. "Nothing, Mommy."

Nothing, my ass.

I'm just about to launch into a tirade when I realize I'm going to throw up. Again.

* * *

Nic arrives first, then Anne, and finally Kris. They stand around the kitchen while I serve the salads and pour the white wine. Anne helps me carry the plates, Kris takes the glasses, and Nic follows with the silverware.

We sit in the living room, picking the comfiest chairs and spots on the sofa to balance our plates on our laps. I was raised to think that a meal wasn't a proper meal if you weren't at the dining room table, but I've broken that rule now that I live alone. I like eating on the couch, like sitting cross-legged with the wineglass just behind my shoulder on the sofa table, not that I'm going to drink my wine tonight.

We've barely begun to eat when Kris dives right in. "So, what's the big news?"

Anne waves her glass of wine before taking a drink. "Does your news have anything to do with you not drinking for the past few weeks?"

The others turn and look at me. That didn't take long, I think. But of course Anne would pick up on the no drinking. Anne and I always enjoyed our wine together. I wouldn't call us drinking buddies, but she and I had no problem opening a bottle of wine on nights our husbands worked late.

I set my plate at my feet. "Yes, it does."

Kris is looking from me, to Anne, and back at me again. She's just got it. Her expression is priceless. Jaw dropped, eyes wide. "You're *pregnant*?"

"I am." There. It's out.

The silence is deafening, and I'd really like to gulp down my wine, but I don't. I'm not drinking, not escaping. Have to do this. "About seven weeks."

"Wow." Kris is shaking her head. *"Wow."*

"Daniel's going to have a fit," Nic says.

I love Nic, but her tendency to state the obvious really gets on my nerves. And yes, Daniel will have a fit. I can only imagine the things he'll say to his parents about me and my lax morals, unaware the kids are hearing every word he says. I know Daniel would never intentionally bad-mouth me to the kids, but the kids have repeated things that their dad has said, which their dad shouldn't have said.

"You've known for a while, then," Anne says quietly.

I nod. "Since I missed my period."

She sets down her wine. "Why didn't you tell us sooner?"

"Because I couldn't take any more criticism or pressure." I sigh, rub my head. "And I needed time to adjust to the news first."

Nic's somber. "So what are you going to do?"

What am I going to do? "I'm having the baby." And then the fight and defiance go out of me. My eyes fill with tears. "I'm having the baby," I repeat, "and I'm really scared."

Kristine leans forward. "Are you feeling as bad as you did with Jessica? You were so sick with her."

"It's even worse." I reach up to wipe the tears dry before they can fall. "I'm sick morning, noon, and night. And I'm so snappy with the kids. All I do is yell right now."

Anne scoots over on the couch, covers my hand with hers. "You always wanted one more baby."

I bite my tongue to keep fresh tears from forming. I'd

been so afraid they'd be angry with me again, so afraid they'd turn their backs on me. I want this baby, but I don't want this baby. I'm thrilled at the idea of a baby and terrified all at the same time.

Babies are so much work. They're exhausting and time-consuming and demanding and expensive. "I don't know if I can do this," I choke out, the tears falling despite my best efforts. "I don't know how to take care of three kids on my own."

"William and Jessica are old enough to help," Nic says. "They'll be a big help, especially William."

I nod and reach for my napkin to wipe my eyes and nose. "Is it fair to the kids, though? Is it fair to bring more chaos into their lives?"

"Is it fair to the baby to just get rid of it?" Nic flashes.

"No." And I want the baby. That's the crazy thing. I'm sick and scared and overwhelmed, but I'm also excited about having a little one again. All the itty-bitty newborn clothes. Setting up the crib. Buying a new stroller. Decorating a new nursery.

I look up at them. "This baby won't ever have as much, not financially."

Kristine reaches out and strokes my hair. "But the baby will have love." She smiles at me through tears of her own. "You're a great mom, Jack. You'll be wonderful with the baby."

"What if I'm not?"

"You will be. And we'll help you," Kristine says. Anne and Nic nod.

"We can take turns helping out," Anne adds. "There's no reason we can't all pitch in. I've missed having a baby around. I'd love to have one afternoon each week where I take the baby. I'll be Auntie Anne and my kids will be your baby's cousins and the baby will have tons of family."

I cover my face with my hands and just cry. They're all touching me. Patting my back, rubbing my knee, squeezing my arm. They're letting me know I'm not alone and they won't leave me behind. They might have been tough on me earlier, but they're also women, and they know how hard life is, how hard it can be.

Finally I get some control. I blow my nose and wipe my eyes dry. "You guys are amazing."

"We love you, Jack," Anne says simply.

And I nod, because I know they do.

"So what's the baby's due date?" Kris asks as we eventually resume eating.

"December thirty-first." I smile weakly. "Can you believe it?"

"You never go full term," Nic says. "Just watch. You'll end up having a Christmas baby."

"That's exactly what Dr. Montgomery said." I'm laughing and crying at the same time. This is *crazy*.

This is life.

In the next week, boxes of maternity clothes show up on my doorstep, as does a dog-eared copy of *What to Expect When You're Expecting,* along with a brand-new pregnancy diary so I can keep track of the new baby's growth.

I had one of these with Jessica but stopped writing in it around week eleven because everything I wrote was so cranky and negative.

· I vow to be more cheerful this time. Even if I'm sicker than before.

I don't need any of the maternity clothes yet, as I'm losing weight, not gaining. I see Dr. Montgomery for my monthly checkup. I'm now eight weeks. He's satisfied with everything except my weight. "Don't starve," he reminds me. "And don't stop taking your prenatal vitamins."

School is nearly over for the year, and I sign the kids up for sports camp and summer activities, knowing I'm going to need to keep the kids busy, especially if I'm not going to feel better anytime soon.

Lisa agrees to work full-time through the summer. I shift some projects around, wrapping up one, turning down another, and postponing a third so I can work a little less and sleep a little more.

June's hot, hotter than normal, and the unusually high heat has me pulling out my Hawaii clothes. I walk around the house in a tiny tank top and beach sarong. I feel silly, but at least I'm cool.

The heat, though, makes me think of Kai. Not that I've ever stopped thinking of him. Or wanting to call him. How could I forget him when I'm carrying his child?

Maybe I don't want to forget him. Maybe I still have this secret fantasy that he'll come to me and we'll have that click of chemistry and connection and we'll find a way to raise the baby together.

We don't have to get married.

We don't even have to live in the same house. We could go back and forth, bicoastal of sorts, and the baby could have the best of both worlds. Hawaii sun and

Seattle rain. Hawaii cool with Seattle cold. I laugh a little. Everything's going to be all right, isn't it?

Late June, while the kids are at tennis camp, I go to University Village for a quick shopping trip. William and Jessica could both use some new summer clothes, and I head to Kids Gap for shorts and T-shirts.

Jessica's in a lime green and orange phase, so I grab her some denim skirts and shorts and wild T-shirts, and William gets his standard blue-and-red athletic-type wear. I'm just about to pay when I see the Baby Gap section at the very back of the store. Suddenly I'm there, touching the soft fleece blankets, the adorable denim and khaki overalls in nine to twelve months, the newborn onesies with yellow giraffes and purple elephants.

"May I help you with something?" the perky salesgirl asks me, one hand on her hip, clipboard in the other.

I almost touch my stomach, thinking of my baby, thinking that soon I'll be setting up a nursery and getting everything ready. But it's too soon now. I'm superstitious that way. "No. Just looking."

"We've got cute fall clothes coming in every day."

"Thanks." She leaves, and reluctantly I hang the fuzzy zipper sleeper back on the rod. I'd forgotten how gorgeous newborn clothes are. I love all the whites and brights, the cheerful patterns, the funky stripes and bold checks.

Impulsively, I take back the zipper sleeper. I'm going to buy it. The sleeper and the matching blanket. I can't help it. They're so soft and yummy, and the baby will love them.

As I pay, the checkout girl asks if I need a gift receipt for the baby clothes. "No."

"Not a gift?" she persists, showing me where to run my credit card.

"No."

"You have a baby?"

I flush, nervous, shy. "I'm expecting."

"Congratulations."

"Thank you."

"Not your first?" she asks, gesturing to the kids' clothes she's just bagged.

"My third."

"Well, that's wonderful." She hands me the shopping bags. "Enjoy."

"I will." I'm humming as I leave Kids Gap. I will enjoy this baby. It wasn't planned, but it's very wanted.

Driving home, I turn on the radio and suddenly I'm back in Hawaii. Brother Israel's "Somewhere Over the Rainbow" comes on.

I love this song and turn it up.

They play this song everywhere in Hawaii, but then, Israel Kamakawiwo'ole is Hawaii.

The first time I heard Brother Iz's version, it was on the catamaran that very first night I met Kai.

And then they played the song the night we ate at Duke's.

And in the shopping mall.

They even play the song on the airplane as the jet taxis from Honolulu, and I cry every time I hear it.

I'm crying now.

You don't know Hawaii until you know Brother Iz's

voice. And you know his version of the song. The song's played at the end of the movie *50 First Dates,* and it's beautiful, so beautiful, just like Hawaii and Kai and the ocean and the dramatic, jagged green Pali.

I miss him. I miss Hawaii. The pang inside me is so strong, so sharp, and it's like being homesick and heart-sick all at the same time.

I've got to talk to Kai. I've got to hear his voice and that husky, sexy way he has of laughing and the way he calls me "girl."

Impulsively, I pick up my cell phone and call his cell. But a voice on the other end of the line tells me his number is no longer in service.

After ending the call, I drop the phone in my lap and clutch the steering wheel, stunned. His number's discon-nected? It never once crossed my mind that his number would change, that I wouldn't be able to reach him.

I *have* to be able to reach him.

He's the father of my baby.

Heart pounding, I pick up the phone again. I call in-formation, get the phone number for Outrigger Reef on the Beach, and ask for the hotel's beach activities desk.

An English accent answers. Tommy, I think. It's Tommy from Leeds.

"Is Kai working on the beach today?" I ask, heart pounding, stomach cramping. I'm afraid. Nervous. I don't know what I'm doing. I don't know why I'm calling. But suddenly I must talk to Kai, must hear his voice, must connect.

"No, he's not. He was here earlier, though. Is this Desiree?"

Desiree. Is that the new girl? The new flavor of the week? I exhale. "No."

"Do you want me to take a message, love?"

"No. That's okay." I hang up, roll down my window, blink away tears.

We can always call him later, I say to the baby. *We've still got time.*

The nurse at my next monthly checkup reminds me it's time to sign up for Lamaze classes, and I do, not that I think I need them. But this is what expectant mothers do, and I did it for the other two, so I resign myself to doing it again.

Anne agrees to be my birthing partner, and I'm just glad December is still a ways off. I can't imagine actually giving birth with Anne at my side. She'd be way too hard-core. She'd tell me to go all natural. No drugs. She'd be kicking my butt until the baby was out.

In the evenings, I sort through the maternity clothes, pulling out skirts for later this summer and then trousers and suits for the fall.

Dutifully I write in the baby's diary. I haven't decided if I'll do the amnio or not, and I think I don't want to know what sex the baby is, either. Boy or girl, I don't care. I already have one of each. I just want the baby healthy.

I have the kids for Fourth of July this year, and Kristine invites us all over for a barbecue and the big fireworks show you can see from her house high on Queen Anne.

Kristine has a killer view of the Space Needle and the Sound, and the kids sit with bowls of homemade peach and strawberry ice cream as the night explodes in green and blue and white. Nic and her husband stand together, his arm wrapped around her, while Kris chases her wild boys around the yard, one boy terrorizing the other with sparklers.

I meet Anne's eyes, and we both smile. This is a perfect night, warm, happy, peaceful. I vow to remember tonight. It's exactly the kind of night I want to remember. My kids are healthy and happy. My friends are with me. Everything is good. Everything is just as it should be.

eighteen

The fireworks finale seems to last forever, a triumph of pyrotechnic technology, and as we head home, the kids are comparing favorites.

I like the loud silver ones.

I like the big red ones that turn blue.

I like the ones that look like rain.

In the house I herd them up the stairs, to the bathroom to brush teeth before changing into PJs and climbing into bed.

Sometime in the middle of the night, I wake, needing to pee.

I stumble my way into the bathroom, hike up my nightgown, and sit on the toilet. I pat the wall to find the toilet paper and tear off a strip to wipe—and I recognize immediately that something's not right. I peer down to look at the toilet paper in the semi-darkness and it's colored. My underwear's colored.

I'm up, flicking on the bathroom light and standing there all by myself, seeing what I shouldn't be seeing. Blood. Lots of it, too.

I feel almost dizzy with dread. It's July 5, and I'm losing the baby.

I sit back on the toilet, my nightgown hiked up, my underwear still around my ankles, and I try to think, try to be calm. I can't be losing the baby. I can't be. It's been the best day. The best holiday. I was so relaxed tonight. So happy.

I press a hand to my eyes, press back the tears and scream of panic.

Maybe it's not over, maybe it's not too late. Doctors can do all kinds of things. I just need to talk to my doctor. Get to the hospital.

Heart pounding, hands shaking, I roll together long sheets of toilet paper to pad my underwear before flushing the toilet and going to my room to find some sweatpants and a T-shirt. I'll go to the hospital. They'll know what to do.

But in the hallway, I freeze. What about the kids? What do I do about them? I can't drag them to the hospital, and I can't just leave them here alone.

I check my watch. Nearly two in the morning.

Whom do I call to come stay so I can go?

Anne would come. So would Kris and Nic. They're all home now. I just saw them all earlier tonight.

I pick up the phone, poised to dial Anne's number. But I can't. It's not fair to her. She has a family, kids. How do I just call in the middle of the night and wake everyone up?

Carrying the cordless phone, I go lie down on my bed, trying to remember what side the doctor said is the best for the baby. The left side helps deliver better oxygen, right?

I call my doctor's pager number, leave a message, and

then hang up. While I'm waiting for him to call, I telephone Swedish Hospital's emergency line and am connected through. I beg the receptionist to please let me speak with a nurse, and the receptionist is sympathetic enough to put a nurse on the line.

I tell the nurse I'm just past twelve weeks pregnant and I'm bleeding. Bad. "I've called my doctor, but he hasn't phoned back, and I don't know if I should come to the hospital or not." I'm trying to be brave. "I don't know what I should do."

"You left a message for your doctor?"

"Yes."

"How long ago?"

"Just now."

"Who is your doctor?"

"Dr. Montgomery."

"He's good. He'll call you back," she says.

"But I don't know if there's anything I should be doing now."

"Are you in a lot of pain?"

I feel vaguely heavy and crampy, but it's not bad, not like period pain. "No."

"How long have you been bleeding?"

"I don't know. When I woke up a little bit ago, I discovered I was bleeding."

"If you feel you're in danger, come to the hospital."

There's a beeping on my phone. Call waiting. Dr. Montgomery is calling me back. "I've got the doctor phoning now," I tell the nurse. "Thank you for your help."

"Good luck," she says.

Dr. Montgomery is more pessimistic. I tell him everything I've told the nurse, and he doesn't sound surprised. "You're probably miscarrying."

Yes. Yes, thank you, Doctor. I know. "But is there anything I can do? Anything I can do if I go to the hospital?"

"No."

"But the bleeding—"

"Nature's way, Jacqueline."

Nature's way, my ass. Mother Nature is a woman, and Mother Nature wouldn't do this to another woman.

"Come to my office in the morning," he says. "We'll take a look. See if the pregnancy is still viable."

If the pregnancy is still viable. I know what that means.

I hang up, set down the phone and lie quietly, on my left side. I muster calm. Strength. Faith. *Come on, little baby. Come on, hang in there. Don't give up, don't quit, don't leave me now.*

It's a long night.

At first I don't sleep, can't sleep. But sometime around three-thirty my eyes close, and when I open them and look at the clock, it's nearly six.

I wait another half hour before limping my way to William's room, where I wake him first. "William, honey, I need your help. I'm sick, and I'm going to go to the doctor soon, but until I go I need to stay in bed."

William's immediately sitting up, eyes wide, serious. "Should I call Dad?"

"No! No. Just help me get Jessica up and ready for camp. Help her with her cereal, and make sure she has her backpack with her swimsuit and tennis racket when you leave for the club. I'm going to go downstairs and lie on the couch, but I really need you to help me so I don't have to go up and down the stairs more than I have to."

"Okay." He's out of bed and dressed in shorts and a T-shirt. "I'll get Jessica up. I'll make her breakfast. You lie down, Mom."

I go to my bathroom, check my underwear. Still bleeding. Change the toilet paper and go downstairs, where I lie—on my left side—on the family room couch so I can watch William and Jessica have breakfast.

Jessica comes over to me, and she's wearing her new favorites, green cargo short-shorts with a pink-and-green Barbie T-shirt. "Mommy?" she says, bending over to look me in the face. She puts her hand on my forehead as if I have a fever. "Mommy, are you going to be okay?"

"Yes." I take her hand, kiss it. "I'm fine. I just can't walk around too much right now. But I'm fine. I promise."

Her blond eyebrows furrow. "William said you might have to go to the hospital."

"I might. Just to be safe."

"Should we call a taxi?"

I almost laugh. "No, we don't need a taxi. I'll call Anne or Kristine and see if they can take me, and if they can't, I can drive myself."

She leaves me to climb up on the kitchen counter to grab the downstairs phone. Jessica hands the phone back to me. "Call Anne now."

"Jess—"

"I won't go to summer camp until you call."

I smile faintly. Jessica can be a pain in the ass, but she's so damn smart sometimes that it's scary. I dial Anne's number, and her voice mail comes on. I leave a

message, ask her to call me, and hang up. "There," I say
to Jessica, "phone call made. Now get your backpack
and meet your van."

My smile disappears as the children walk out the door
for the van that picks them up every morning for their
summer camp.

I can't lose the baby. I won't lose the baby. Please
God, don't let me lose the baby.

I drive to the doctor's office and present myself to the
receptionist the moment their door opens. "I've no appointment," I tell her, "but I'm pregnant, and I'm bleeding, and I have to see Dr. Montgomery."

"Are you in pain?" the receptionist asks.

"No."

"How long have you been bleeding?"

"Since around midnight."

The receptionist doesn't say anything. She doesn't
have to.

I sit down and wait to be called, leaning heavily to my
left side as if I can somehow protect the baby, keep the
oxygen flowing.

Thirty minutes later, my name is called. My doctor is
delivering a baby right now, but his partner will see me.

Dr. Jenkins asks me a few questions and then says
we'll do a vaginal ultrasound.

I slide in my paper gown down the bench and put my
feet in the stirrups and feel tears fill my eyes.

This isn't going to be good, I think, even as I pray,
Baby, be there, baby, be there.

I look at the doctor, who is looking at the little screen.

Bless the doctor. No expression at all. A consummate professional.

"Mrs. Laurens—"

"Ms. Laurens," I correct.

"There's no heartbeat."

There's no heartbeat. I blink, feel tears slip down the sides of my face into my hair. "Are you sure?"

"Yes."

She rolls back on her chair and returns the ultrasound wand to wherever it goes. I smooth the paper gown over my stomach, toward my legs, and then lower my legs one by one.

"I'll have your doctor follow up with you."

I nod. Sit up.

"Right now we just let nature take its course, but if there's pain, or the bleeding continues, we might want to schedule a D and C. But Dr. Montgomery will discuss that with you when he calls you later today."

I nod.

Dr. Jenkins stands, extends her hand, and touches my arm. "I'm sorry."

It's over.

It's over, and all I can think is, Thank God I never told the kids.

Thank God I lost the baby before I showed. Not because I care what anyone thinks, but because the kids have hurt enough. They don't need to know about the half baby brother or sister who now will never be. They don't need to be troubled or confused. They don't need to feel how I feel.

I curl up in bed and cry.

My God, could this year be any harder? Any worse? Could I just please get something good, something easy, something right?

My friends almost live at my house. They're taking the kids out, inviting them for dinner and play dates, trips to the park and the movie theater. They're bringing me my favorite lentil soup from Cucina Cucina and chicken enchiladas from Ooba's. There are flowers next to my bed and more on the kitchen counter. And even if Kris and Nic and Anne gave me hell for seeing Kai, they're also being incredibly gentle with me now as I try to deal with the wild emotions and even wilder hormones.

I really wanted this baby.

I really got excited about having a one-last-chance baby, an unexpected, unplanned, and miraculous little human being in my arms again. A baby at forty.

I cover my face as the tears start all over again.

I've miscarried before, twice before, but it doesn't help, doesn't ease any of the shock or the grief. Making babies has never been easy for me, but somehow the hard work, the morning sickness and aches and cranky moods, just made the wonder of delivering a baby all the more incredible. To think something so good can come from so much yuck.

I try to catch my breath, the relentless tears making it hard to breathe. I have to get a grip. Have to accept it. But I can't. Not yet.

I want to mourn for this baby. I want to mourn for me.

I want to be angry that I've no control now, no control over the end. It's not fair. It's not fair that love dies, and marriages fail, and babies can't go full term. It's not fair that we have to just suck it up and adapt, accept. It's not fair that life hurts.

I drag my pillow over my head. My God, I'm worse than the kids.

Oh, who am I kidding? I am a kid, just with wrinkled skin on the outside. I've never grown up, and you know, I don't know that I ever want to grow up if it means losing the part of me I love best. And what this last year taught me was that I'm just a girl in a grown-up body. I'm silly, sarcastic, romantic, optimistic.

This year has taught me I'm alive, not dead.

This year has been both the best and the worst year in recent memory.

Slowly, I drag the pillow off my head to hold it close against my chest instead.

Losing the baby makes everything easier.

Losing the baby makes life tidy again.

I should be glad for that. No difficult explanations to family and friends, no awkward answers to strangers, no disgust from Daniel, no financial burden or struggling on my part.

No, the future is familiar again. The unknown has become more known. I'm traveling the path already traveled.

After climbing from bed, I turn on the shower and strip off my tired sweats. The water hasn't quite warmed yet, and I stand beneath the stream, shivering. And crying.

Crying.

It's the hormones. It's just the body resetting its clock. I'm not really this sad, not this much of a mess. I'll even out soon, even out and move forward, move back into the groove, whatever the hell the groove was.

I didn't love Kai. I was infatuated. Intrigued by a life I'd never lived and possibilities that were more of an escape than a mature acceptance of life. People who move to Hawaii are running away from something, running from truth, responsibility, maybe even themselves; and if I'd gone to Hawaii, I would have just been running from me.

Now I have to confront that me, the woman I am and the woman I've become.

I squirt shampoo into my hand and lather my hair, thinking this is the first time I've washed my hair in nearly a week.

I'm glad I never told Kai about the baby.

I turn off the water, giving up on the shower before getting around to conditioning and shaving.

I'm done.

There won't be any more babies. The baby oven is closed. I'm single, forty. I can put all the lotions and potions I want on my skin. I can get my boobs done and my tummy tucked. Can color my hair every three weeks. But I can't fool my ovaries. They know the truth.

I'm out of time.

The eggs are old.

Whether I like it or not, the fertility game is up.

A month after my miscarriage, Kristine plans a girls' day out. She's booked us all spa manicures and pedicures at Frenchy's and then downtown, where we're going to shop, have drinks, and eat fattening appetizers.

It's not until we're at Frenchy's that it hits me. August 18. Kristine's birthday. Her forty-third.

"It's your birthday," I say. "And you planned your own party!"

"It's not my birthday party, it's just a girls' get-together. I thought we all needed some fun and a chance to play a little before the summer ends."

Nic's feeling just as bad. "We forgot your birthday." She gulps. "Again."

And it's true. We forgot her birthday last year, too.

Kristine waves her hand. "I don't care if you remember or forget. The great thing about being forty-three is that I'm comfortable throwing a party for myself."

I give Kristine a hug. "We're terrible friends. And I'm sorry. But happy birthday, baby!"

We all cheer her with our bottles of polish, but Kristine one-ups us again. She's brought along a bottle of champagne that's already been chilled and four acrylic flutes.

We pop the champagne and make a proper toast to Kristine and then another to girl power and great friends.

Kristine is in an unusually frivolous mood, and as she tops off our champagne, she makes lots of jokes. Nic laughs at everything, too. And with Anne sitting to my right, whispering to me that she's honestly, seriously, going to get that boob job, even if she has to go to Philip's best friend behind Philip's back (which I know she'd never do, but I let her talk), I realize I'm really very lucky. I know the best women in the world.

This day is exactly what I needed. I haven't dressed up and gone out, not even for cocktails, in months. I didn't drink in the three months I knew I was pregnant and haven't wanted to drink since the miscarriage. Now the champagne goes straight to my head.

Nic, who rarely drinks more than a glass of anything and doesn't even finish her champagne at Frenchy's, becomes our designated driver, as usual. We stop shopping, go straight to the restaurant, and order cocktails and appetizers and, later, dessert.

On the way home, Anne asks me how I am. I tell her I'm fine.

"No, really," she says, holding my chin in her hand and giving me her penetrating Earth Mother gaze. "How *are* you?"

She's drunk, but that's okay. We're all a little loopy (except for Nic). "I'm *fine*."

"Do you ever think about your surfer guy?"

This is the first time Kai's been mentioned since . . . well, the intervention, and I notice everyone has gone quiet. "Yes."

It's true, too. Every now and then I see someone, something, that makes me think of Kai and Hawaii—a pair of Maui Jim sunglasses, Reef flip-flops, a certain tattoo, or a really dark tan—and I get this funny fluttery kind of pain. But I can't live like that, feeling bad. That wasn't Kai, and that wasn't how Kai made me feel.

Nic appears to concentrate on driving, but I know she's listening just as intently when she asks, "So what made Kai so special?"

I'm sitting in the backseat next to an open window. It's a hot, sunny August afternoon, and my hair is blowing just the way it did in Kai's truck. I catch my hair in my hand, hold it away from my face, feel the bittersweet ache inside me, the ache extra poignant because for a brief moment in time I was pregnant and carrying his baby.

"Everything," I say at last, turning from the sun and Hawaii back to Anne and my friends. My shoulders rise and fall and my smile's crooked because it still hurts. "He made me feel good about me." I hold Anne's gaze and try not to cry. "And I felt so good with him."

"I'm sorry." Anne takes my hand. "I'm sorry I didn't make it easier for you. I think I was jealous—"

"Jealous?" I interrupt, incredulous. "But why?"

"What's not to envy?" Anne drops my hand, pushes her hair back from her face, tears in her eyes. "A young, hot, hard body totally digging you? Wanting to jump your bones, keep you in bed?" She makes a little hiccup of sound. "I can't even get Philip to look at me, much less make love!"

Kris is nodding in the front passenger seat. "We're kind of stuck in the same old routine—"

"Damn rut is more like it," Anne mutters. "And you've had these trips to Hawaii and this romance and this guy . . ." She makes a little face. "You got to do something we can't. We won't." She shrugs. "I just wish it had ended more happily for you."

So do I. I wipe the tears away quickly. But my life is good, and I love my kids and I have great friends. "I'm all right," I say, and I mean it because I *am* all right. "I've no regrets. I'm glad I went to Hawaii . . . met Kai. Think about it. *Me* on a surfboard. That alone was an adventure."

Anne laughs. "But still. I was wrong. And Jack, the next time you meet a hottie, go for it, girl."

Two weeks later, Anne and Philip are having an end-of-summer barbecue, the day before Labor Day sort of barbecue, and have invited me to join them, as they know Daniel has the kids and they're off in Santa Barbara.

Nic calls me before the party to let me know her sister's having a crisis and she's heading to see her tonight.

"I'll miss you at the party," I tell her. "And please drive safely."

"I will." Nic hesitates. "Um, Jack, how do you feel about dating?"

"Why?"

"Philip and Anne have invited a single doctor to the barbecue tonight. I think they're going to try to set you up." Nic sounds guilty. "I wasn't supposed to say anything, but I was worried Anne's matchmaking attempts might upset you."

Just as Nic can be so obtuse, she can also be incredibly sensitive. "Thank you, Nic. I appreciate the heads-up."

"You're still going to the party, aren't you?"

"Oh, yes." I laugh. "I don't get invited to many parties these days. It's important to show up when I am included."

"Jack . . ."

"What?"

"I don't know how you do it."

"Do what, Nic?"

"You're amazing." She takes a little breath. "And I admire you more than you know."

Knowing I'm possibly being set up, I dress for the barbecue with a little more effort than I might have put in otherwise. I flat-iron my hair, do my makeup, find the right necklace to go with my white gauze top and sage green linen skirt. I don't know if this doctor is short or tall, so I play it safe and wear pretty flats. My toenails still look great from the Frenchy's spa day, and as I look in the mirror I think I look okay.

No one would know about the pregnancy or the miscarriage. No one would know about Kai. Or Daniel.

I just look like an attractive woman going to a party at a friend's house.

When I arrive, Philip is at the barbecue busy pulling tequila-marinated shrimp kebabs off the grill. He shouts for an extra hand to take the plate, and I oblige. But as I take the plate, another man reaches for it, too, and that's how I'm introduced to the single doctor. James McKee is his name, and he's a recent transplant from Texas.

"Can I get you something to drink?" James offers once he's passed on the shrimp appetizers. "A glass of wine? A cocktail? I think they're making mojitos in the kitchen."

"Wine would be great."

"Red or white?"

"Red, if it's open." Nervously, I stand by Anne's new fountain—she just recently relandscaped the backyard—and wait for James to return.

Relax, I tell myself. Smile. Just be yourself. Anne and Philip wouldn't be introducing you to someone they didn't like.

James returns and hands me the goblet. "They've got some nice wine in there."

"Anne and Philip are wine snobs," I say with a smile. "Sadly, I'm one of those that know nothing about wine but like whatever I get to drink here."

James laughs, tips his bottle of Heineken in my direction. "I'm with you. I don't know much about wine, either, but I think I've got my beer sorted out."

We stand there a moment, and I'm feeling even more awkward, so I make a stab at conversation. "You work with Philip?"

"Yes. I've just moved here from Baylor. Renting an apartment in Belltown."

"How do you like it so far?"

"Weather's amazing. I don't know what people complain about."

"You moved here in summer, didn't you?"

"Late June, but there's only been a couple days of rain in sixty-plus days."

"We do have gorgeous summers. Fall is even nice. It's the other seasons that get folks down."

"Does the rain bother you?"

"Not usually, no."

"But . . . ?"

"This was a hard year." I immediately tense. I wish I hadn't said that and then grab the first possible topic I can think of. "Are you a Texas native?"

"No. From Colorado, originally."

We fall silent again. Now it's James's turn to try. "I hear you're a designer."

"Yep. It's how I pay my bills."

"Philip says you're good. That some of your homes have been featured in national magazines."

"Regional magazines. *Northwest Home* and *Seattle*."

"That's wonderful."

"I'm still hoping to get *Architectural Digest* someday."

"It'll happen."

Again silence stretches. Then James looks up at me. "This is awkward."

I nod. "A little."

"They said you were pretty but—wow. You're beautiful."

I look down, feel my cheeks warm. That was the last thing I expected him to say. "Thank you."

We fall silent again. He looks up at me and grimaces. "I'm striking out here, aren't I."

I look at James, note the sweep of medium brown hair, the light blue eyes, the clean lines of his face. I bet he's Irish. Probably went to Catholic school. Scored brilliantly on his SATs.

"You're not striking out," I say gently. "I'm just not exactly a chatterbox tonight."

He nods, glances around, sees the appetizers being passed. "Hungry?" he asks. "Hunkering for a shrimp kebab?"

"No. You?"

"I might chase one down."

"Go for it," I say.

James doesn't return immediately, and I think I've offended him. But he finds me when dinner's served, and we sit together at one of the round tables on the patio.

All my initial impressions of James are correct—intelligent, pleasant, attractive man. I can't think of one offensive thing about him, so when he asks for my phone number I give it to him. But not long after that, I slip into Philip and Anne's bedroom, grab my purse off the bed, and head home. It was a nice barbecue, and James—Jim—was a really nice man, but being there tonight, surrounded by all those familiar couples, made me realize I'm doing good, but I still have a long way to go.

Anne stops by my house the next morning with a plastic container of leftover chicken and ribs. "We had way more food than we needed. I don't think people even had seconds," she says, shooting me a dark look as she slides the plastic tubs into my refrigerator. "I know you didn't. You were out the door in record time."

"I was tired."

"Huh!"

"I was, but I had a great time, and I thought your garden looked great. I love the new patio and fountain."

"You're just kissing up to me now."

I laugh and take the pitcher of iced tea from the fridge and pour us each a glass.

Anne sits on one of the bar stools. "So, what did you think of Dr. McKee?"

"He seemed very nice."

"Just nice? He's gorgeous."

"He was attractive, yes, and polite. A nice man."

She groans. "You keep using the word *nice*."

"Well, he was."

"You didn't like him."

"I didn't dislike him."

"If he calls, will you go out on a date?"

"Yes."

Her jaw drops. She's elated. *"Really?"*

I can't help but smile at her enthusiasm. *"Really."*

"Why?"

"He's a nice guy."

"So nice is good."

I laugh at her craziness. She thinks she's got her head on so straight, but every now and then she's actually crazier than me. "Anne, nice is great."

That afternoon, Daniel drops the kids off on their way home from the airport and we have our own little barbecue together—steaks on my gas grill, baked potatoes, corn on the cob. It's been a perfect summer day here in Seattle, the kind of day that lasts forever, the sky still light until nearly nine p.m. Nights like this it stays warm, but not too warm. Lawns are green. Children run around in swimsuits, carrying melting Popsicles. The idyllic kind of summer that makes childhood extra poignant.

But finally it's time for the kids to come in, and take a bath, and get ready for bed. Tomorrow's the first day of school, and the first day is always a big deal. Jessica has laid out her clothes. William hasn't set anything out but I know he's thinking about school. His backpack is already by the front door.

They go to bed, and I can hear them whispering to each other across the hall. I head downstairs, go outside, and collect the Hula-Hoop and basketball from the driveway before locking up the house for the night.

James McKee called while I was making dinner earlier, wondering if I wanted to go to a Mariners game this coming weekend. The Mariners aren't in last place the way they were last season, but I'm not sure if a game is the right first date. Daniel and I used to attend lots of games together, and then once we had the kids, it became a big family thing. I think attending a game would still be hard for me. Too reminiscent of the married years.

Maybe James can just meet me for dinner somewhere. Palace Kitchen. Or Thai Ginger.

It'll be a nice evening—not like my dates with Kai, but no one is like Kai.

I draw the curtains in my room and head for the bathroom to wash my face.

I don't talk about it with anyone, but I still dream about Kai at night. Not as often as I used to, but there are mornings where I wake and feel really, really good, really warm and happy and safe, and then I remember my dream, and Kai and I were together. Unrealistic, I know. But still, a girl does dream.

nineteen

It's good having the kids back in school. We all settle into a routine, and things are so much easier than they were this time last year. So much easier than they were even last spring. We're all just calmer, more settled, and I mean that in the best sort of way. The kids have grudgingly accepted the new two-household thing, and even if Jessica sometimes frets at going back and forth, there are no more heartbreaking scenes where she cries in my arms.

I'm happier, too, and grateful for all my blessings. Like my kids. My amazing friends. The charming little shingle house we live in.

When I think back to last fall, it's just a blur. The only thing I know for sure is that I'm not going to struggle through the holidays the way I did last year. In fact, I won't actually have the kids for Christmas this year, but even then, it's not going to be the big drama it was last December. I'm scaling everything back, including my expectations.

Maybe the kids and I need to come up with some new

traditions, less stressful traditions, ones that we will all enjoy.

Driving William home from football practice Tuesday night, I ask him what he likes best about Christmas.

"Being with family," he says, wearily clutching his battered football helmet.

I smile as I glance in the rearview mirror. I can always count on him for the warm fuzzies. "What about you, Jess?" I ask.

She looks out the window for a long minute before sighing. "The presents."

I knew that was coming. My smile deepens. Thank God some things never change.

It's two weeks later and the end of September. We're still getting these magnificient sunsets where the sky is rich with layers of red and gold. Sunday night I sit with the kids on the couch, watching yet another episode of *SpongeBob* and *Teen Titans*.

Tonight we got lazy (I got lazy) and ordered pizza for dinner. As the sky darkens, deepens, William takes another piece of pizza and Jessica begs for a Popsicle. I say yes to everything, still savoring my indulgent mood. All day I've been thinking about life, my life, the past few years, and all the stuff I still want to do.

As I wipe up a drip from Jessica's purple Popsicle, I'm thinking how glad I am that I went to Hawaii in January. Meeting Kai changed me. Made me realize that growing up doesn't have to mean growing old.

I want to surf again. Snorkle. Play on the beach. I want to date younger men, too. There's no reason I have to date guys my age. No reason I have to go for balding, heavyset, and Viagra. If a younger man finds me attractive, why can't that be okay?

Why do women have to follow the rules?

And whose rules are they, anyway?

Fired up by my own rant, I toss the crumpled paper towel and grab a notebook and pen to start a list of all the things I want to do in the next few years.

Sitting on the couch, I scribble down my ideas in no particular order:

Go to Argentina.
Learn to tango.
Belly-dance.
Take a wine-tasting class.
Climb Mt. Rainier.

I go back, cross out "Climb" Mt. Rainier for "Visit" Mt. Rainier "Park."

I consider the list for a few minutes, tap the pen against my teeth, and then pick up where I left off:

Visit Mt. Rainier Park.
Sail the Greek islands.
Go to the Cannes Film Festival.
Get invited to Bill Gates's house.
Get some muscle definition in my arms.
Get a tummy tuck.
Take the kids on a cruise.
Get my second house in *Northwest Homes*.
Get my first house in *AD*.

Design my first restaurant interior.
Adopt a baby.

I go back again, scratch off that last one. I don't need another baby. I just need to laugh and play more with the two I've got.

A week later, I take out my list and make the leap. I'm going to Argentina for Christmas. Daniel gets the kids this year, and I'll die if I have to be in my house alone, without them for the holidays. Going to a friend's house won't help, either. I don't want to be around children if I can't be with mine.

I call my travel agent, the one who booked Anne and me into the Halekulani that first Hawaii visit of mine, and tell her I want to go to Buenos Aires for Christmas. I've got ten days, and I want to see as much of Argentina as I can. She promises to get back to me with prices soon.

In the meantime, I sign up for tango lessons. If I'm going to go to Argentina in ten weeks, I might as well start learning about their culture. From now until my trip, I'm going to drink only Argentinean wine and read books by Argentinean authors.

Not that I know any Argentinean authors. But I can learn, right?

Halloween is still weeks away, but Jessica must be putting on her costume at least three times a day. I've already had to mend it, and it's one of those supercheap silky princess costumes that still manages to cost a fortune. Tonight is my first tango lesson, and I'm nervous.

This is so silly, I think as I finish dressing. I'm going to make so many mistakes, and so many things could go wrong.

What if I'm the only one there on my own?

What if no one wants to partner with me?

What if I have no rhythm and three left feet?

What if I fling my arm up and poke some man's eye out?

Oh well. I guess I'll soon find out.

I go through my purse again. Wallet, keys, cell phone. Heeled shoes for dancing, and I'm already wearing a swishy skirt.

My hands are clammy as I turn off my computer. I don't really want to be doing this tonight. I won't know anyone, and I won't remember the steps— I break off, laugh at myself. I'm back in panic mode. Some things never change, do they.

At my desk, I scribble a note to my new sitter—Lisa's new roommate at the sorority—letting her know that I'll be back a little after seven.

I get through the class okay. It's exactly what I feared—mortifying. I'm not, and never have been, a dancer, and all night I feel as if I *do* have three left feet. But the instructors, a couple from Buenos Aires, are fascinating, and I'm in love with their language, the music, the history of the tango, and the way they move together.

I might not ever be a great dancer myself, but with even one class I already appreciate the art form.

I'm just glad the next class is six and a half days away.

At home, I pay Kerry and she pockets her cash. She's

on her way out the door when she turns back. "Oh! You had a call tonight from someone named . . . Kai?"

I sag against the kitchen counter, my legs all wobbly and weak. *Kai called?* "When?"

She nods, shrugs. "Earlier. A couple hours ago."

My body goes hot and cold. "Did he say anything?"

"Just to tell you he called."

"That's it?"

Kerry pulls her purse higher on her shoulder. "Yeah."

I look around for a slip of paper. "Did he leave his number?"

She turns her head and then shakes it once. "No." She sounds confused. "You don't have it?"

"No." My heart's racing, and my hands shake. I'm already reaching for the phone, but I don't know where to call. It's ten now my time. Even with the three-hour time difference, the beach desks would all be closed. "Did he say he'd call back?"

"No."

"Dammit." Tears fill my eyes, and it's ridiculous. I don't know why I'm getting so upset. There's no point in getting upset. I can always try to call the surf school tomorrow.

But Kerry sees my expression and is frowning. "I'm sorry. I thought you'd have his number."

"It's okay." I turn away, rub my forehead, and try to calm down. I'm acting like a sixteen-year-old kid. This is silly.

Kerry leaves. I lock the door. Turn out the light and then stand there in the dark entry, feeling my heart still pound. I stand there until the adrenaline rush fades and my pulse is steady again. Then I climb the stairs in my swishy dancing dress, trying to be calm, trying to be grown up.

At least he didn't forget me completely.

Late the next morning, I call the beach desk and ask for Kai, but he's not working today.

"Is he on the schedule tomorrow?" I ask.

I get a vague, noncommittal reply.

"I don't suppose you can get a message to him for me?" I persist.

The girl on the phone tells me she doesn't have his home number. She'll take a message, though, in case he checks in. I leave my name. "Jackie," I tell her. "Let Kai know that Jackie returned his call."

I wait a day and then another for Kai to phone, but he doesn't. Then it's Saturday morning and crazy busy.

Jessica's soccer game is at nine, and although it rained all night, it's finally stopped now. I'm the snack mom this week, so I cart boxes of doughnuts and juice boxes onto the muddy field.

Jessica's team wins for a change (thank God), and as soon as the snacks are doled out, we hustle back into the car for the drive to Edmonds, where William's football game begins at one. He changes into his pads and uniform in the car—not safe, I know, but he does do it with his seat belt on—and lunch is a drive-through hamburger.

I'm grateful that despite the gray clouds overhead, the rain has held off. At the stadium, Daniel and I nod politely at each other and Jessica goes to sit with her daddy while I take a seat in the bleachers as the players line up for kickoff.

William, my lovely, handsome, husky lineman, takes a few big hits early in the first half, gets yelled at by the coach after missing a key block, and looks up at me once where I sit in the stands.

I can't really see his expression, but there's no lightness in him. Despite his huge shoulder pads, he seems to sink, and I feel his worry and frustration. William is already so hard on himself that it doesn't take many strong words from a coach to weigh his heart down.

I wish I could go scoop him up in a hug, but he's ten now, and mothers aren't allowed on the field. Instead I give him a big thumbs-up, and he stares at me another long moment before turning away.

Being a mom is the best and worst job in the world. You love them so much, it hurts. You love them so much, you can't even begin to express it.

The game ends in a disappointing loss, and the kids go home with Daniel. I wish, though, they were going home with me. I've a touch of the lonelies today, nothing super serious, just the feeling of too much time, and emotion, on one's hands.

Traffic from the Washington Huskies game snarls the freeway traffic, and it's nearly dark by the time I reach my house.

Inside I flick on the kitchen light, head to my room, turn off the TV in the corner, and am just about to strip and take a shower when the doorbell rings.

Running a hand through my hair, I head for the front door, feeling grumpy and vaguely blue. I turn on the front porch light, as it's twilight and getting darker earlier every night, and open the front door.

We think we know life, can predict life, control life. We think we're prepared for the worst, and expect to be disappointed. And then life happens, and life is handsome, tan, muscular, clothed.

Kai.

Kai's here. Right here. Not in Hawaii, not at the surf desk, not on a surfboard, but here. In Seattle. On my doorstep.

I can hardly breathe. Definitely can't speak. Instead I just look at him, drinking him in, thinking, This isn't real, can't be happening. Not after so many months.

It's been a long, long time. Five months. Six?

He's wearing baggy jeans and a gray sweatshirt-style sweater, and I don't think he's ever looked so good.

Or so young.

Or tan.

"Do you still have all your muscles under there?" I ask, my voice shaking.

His blue eyes hold mine, and he grasps his sweater by the hem and lifts it up, showing me the flattest, hardest tan abs in the world. The tight, cut, six-pack kind. But I see more than abs. The bulldog tattoo is still there, too, right where I last saw it, between his navel and crotch.

I'm breathing funny. "Are you real?"

"Security at the airport said so."

I wish my heart would stop racing like this. "You got the special screening?"

"Pat-down and everything."

"They're just doing their job."

"Thoughtful of them."

I can't look away. He is real. And he is here. And he

can breathe on the mainland, not just his island. "I didn't think you left Hawaii."

"You didn't come back."

My eyes suddenly burn. My heart hurts worse. "I . . ." My voice fades. He'll never know how much I missed him, and even if I tell him, what do I tell him about the baby? Should I even tell him I was pregnant? "I . . ." I shake my head, overwhelmed.

He jams his hands in his jeans pockets, dragging the jeans even lower on his lean hips. "How are you, girl?"

Girl.

Girl.

I'd so wanted to be his girl but couldn't make it happen. "I'm good."

We're standing on opposite sides of the door, and leaves swirl outside, past his legs, red and brown and gold, huge maple leaves, leaves bigger than my face, my hand.

His gaze travels over me. "You look beautiful."

I'm wearing game-day clothes—jeans and a turtleneck and boots. It's Mom wear and far from sexy. "I don't look beautiful."

"You do. But then, you always look beautiful to me."

I bite the inside of my lip, my heart hammering with staggering force. "When did you arrive on the mainland?"

"Today."

"I didn't think you'd ever leave the rock."

The corner of his mouth tugs, a reluctant smile. "I guess I was wrong."

My heart swoops low, and I touch the door frame, trying to figure out if this is right, if this is true. If maybe it's night and I'm asleep and dreaming. Because this wasn't supposed to happen. This was never going to happen. He didn't leave Hawaii, and he wasn't going to come here. . . .

"Who'd you come to see?" I whisper.

He gives his head a shake. "You're such a silly girl." He takes a step toward me, draws a tendril of hair from my eyes, smoothes it back from my cheek. "Who do you think I came to see?"

"Me?"

"You're my girl, aren't you?"

Tears fill my eyes. I blink. Concentrate on the neck of his sweater. "What about work?"

"It's slow season for us right now. I took a couple weeks off."

I blink, and tears fall. "Why didn't you come sooner?"

He wipes away one of my tears and then another. "It took me a while to save up the money. Had to pay off some bills and take care of rent so I'd have a place to come home to."

"You're only here for two weeks?"

He laughs now. "You're still such a princess."

"I'm not."

"You are." But then he cups my face and lifts it and kisses me. "But that's okay. I love everything about you."

I kiss him back. I can't help it. But the kiss finally ends, and I smile, touch my finger to his mouth. "So what are you going to do in Seattle for two weeks?"

He shrugs, hunky shoulders shifting. "I guess I'm having an adventure."

An adventure. With me.

I bite my lip again but can't hide my smile of pleasure. "You say all the right things."

His expression gentles. "I say nothing I don't mean."

I'm still standing there, staring at him, feeling like that caterpillar who has turned into a butterfly. "Do you want to come in?"

"Are the kids here?" he asks.

"They're at their dad's."

"You're all alone?"

"Yes."

He nods, lifts his bag, and I stand aside. I watch as he enters my house, and I like him here in my foyer, handsome, sexy, casual. I'm still grinning as I shut the door.

"So what have you been doing, girl?"

"Not much." And then I reach for him, take his sweatshirt in my hand, and tug him toward me. "Just growing up."

epilogue

~~~~~~~~~

I f you read *People* magazine, you know celeb couples rarely go the distance and happy-ever-after endings are popular in movies but not in real life.

I do wish *People* magazine would call me. I'd like to tell them that happy endings are possible and sexy surf instructors really do fall in love with soccer moms.

It's a year since Kai showed up on my doorstep, and we're still seeing each other and still very much together, although "together" means sometimes we live apart. He's still a surf instructor in Hawaii, and I'm still a mom in Seattle, but we have this incredibly hip and implausible lifestyle where we go back and forth between the two.

But we don't limit our adventures to Hawaii and Seattle. We've been taking other trips together, like the Argentina trip last December. Kai went with me for Christmas, and we had the most romantic ten days imaginable. Right now we're planning another trip for this summer, a Greek island cruise with William and Jessica as soon as they get out of school in June.

My friends—surprise, surprise—all really like Kai.

Nic and Kris and Anne find him really easy to talk to, and my kids think he's beyond cool. As Jessica says, Ashton Kutcher has nothing on Kai Carson. I just laugh and pray she doesn't repeat that one to her daddy.

Daniel's still not thrilled with me and my younger guy, but I can't help that. He has his life to live and I have mine. And eventually Daniel will get used to Kai being in my life, because Kai's going to be around awhile.

Kai's talking about a beach wedding in Fiji.

I'm holding out for Greece.

And it's no real secret that I'd still love just one more baby.

about the author

Turning forty was a revelation. I confess, I dreaded it for years, agonizing at thirty-five because I was halfway through my thirties and approaching that awful number suggesting old, signifying middle age. Then somehow, before I was ready, I was forty—and single. Imagine my surprise when I discovered that I *liked* being forty—forty felt smart, sexy, competent. Being divorced is difficult at any age, but being forty I didn't have to ask permission from anyone anymore. I knew who I was, knew what I wanted, and knew what I didn't want. I didn't want to continue on the same path. I wanted the path not yet taken.

Five months after my fortieth birthday, I was in Hawaii on business, and much like my character Jacqueline in *Flirting with Forty*, I decided it was time to try something new. Completely out of my comfort zone, I donned a rash guard over my conservative one-piece suit, lathered on sunscreen, and took a private surf lesson. It was frightening, exhilarating, and exhausting, and yet the view of Waikiki with the green mountains behind the city and rugged Diamond Head off to the right showed me a

Hawaii I didn't know existed. Hawaii suddenly wasn't tourists and fruity tropical drinks, but a place of spirit and sun, water and mountain. It was one of those epiphany moments: I realized that the world is bigger and more interesting than we know and there's so much more possibility than we let ourselves see. I returned to Seattle a changed woman. Not only was I coming home with an idea for a new book, but I was determined to be more positive and no longer limit myself with preconceived ideas of what I could or couldn't do.

I never expected a single surf lesson—or conversations with a sexy young surf instructor—to change my life, but the lesson and conversations did. I'm still not a great surfer. I don't charge the waves the way competitive athletes should. But I do paddle out, and I jump up to my feet, and enjoy the ride.

For more on Jane and *Flirting with Forty*, visit her at her Web site, www.janeporter.com.

5 Things Surfing Taught Me About Life

1. Never Turn Your Back on the Ocean
Be smart about life and risks; don't turn your back on danger.

2. Paddle Through a Channel
When paddling, don't paddle against the big waves; look for the smooth channels between. Why make life harder than it has to be?

3. Waves Come in Sets
There's a natural rhythm to life; go with the flow and use momentum when it's on your side. When the waves are flat, use the down time to rest.

4. Look Where You Want to Go
Your surfboard will go in the direction you're facing. Make sure you know where you want to go in life. Keep your eyes on your goal.

5. Stay Loose to Keep Your Balance
Tensing up won't help you keep your balance or handle life's ups and downs. Relax. You're okay.

one

~~~~~~~~~~~

Zooming into the country club parking lot I snag a spot close to the club pool. Okay, technically it's not a spot, but there's nothing else close and I'm late.

Nathan says I run late often, and yes, sometimes I do, but not always. It's just that my schedule all summer has been ungodly. I've always been busy, but in the past year I've taken on way too much, sat on far too many committees, agreed to assist too many organizations.

The problem is, everyone needs help, and I hate inefficiency, I really do, which is how I got to be on so many committees in the first place.

I know how to get things done. I've always known how to get things done and for me, it's relatively easy organizing functions and raising money. And as we all know, everything these days is about raising money. As well as improving the quality of life for the kids.

The kids. It really is about the kids, isn't it?

I sign in quickly at the pool house's front desk and wave at a passing mother—never do remember her name, though—and emerge into the late afternoon light that already streaks the pool.

Scanning the pool for my girls, I tug my top over the waist of my white tennis skirt. I wish I'd showered and changed before heading to the pool but I was afraid of being even later. It's Friday, Labor Day weekend, and my nanny hoped to leave early today to go camping with her boyfriend.

I feel badly that Annika didn't get to leave at three thirty as requested (it's nearly five now) but today was hellacious. Morning pilates, two-hour auction committee meeting, afternoon on the tennis court before quick grocery shopping. Then it was a rush home to get the salmon steaks into the bourbon marinade for dinner before another rush out to pick up the girls from the club.

Pushing my sunglasses up onto the top of my head, I spot the girls. Tori's in the baby pool, Brooke's lying on her towel on the lawn, and Jemma's swimming in the deep end with her friends. Annika, our Finnish nanny, sits in the shade near the baby pool, her purse on her lap. She's ready to go, which annoys me.

I don't like being disapproving but I do resent being made to rush, and then feel guilty. It's Labor Day weekend. She has Monday off. It's not as if she won't have three full days vacation.

Annika spots me, I lift a hand, letting her know she can go. She leans down, kisses Tori and with a nod at me, leaves. Quickly.

"Taylor!"

It's Patti calling my name. I turn, spot her and a cluster of women at one of the pool's round tables, and indicate that I'll join them in just a moment. First, I have to get something cold to drink.

Something preferably with alcohol.

A few minutes later I collapse in the poolside chair with my gin and tonic. Nice. Sliding my sunglasses on, I sip my drink appreciatively. Day's almost over. I'm almost free.

Suddenly Annika, my nanny, reappears on the pool deck, dashes to a table near the baby pool and rifles through the stack of beach towels they brought earlier. She's looking for something and it's got to be her car keys or her cell phone—she couldn't survive without either.

It's her cell phone.

I'm not surprised. What twenty-two-year-old girl doesn't live on her cell?

Annika leaves again and I watch her dash back out. She's worked for me for over a year now and we almost never talk. I leave her to-do lists and when she goes home at night she leaves the lists behind, everything done, all the chores checked off.

Sometimes I feel a little guilty for not ever having a proper chat, but what would we talk about? My girls? My house? My laundry? No, thank you. I have enough on my mind without having to discuss the above with a foreign teenager.

What a day. Not bad, just long, and busy. Pilates nearly killed me, I killed my opponent in tennis, and the committee meeting—well, that went so much better than I expected.

"Have you been here long?" I ask the group at large, dropping my sunglasses back onto my nose.

"An hour," Patti answers.

Monica grimaces. "Since two."

"Noon," Kate adds.

Noon? I make a face. I can't imagine sitting here for five hours. My God, doesn't she have anything else to do?

"You should have gotten a sitter," I say, glancing at my children, praying they'll be content for another half hour at least, an hour if I buy them an ice cream. Tonight I would buy them ice cream, too, if it meant I could just leave my feet up for a while and relax.

Kate sees my grimace. "I couldn't get a sitter," she explains. "Labor Day weekend. Everyone's going away."

True. We were going to go away, too, and then Nathan begged off at the last minute, said all he wanted to do was stay home, enjoy the girls, and maybe get a round of golf in.

"Actually," Kate continues, crossing her legs, tugging down her straight twill skirt, a skirt that looks like Eddie Bauer but I know is Ralph Lauren, "I feel like I got off easy. The kids really wanted to go to Wild Waves, but I convinced them they'd be better off just spending the day here and saving the money."

Saving money? *Kate?*

I struggle to keep a straight face. Kate Finch is loaded, one of the area's old money and then she married Microsoft money—and not one of the little Microsoft millionaires that pop up everywhere—but Bill Finch, head of the Games division, so the Finches are set for life.

"How did you convince the kids to do that?" Patti asks, leaning forward to get out of the sun's rays. Petite and brunette, Patti Wickham has endless energy, a vivacious personality, and the ability to not take no for an answer.

"Bribed them." Kate sniffs. "Told them I'd give them the cost of the admission ticket, and what I would have spent on gas if we could just come here. Worked like a charm."

Thank God for money.

Hate to admit it, but I'd do the exact same thing. Who'd want to make the drive from Bellevue to Federal Way—what is that, forty minutes each way?—and then spend hours worrying about the kids getting lost or abducted before driving back home in rush-hour traffic. No, Kate's right. Far better to take advantage of the Points Country Club pool before it closes for the summer.

My youngest daughter, Tori, who has only just recently turned four, remembers I'm at the pool and comes running over to give me a wet hug. "Mama, Mama, Mama! I missed you!"

I hug and kiss her back. "Having fun?" I ask, rubbing her bare tummy.

She nods, her blond curly ponytails like piggy corkscrews in the sky. "I'm hungry."

"We're having dinner soon."

"Can I have some French fries?"

"We're going home in twenty minutes—"

"I want French fries."

"Honey."

"I'm starving." Her lower lip thrusts out. "*Starving.*"

Oh, why not? It's Friday. Labor Day weekend. I'm tired and don't want to get up. If French fries will keep her happy, let her have them. "Tell Brooke to go with you to order. She's right there, in the shallow end."

"'Kay."

"Kay."

Tori runs off in her pink two-piece, her still-chubby thighs making little slapping noises. "Is that bad?" I ask, looking at my friends. "French fries right before dinner?"

"It's the end of summer," Patti answers with a shrug.

Exactly. Kids will be back in school in just days and it'll only get harder, what with homework and sports and meetings. Being a mother is a full-time job. I couldn't work outside the home even if I wanted to.

"Mom! *Mom! Taylor Young!*" My middle daughter, Brooke, shouts at me from the pool, resorting to using my name when I take too long to answer.

I put a finger to my lips, indicating she's too loud. "Come here if you want to talk to me," I stage-whisper. "Don't shout across the pool."

With a sigh, Brooke drags herself out of the pool and splashes her way to our table. "Did you tell Tori I had to go order her French fries?"

"She's hungry." I'm not in the mood to deal with Brooke's attitude now. For a middle child Brooke is extremely strong-willed. "You can share her fries."

"I don't want fries."

"What do you want?"

"Ben and Jerry's ice-cream bar."

"No—"

"You said." She gives me her I'm-seven-and-going-into-first-grade look. "You did, Mom."

"What about a Popsicle?"

"Why does Tori get fries and I have to have a Popsicle? Why does she always get everything she wants? Because she's the baby? When I was her age I could order my own fries—"

"Fine. Get your ice cream." I give up. I just can't do this today, tonight. Not without another drink. "Help Tori and get what you want."

She flounces away and I see the face she makes at me. I don't call her on it, though. I'm too tired and as the parenting experts all say, you have to pick your battles. I want them to get good grades so I suppose I've picked mine. Besides, they're not as lippy with Nathan. They wouldn't be. He doesn't put up with it, not like I do.

"Good meeting today, Taylor," Patti says as Brooke grabs Tori by the shoulder to haul her into line at the snack bar.

Patti's co-chair with me for the Points Elementary School auction and we held our first meeting of the year this morning at the Tully's on Points Drive.

I was worried about the meeting but I needn't have been. Our committee of seven is amazing. We've got the best parents this year, the best moms hands down.

"I heard so many great ideas during our brainstorm session," I say, squeezing the rest of my lime wedge into my gin and tonic. "I have a hunch that this year's auction is going to just blow everyone out of the water."

And it will with what we're planning.

We've got some *spectacular* live auction items already lined up, including a trip to Paris—first class on Air France, and a week on Paul Allen's private yacht . . . in *Greece,* no less. I suppress a shiver of excitement.

Corny as it is, I get goose bumps just thinking about it. "Patti, we can make this happen."

"We are making it happen," Patti corrects. She might be tiny and pretty, but she's a workhorse. "We've already got chairs for each committee and everyone's experienced—"

"On the *ball*," I add.

"And as we know, experience makes all the difference."

Isn't that the truth? I just love Patti. We're on such the same wave length. It's not just that we're friends, but we've served on practically every school committee possible, and there's no way I would have tackled the school auction if Patti hadn't suggested we co-chair it together.

The school auction is Points Elementary's biggest annual fund-raiser. The phone-a-thon, walk-a-thon, and wrapping paper sales all bring in money, but they don't come close to generating the kind of money the auction does.

A strong auction nets a quarter million dollars. A fabulous auction nets a hundred thousand more.

Patti and I think we can hit four hundred thousand this year. At least that's our goal.

"Anything juicy happen at the meeting?" Kate asks, pulling up another white chair to stretch her legs on. Her legs are thin and tan, but they're always tan. Kate plays a lot of golf and she and Bill routinely sneak off to Cabo.

Patti and I look at each other, try to think. There wasn't a lot of chitchat. We were pretty organized and the auction meeting isn't the place for gossip. It'd look bad. Unprofessional.

"I know something juicy," Monica chimes in eagerly.

I shoot Patti a here-we-go-again look. Monica Tallman irritates me. She isn't poor, and she's not unattractive, but she's pathetically insecure and compensates for her feelings of inferiority by trying too hard.

The truth is, Monica needs a life. And she needs to stop copying my hairstyle.

Monica throws a hand into her hair, showing off her most recent highlights, which are nearly identical to mine. "The Wellsleys separated this summer," she announces loudly.

"The Wellsleys?" Kate gasps.

Monica nods, sips her wine cooler, pleased to be the bearer of horrible news. "Apparently Lucy was having an affair."

"*What?*" We all turn, shocked, to stare at Monica.

Patti frowns, a deep furrow between dark eyebrows. At least I know she doesn't do Botox. "I don't believe it," she says. "I can't believe it. Lucy would never do that. I've known her for years—"

"She's on the altar guild at St. Thomas," Kate adds.

Monica shrugs, lips curving. "Jesus loves a sinner."

Unbelievable. I drain the rest of my gin and tonic and immediately crave another. Too bad I can't send one of my girls for the drink but they don't sell liquor to minors here.

Monica gives her wine cooler a twirl. "Pete's going after custody."

"*No.*" Now this is going too far. It really is. I know Lucy, too, and she's a great mother, a good wife, and it'd destroy her not to have the kids. Kids need to be with their mother, too.

Well, unless their mother's a nutcase.

Like mine was.

"Pete thinks he's got a case." Monica sounds smug.

I hate it when she's so smug. I really think she needs to work out with her personal trainer a bit less and volunteer a lot more.

"You can't take children from their mother," I defend. "Courts don't do that. I know it for a fact. Are you *sure* she's having an affair?"

"I imagine it's over now that Pete found out, but Pete's embarrassed. He paid for her lipo, the implants, the tummy tuck, the eye job, the laser skin treatments and now he finds out it wasn't even for him? Fifty thousand later he feels a little cheated."

Patti's outraged. "Lucy didn't even need the work. She did it for him. He's never been happy, especially with her."

I nod my head in agreement. Lucy was really attractive, even before all the surgeries, and you know, you couldn't tell she had that much work done because it was subtle. *We* knew, because she'd told us, highly recommending her plastic surgeon to us. And in the plastic surgeon's defense, he was very, very good and the only way I knew Lucy had done her eyes (before we knew about the plastic surgery) was because she just *looked* happier.

Apparently she was happier.

She was getting laid by someone who wasn't her fat husband.

That's not a nice thought, and I shouldn't think thoughts like that, but Pete *is* big. He's gained at least thirty-five or forty pounds in the last year or so. Maybe more. When I saw him at brunch a couple of weeks ago I almost didn't recognize him, and Nathan, who never notices anything like that, even leaned over to me and said Pete was a heart attack waiting to happen.

Did that stop Pete from filling up his plate at the buffet? No. In fact he went back for seconds and thirds—piles of sausages, cream-cheese Danishes, eggs Benedict, blueberry and sour cream crepes, strawberries covered in whipped cream. You could hear his arteries hardening as he lumbered back to his table.

I can't blame Lucy if she didn't want to sleep with Pete. I wouldn't want to eat with him, much less do the down and dirty, but an affair . . . ?

I wonder if the sex was good. . . .

God, I hope it was, especially if she's going to lose the kids.

Shaking my empty glass, the ice cubes rattle. I want another drink but can't make myself move. Not just because I'm tired (which I am), but if I go get another drink, it's more calories.

I weigh the pros and cons of another drink knowing that I'm in good shape but it's something I work at. Image is important and the closer I get to forty (O God) the more I care about my appearance. It's not enough to be fit. You've got to look young and that's some serious time and money.

Lately I've been thinking about getting some work done. Nathan says he loves me as I am, thinks I'm perfect and doesn't want any artificial bits of me, but if it'd make me better, wouldn't the pain be worth it?

I tune back in and realize they're still discussing Lucy

and Peter. "—says he feels like she humiliated him in front of the whole community."

"Well, I didn't know until now," Kate says.

Me, either, and my fingers itch to take my phone and call Nathan and see if he's heard. He used to be in Rotary with Pete. They were both in the Friday morning group that met for breakfast at the golf course across town.

Patti's frowning. "She's like us, a stay-at-home mom. So who could she be sleeping with? A UW student? A pool boy? Who?"

"Someone's husband." Monica looks like a cat. She's so pleased with herself that even her ears and eyes are smiling. "Apparently Pete has told the wife, too, and so that's two families wrecked."

Wrecked.

The very word conjures up horrible memories and I suddenly touch my stomach, checking to see if it's flat. It is. I can feel my hipbones. Good.

The thing to know about me is that I hate fat almost as much as inefficiency, which is why I'm always hungry. I want to eat, but I don't. Nathan thinks I'm too thin, but he doesn't know what it's like always having women look at you, compare themselves to you.

"So where is Lucy now?" I ask.

"I think she's still in the house. Pete tried to kick her out—and she left for a couple nights—but she returned. Said she wouldn't leave, that it was her home, so Pete took the kids and left." Monica stretches, yawns. "God, it's a gorgeous day. Can you believe this beautiful weather?"

Kate and Patti exchange glances. "So where *are* Pete and the kids staying?" Kate persists.

"Their place in Sun River."

But they've got to be coming back soon. School starts on Tuesday and Pete has to work.

Those poor kids. They must be so scared and confused.

I look around the pool for mine. My girls are just yummy. I really shouldn't brag but all three are beautiful— you can tell they're sisters, they all have the same golden skin, long honey-blond hair and big blue eyes. People are always stopping me, telling me the girls should be models. Maybe they will. I don't know. We're just so busy as it is.

"Mom! *Mommy!*" Tori wails tragically at the edge of the grass, her big beach towel bunched at her feet, her paper plate upside down in her hands. "I dropped my French fries!"

I sigh. My friends chuckle. They know what it's like, they know what I'm going through. "Go get some more," I call to her. "They'll remember you at the counter."

"Come with me," she pleads.

"You can do it. Besides, Brooke's still over there. Catch her before she leaves. Tell her Mommy said to—" But before I can finish, Tori's running past me.

"Daddy!" she screams, rushing toward Nathan, who has just appeared at the pool.

Smiling, I watch Nathan swing Tori up into his arms. We've been married eleven years, twelve on Valentine's Day, and I still think I married the sexiest, greatest man. It's not just because he has money, either. We're *happy*. We have a great life together. I'm lucky. Blessed. Really and truly.

Nathan's a wonderful father, and an amazing provider.

You should see our home—as a little girl I dreamed of someday living in a house like ours—and our three little girls are gorgeous and Nathan spoils all of us. Constantly. So much so that I feel a little guilty sometimes.

"There's my beautiful wife," Nathan says, walking toward us with Tori still in his arms.

Nate is a vice president for Walt McKee's personal holding company, McKee being the founder of satellite communications and that's the name of the game here in Seattle. Technology. Bill Gates, Paul Allen, Steve Balmer, Walt McKee, are all practically neighbors, and if not close friends, acquaintances. I'm not trying to name-drop, it's just that this is my world, the one I live in. I see the Gateses and McKees and Balmers everywhere. Our kids play together on the same sports teams, dance at the same ballet studios, swim at the same country club pool, and sometimes attend the same school.

Nate leans down, kisses me before turning to greet my friends. In the late afternoon light, Nathan looks even more golden than usual, his brown hair sun-streaked from swimming, surfing, and playing golf, his warm brown eyes almost bronze. I think he's more handsome now than when I first met him.

"Hello, honey," I answer, reaching out to capture his fingers. "How was your day?"

"Good." He shifts Tori to his other arm, oblivious that Tori's damp little body has left his shirt wet, as well as stained with a splatter of ketchup.

Tipping my head back, I smile up at him. "I didn't think I'd see you for another hour or two."

"Escaped early." He puts Tori down, glances around. "I see Jemma. Where's Brooke?"

"Eating something somewhere," I answer.

He nods and pushes a hand through his thick hair— I'm so glad he still has his hair. "I'm going to get a beer. Anybody want anything?" he asks my friends. "Kate? Patti? Monica?"

They all shake their head but I can see their eyes feasting on him. I can't be jealous, either. Let's face it. Nathan's feast worthy. Six three, very broad shouldered, and with very nice abs. He works out daily, always has.

"How about you, darling girl?" he asks, turning to me. "Gin and tonic with lots of lime?"

I smile up at him. "I love you."

"I know you do."

I watch him walk away, thinking again that I'm so lucky that it sometimes makes me feel guilty having so much. I certainly didn't have any of this growing up. Growing up . . .

Growing up was a nightmare.

I shudder, push the thought away, telling myself to focus on the here and now. Everything's good today. Everything's great. And it's not as if I just fell into this amazing life. I worked to get here, worked to make it happen. Now if only I could relax and enjoy it more.

"Oh my God." Monica leans forward, grabs Kate's arm. "Lucy's here."

"What?"

Monica nods across the pool. "She just walked in, and she's got the kids."

Our heads all swivel toward the pool entrance, and

Monica's right. Lucy Wellsley is walking around the deep end of the pool, a beach tote bag over her shoulder, a stack of colorful striped towels in her arms as her three kids, two boys—fraternal twins—and a little girl, all run ahead.

"Should we invite her to join us?" Patti asks, glancing at me.

"I don't know." I mean, I feel bad for her, but infidelity? Affairs? This is bad. Really bad.

"She's brave," Kate mutters. "I wouldn't show my face here."

"Well, I don't think we have to worry about extending an invitation," Monica practically purrs. "Because Lucy's on her way over here now."